I0556435

# Lady in White

### David McCurrach

Lazy Day Press

2022

Published by LAZY DAY PRESS, 2022
North Fort Myers, FL
Cover Design by Chris Andruskiewicz, Sparrow Graphics

ISBN: 979-8-9856506-1-7

davidmccurrach.com

# Table of Contents

# Part One

# Rough Waters

# Chapter One

I couldn't believe my eyes. There she was. At the bar. Alone.

I blinked a couple of times to make sure I wasn't imagining her. The only other time I'd seen her was a couple of nights ago.

I passed through the Atrium at midship. Some sort of competition captivated the crowd. Could have been anything—Name That Tune, Sing the Next Line, or some other silliness. I wasn't interested enough to even look.

Until the white dress caught my eye. The gown was far more elegant than the typical cruise attire. In fact, as soon as I saw her, the people around her faded into oblivion. The dress was so dazzling it overwhelmed everything, except for the beauty of the woman wearing it.

I wished I'd taken a moment to absorb all her loveliness, but I didn't. I thought about it but continued on to wherever I was going. Of course, I didn't even remember where that might have been. All I remembered was the lady in white.

And yet, here she was again. Sitting at the bar, by herself, enjoying an evening of solitude. I'd really thought every guy in the bar would be hitting on her, but she was alone. Maybe she was so exceptionally beautiful, they realized they didn't stand a chance.

My wife had sent me to the bar for a Coca-Cola with crushed ice. Ever since the ship left the pier, she's been suffering from sea sickness. The Dramamine helped to a certain extent, but it made her so sleepy she couldn't function. The Coke was a compromise and, although not as effective, did seem to calm her stomach.

I'd gotten the Coke, but instead of leaving, I just stood there. I didn't feel conspicuous at first, but when the bartender asked me if I needed anything else, I thought I should order something.

I asked for a Corona—that was what she was drinking—and sat down on the stool next to her. She didn't seem to notice. I still had the glass of Coke when the bartender set down the bottle of beer.

"Do you want a glass?"

"No, thanks."

I felt a little stupid as I sat there contemplating my beer. The bottle was interesting, but not nearly as fascinating as the incredible woman sitting beside me.

Her silky-smooth skin glowed with a modest tan; her soft blond hair curled stylishly just beyond her bare shoulders; her scent gave off a blend of jasmine and exotic spice; her makeup was minimal except her lips, which were a bright, shiny red; her beauty was undeniable.

I sipped my beer, thinking if I gave her enough time, she'd say something. But she seemed perfectly content to sit there in silence.

In desperation, I blurted out, "Are you enjoying the cruise?"

She didn't even acknowledge my question. Maybe she thought I was asking the bartender, or maybe the obese man on the barstool to my other side.

Finally, I decided to be a little more direct. I didn't know why I felt the need to speak to her, but since I did, I gave it another try.

I moved my body so I faced her. "Excuse me, Miss."

She looked at me like I wasn't even there. Then she turned back.

I repeated myself. "Excuse me, Miss."

She turned again. This time she looked angry and barked, "What do you want?"

That was a good question. What did I want? I had no idea.

I was on a cruise with my wife, celebrating our twentieth wedding anniversary. Pretty special, right? Granted, she spent most of the trip either moaning or vomiting. At this point, I avoided our cabin at all costs. She seemed fine with that.

The blonde repeated, "What do you want?"

I thought a minute. "Someone to talk with."

"What about the hippo sitting on the other side of you?"

Apparently, he heard her remark and took exception to her use of the term *hippo*. He rose up to have a word with her. I gently pushed down his shoulder and eased him back onto the barstool.

I said, "That wasn't necessary."

"I know. Why do you want to talk to me? Are you lonely?"

I thought *I'm pathetic* but replied, "Yes."

"Are you on the cruise by yourself?"

"No."

"Who are you with?"

"My wife."

"Not that it's any of my concern, but why don't you talk with her?"

"She's seasick and can't leave our cabin."

With that, her demeanor changed. She truly saw me for the first time. "I'm sorry to hear that. Is there anything I can do for her?"

She had me there. I could think of many things she could do for me, but I didn't think I'd be comfortable with the lady in white helping me care for my wife. Best to let that go. Anyway, I needed to get her Coke back to our cabin before all the ice melted.

I said, "That's kind of you, but I think I've got it covered. Thanks for talking with me." *Definitely pathetic.* "Maybe we'll see each other again."

To my surprise, she replied, "I hope so."

# Chapter Two

When I got back to our cabin, my wife was sitting on our balcony. I thought out loud, "Maybe the fresh air will do you some good."

"I got bored waiting for the Coke. What happened to you anyway?"

"Nothing. The bar was busy and it took the bartender a while to get to your drink."

"You know, they only have like nine bars on this ship. Could you have found one that wasn't so crowded?"

What could I say? Probably, but I'd miss my chance with the lady in white? I should be realistic—my chance with the lady in white was zero, so I wouldn't have missed anything. Besides, I was madly in love with my wife. What was I even thinking?

In the interest of not causing any further stress for her, I replied, "Yes, dear," and sat down.

After a few minutes, I said, "You know, it's relaxing out here." When she didn't respond, I turned towards her. She was racing to the bathroom with a mouth full of you-know-what.

After a while, she rejoined me. I gently took her hand as we enjoyed the myriad of stars and the refreshing sea breeze.

I asked her a little later if she wanted another Coke. She said no. I read awhile and then we both went to bed.

The next morning, I was up bright and early—off to the breakfast buffet. I'd offered to bring something back for my wife or to order room service for her, but she declined and said she'd be fine. I was concerned because I didn't think she'd eaten in days. I'd try again, later.

Personally, I was looking forward to breakfast and to the possibility of seeing the lady in white again. Of course, this morning she probably wouldn't be wearing the white gown. Today, she'd probably be the lady in the string bikini—even better. I didn't see her for breakfast and decided to take a couple of laps around the tanning areas for a little exercise after my meal.

No joy. That's Air Force lingo for "I don't see anything." In this case, the words would be just as descriptive of how I felt.

I took my coffee back to our cabin. My wife was out on the balcony again. I joined her.

She felt a little better. "I love looking at the sea, feeling the sun warm my body and the breeze caress my face. Do you think there's any way I could move one of the beds out here?"

I thought *Are you kidding me?* but said, "I'll talk with our steward."

She asked, "Do you mind getting me a glass of Coca-Cola with crushed ice?

I replied, "Of course not."

I went back to the same bar. It was closed. Probably a little early for serious drinking, even on a cruise. I then decided to take the elevator up to the poolside bar. Of course, it was packed. As I waited to place my order, someone behind me asked, "How's your wife feeling today?"

I whipped my head around. There she was—the lady in white. This morning, the white dress was replaced by the skimpiest of white bikinis, a sheer white wrap, big sunglasses and a straw hat.

This girl had to know white was her color. I tried not to stare at her perfect body. She'd replaced the bright red lipstick with some shimmering light brown gloss. Her lips were just as inviting as they were last night.

I replied. "She seems to be feeling a little better this morning."

"Maybe she'd like to do something with me."

I thought, *Maybe I'd like to do something with you,* but said, "I don't think she's quite up to that yet, but I'll certainly let her know that's an option."

"Thanks. I'd really like a friend."

"Are you lonely?"

"No. Not at all. I'd just like a girlfriend to do things with."

The bartender asked me, for the third time, what I wanted. I turned and ordered a Coke with ice. When I turned back around, she was gone.

To be honest, I don't know if I'd imagined our brief exchange or if it had really happened. Elusive—that was the lady in white. She was so extraordinary that many times, I wondered if she was even real.

Maybe she was just a figment of my imagination. Surely no one this stunning was real. Everyone had their flaws—something about them that wasn't quite up to par. Maybe the lady in white did as well, just nothing I'd noticed. Or maybe there was no lady in white. Crazy thought.

For the next couple of nights, I made multiple trips to the first bar where I'd seen and spoken with her. She was never there.

On the third night, I checked out the other bars—no lady in white. Maybe, I'd simply imagined her.

My wife was still sick. We even took her to the ship's doctor. He thought she might have norovirus and wanted to quarantine her. I reminded him she had hardly left our cabin. He acquiesced, but I got the feeling he still suspected the virus.

# Chapter Three

The next stop on our itinerary was the island nation of Grenada. We were scheduled to arrive in another two days. I suggested we might want to fly home from there. My wife would have no part of that. She said we paid for a two-week cruise and by God that was what we were going to do. Besides, the flights home from Grenada were ridiculously expensive. I knew she was practical and, sometimes, a glutton for punishment.

That night, she casually mentioned, "Daphne came by the cabin today."

"Who's Daphne?"

"Your lady friend. She'd heard I wasn't feeling well and she was concerned about me. There's no one she could have heard that from besides you."

Daphne. I would have never guessed that was her name. How could she have known my cabin number? I never told her. I thought the cruise ship protected that kind of information—like a hotel or resort.

Now that I thought about it, how had she avoided me all these days? I had to admit, I'd been looking for her everywhere.

Oh, well. Time to defend myself. "First of all, she's not my lady friend. I didn't even know her name. In fact, I'm guessing she was the woman I talked to while I waited in line to order your Coke. What did she look like?"

"The most beautiful and alluring woman I've ever seen."

I knew I'd have to be especially careful here. I couldn't really agree with that statement but had to say something. "Did she have long blond hair?"

"I couldn't tell. Her hair was pulled up into a bun."

Maybe that was how I'd missed her. Maybe I didn't recognize her with her new hairstyle.

"Was she young?"

"Yes, way too young for you."

"Hold it just a minute. If she was the woman I talked to in line, I doubt we'd even recognize each other if we crossed paths again."

"How did she know my cabin number and that I wasn't feeling well?"

"I have no idea. I'm just as much in the dark as you are."

"If you're telling the truth, then all this is a little creepy."

"I am telling the truth"—*for the most part*—"and I agree, it's definitely creepy. What could she be up to?"

"I don't know, but I'll be a little more cautious if she comes back."

"As will I, if I see her again."

"I thought you said you wouldn't even recognize her if you saw her again."

"True, true. Maybe I should just stay here with you and never leave the cabin."

"That would be a little much for both of us. I'm sure everything's alright. Forget I said anything."

Gladly. But I had to admit, this was all a little strange. Later that day, the steward recruited a buddy and moved Lilly's bed to the balcony. I told her I was worried she and her mattress might roll into the sea. She insisted the railing would stop her. I wasn't so sure. Either way, she felt a little better breathing the fresh salt air.

The next morning, I invited her to join me for breakfast. She said she wasn't quite ready but might be the next day.

I headed for the buffet. As always, I enjoyed a bacon and cheese omelet and an English muffin with orange marmalade. I found a table overlooking the sea. I was about halfway through my meal when someone asked, "Do you mind if I join you?"

I looked up midbite. Of course, it was the lady in white. Today, she wore a yellow bikini with a coordinating sheer wrap. My mouth was full of omelet and I couldn't speak, so I just motioned for her to sit down.

She made herself comfortable. Her plate was filled with various types of fruit. She also had a small container of low-fat yogurt.

I continued eating my breakfast, expecting her to say something. She didn't utter one word. Every time I looked up, she smiled.

Once I was done, I said, "Lilly enjoyed your visit."

"Who's Lilly?"

"Lilly's my wife. She said you visited her yesterday in our cabin."

"How could I possibly know your cabin number?"

"That's what I thought. She said your name was Daphne."

"That explains it. My name is Erica. Her visitor must have been someone else. Do you know a Daphne?"

"No, I thought that was you."

"Not me. That's strange."

"I agree."

With that, Erica stood up and put her sunglasses and hat on. "I'm going to get some sun. Feel free to join me if you like. Enjoy your day."

If Daphne wasn't Erica, the only way she could have gotten our information would be from the ship's medical office. Maybe, Daphne helped the doctor by following up with guests that didn't feel well. I can't imagine how else she would have known about Lilly.

# Chapter Four

I took a cup of coffee back to our cabin and found Lilly sitting on the balcony. I asked her if she felt like getting out today. She said, "No, maybe tomorrow."

I changed into my swimsuit and headed to the pool deck. I walked around it twice, looking for Erica—she wasn't there. I took the stairs to the uppermost deck, which was filled with lounge chairs and sun worshipers. About half the girls had their bikini tops undone and were lying on their stomachs.

Even though I still hadn't found Erica, I decided this was the group for me and grabbed a lounge chair. I must have fallen asleep, because when I woke up, Erica was lying down on the lounge beside me.

As soon as I got my wits together, I said, "I've been looking everywhere for you."

"You looked like you were sleeping to me. Maybe the search was a dream."

"Funny. How long have you been lying there?"

"I'm not sure. I was in another chair until the sun passed. Then I moved over here. You're looking a little pink. Would you like me to rub some sunscreen on you?"

"Yes!" I replied, maybe a little too enthusiastically.

I laid down on my stomach and Erica started rubbing. Oh my God, that felt so good. She worked her hands into my body, relaxing every muscle she touched. I caught myself just before I dozed off again.

She said, "That's good. Turn over and I'll get the other side."

I rolled over on my back. She began with my legs, then went to my feet, then my arms. This was one of the best massages I'd ever had. She continued rubbing the lotion into my chest and then clapped her hands together. "You're done. Now it's my turn." She handed me the lotion, laid down on her stomach, and undid her top.

I hardly knew where to start. I figured I'd begin with her feet and work my way up. Her bikini bottom was a thong. I wasn't sure how to handle that area, but I knew it definitely needed a thorough coating of sunscreen.

I gently squeezed a little lotion on my hands and started rubbing. After a few minutes, she said, "I'd say you've gotten my buns just fine."

With that, she reconnected her top and turned over. I surveyed her perfect body and decided to start with the feet once again. I worked the thighs especially well. Her arms and her stomach received similar treatment. When I got to her chest, I froze.

She noted my hesitation. "Give me the sunscreen and I'll take care of my boobs."

I've got to admit I enjoyed watching. After the lotion experience, I had an even greater appreciation for Erica. By the time I got back to my cabin, I could think of little else.

As I shut the door, Lilly said, "I'm so glad you're back. You won't believe what happened."

I was worried. "Tell me."

"Daphne came back."

"What time?"

"I'm not sure. Maybe an hour or so after you left."

"You let her in?"

"I know I shouldn't have, but I did."

"Why did you?"

"I'm not sure. She has a kind voice. I almost felt like she hypnotized me."

"What did she do? What did she say?"

"She said she'd brought a pill that would help me feel better."

"A pill?"

"I know. She handed it to me with a bottle of water."

"Surely you didn't take it?"

"I did. Like I said, I almost felt like I was under her spell."

"How did the pill make you feel?"

"All my senses intensified. I felt a heightened connection with everything around me. I experienced a deeper level of feelings than I'd ever thought possible."

"What happened then?"

"She told me to lie down and she rubbed my back and legs."

"You let her do that?"

"I didn't feel I had a choice."

"And then?"

"She rolled me over and kissed me while continuing her massage."

"Oh my God!"

"I know. I couldn't control myself. She touched me in ways I've never been touched before."

"She raped you?"

"No, not rape, totally consensual."

"But you don't know what was in the pill."

"Right."

"It could have been a date rape drug."

"Maybe."

"How do you feel now?"

"I'm a little embarrassed to say."

"Just say it."

"I feel exhilarated."

"That does it. I'm going to find out once and for all who this woman is and what she wants with you."

Lilly relented. "If you must."

I stormed up to the customer service area and asked for the head of security. A man named Thomas said he could help me.

I relayed everything Lilly told me. He asked me to describe Daphne. I told him I'd never seen her. He asked for my cabin number and wanted to meet with Lilly and me later that afternoon. We agreed to four p.m.

Lilly and I were both sitting in our cabin when someone knocked on the door. I checked my watch—four p.m. I opened the door and Thomas came in. He had another officer with him to witness Lilly's statement.

Thomas asked her about the events of the morning in even greater detail than I had. Lilly's memory was still a little foggy. He suggested a blood test to try to determine the nature of the drug. We agreed and he called the dispensary. About ten minutes later, there was another knock at the door.

A nurse came in and drew some of Lilly's blood. Thomas explained their laboratory facilities were limited on board, but they would do a preliminary scan. After that, the sample would be sent to the nearest full-service lab.

Lilly still had a great deal of difficulty trying to describe Daphne. She said her hands and her lips were incredibly gentle. I cringed at the thought.

I invited Lilly to dinner and she said she felt well enough to go. We went to the dining room and I, for one, had a great meal. The best Lilly could do was drink her Coke and pick at her food.

# Chapter Five

That night, Lilly planned to sleep on the balcony again. She asked me to get her a Coke with crushed ice. Lo and behold, who did I see sitting at the bar but Erica.

She wore an exquisite red dress. When our eyes met, she smiled and motioned me over with a wave. I ordered a Corona and told her what happened to Lilly this morning.

She was shocked. "I can't believe something like that could happen on this ship. Did you file a report with ship security?"

I replied, "Yes. They're looking into it."

"With all their resources, they should be able to locate Daphne quickly."

Then she surprised me. She set down her drink and grabbed hold of my hands. "There's something I have to tell you."

She looked down and then back up. Her beautiful blue eyes consumed me. Finally, she said, "The captain is my boyfriend. I'll ask him to look into the investigation and get us any information they may have discovered."

This actually explained a lot. I was sure the captain was extremely busy assuring we reached our destinations safely which was why a beautiful woman like Erica spent so much time alone in the bars at night and tanning during the day. Maybe it even explained her interest in me. Being the captain's girlfriend meant she was alone most of the cruise.

We sat and drank well into the night. The ice in the Coke melted. I was on my fifth or sixth beer. Erica was even more intoxicated.

All of a sudden, without any warning, the ship tilted sharply to the right.

Everything went flying. People, tables, and chairs all flew towards the bar. Liquor bottles fell off shelves. Broken glass covered everything.

Just as quickly as all that happened, the ship straightened back up. Erica grabbed and kissed me. I was drunk enough to go along. After a few minutes, she backed away. "If we were going to sink, I wasn't about to die without you knowing how I felt."

I told her, "I think we're fine."

She looked around, regained her composure and shyly said, "Oh. I thought the ship was going down and that would be the end of us."

I looked around and noticed a number of injured people. Erica and I quickly rushed to their assistance. It was after midnight before all the wounds were bandaged and the debris cleaned up.

I told Erica I was exhausted and going back to my cabin to make sure Lilly was alright. She pulled me towards her and gave me another kiss. "Thanks for being there for me."

I had no idea what she was talking about, but I was anxious to check on Lilly. When I opened the door to our cabin, I was shocked—all the furniture was crammed up against the sliding glass door.

I panicked and threw each piece to the other side of the cabin. I called out for Lilly and heard nothing. I desperately wanted to find her in this pile of debris.

She wasn't there. I pulled back the slider to the balcony. The chair was gone, as well as the mattress and bedding. The naked bedframe was all that remained. I called for Lilly again and looked over the railing.

Chairs, tables, and cushions bobbed in the water. The crew had a massive rescue effort underway. The entire area was brightly lit. Lifeboats cautiously maneuvered through the water. Men and women stood on top of the boats with long poles, trying to find bodies and anyone still alive.

How could something like this happen? This cruise was supposed to be fun—relaxing, enjoyable—not a disaster that almost reached the scale of the *Titanic*.

I was tempted to jump into the water and frantically search for Lilly myself. I knew that would be foolhardy, but leaning over the railing, I felt helpless. My eyes searched the sea from one side to the other, from the edge of the ship to as far away as I could see.

Every now and then, someone on a lifeboat would snag a survivor or a body. All I could do was hope and pray for my dear sweet Lilly.

I momentarily closed my eyes in prayer when I sensed someone standing next to me. I straightened up, somewhat startled. Then, I saw the red dress.

I said, "Erica, what are you doing here?"

"Same as you, hoping against hope they can find all the people they lost overboard."

"What about the captain?"

"He's been relieved of duty and arrested."

"Why?"

"He was at the helm and spotted a large rock outcropping directly in front of the ship. He took manual control and made an abrupt turn. You know the result."

"Did we collide with the rocks?"

"Yes. They're still checking the ship to assess the extent of damage. Even though he averted a head-on collision, I'm told the rocks tore a large gash in the side of the ship. Several compartments are taking on water."

"Are we going to sink?"

"Maybe."

"Good God. I can't believe it." Even with the impending disaster, I had a nagging question. "How did you find my cabin?"

"I overheard you give your name and cabin number to the bartender."

"Are you Lilly's mysterious visitor, Daphne?"

"Of course not. Let's straighten up your room, put on our life jackets and listen for instructions."

Sounded like a good plan to me. We righted all the furniture and set the television back on the counter. We quickly located the ship channel and sat awaiting instructions.

Occasionally, I got up and walked out on the balcony. Few survivors were being found. Now, almost everyone they pulled from the sea was dead.

The first mate came on the public address system. "Ladies and gentlemen, please remain calm and stay in your cabins. We encourage each one of you to put on a life jacket. As you know, we've lost several guests overboard in the abrupt turn to avoid colliding with a rock formation just below the surface.

"We believe we've already rescued all the survivors. As soon as we identify each person, we will call their cabins to let everyone know they're alive. After the ship doctor checks them out, those that are able will be allowed to return to their cabins.

"Even though we avoided a head-on collision, we suffered significant damage to the port side of the ship. We will keep you apprised of the progress of our repairs. At the present time, all ship services are suspended. In consideration of our guests, we are offering free minibar access. Please stand by for further instructions. Thank you."

Erica stood up and took off her life jacket. She said, "These things are unbelievably uncomfortable unless you're floating in the water. How about a beer?"

I wasn't in the mood but reluctantly agreed. She grabbed one for herself as well and sat back down next to me on the couch. "I'm worried sick about Lilly. She sounds like she's such a sweet person. Do you two have any children?"

"We do—a son, Robert, nineteen, and a daughter, Anna, eighteen."

"Hopefully we'll hear from Lilly soon."

We both waited. Around two or three, we fell asleep.

# Chapter Six

Around five a.m., we were rudely awakened by seven short blasts followed by one long blast from the ship's horn. Erica confirmed my worst fear—the blasts signaled us to abandon ship. The noise was deafening. Our anxiety levels were off the charts. We both shook uncontrollably.

The PA system immediately crackled, followed by the first mate's voice. "Ladies and gentlemen, I'm sorry to disturb you, but the ship's status has taken a turn for the worse. We are asking all passengers to put on their life jackets and proceed to their muster stations in a calm and orderly manner. The lifeboats for muster stations four and five were launched for the rescue effort. If either of those was your muster station, please proceed to deck two and follow the crew's instructions."

Erica was still here. "What number is your muster station?"

I replied, "Four."

"Let's use the john, grab some water and snacks and head down to deck two."

Sounded like a plan to me.

Erica hesitated. "What size does Lilly wear?"

I was clueless but found a pair of shorts and a knit top for Erica. She took off the red dress. My heart skipped a beat. All she had on was a pair of tiny lace panties. She quickly got dressed and we were ready to go.

The evacuation was total chaos. The stairs were backed up several decks. People yelled and screamed as they pushed and shoved down the narrow stairways. I thought I lost Erica a couple of times.

With some effort, we finally made our way to deck two, and then onto our lifeboat. We were packed in like sardines. I barely had room to breathe.

Once we were fully loaded and pushed off, a crewmember updated us on the current situation. "The ship is in imminent danger of sinking. There's a giant crack along the port side, and water is pouring in faster than we can pump it out. Right now, we are racing to get far enough away from the ship so it won't pull us under when it sinks."

How could this be happening? And what about sweet Lilly? I had no idea if she was dead or alive. Even though, I was sitting here with the most beautiful woman I could have ever imagined, I was miserable.

The crewmember continued, "We are trying our best to identify any nearby ships and alert them to our dire situation. Maritime law requires any vessel in the vicinity to render aid. We will give you more information as it becomes available."

Erica asked, "Did you see the fog when we boarded the lifeboat?"

"I did. It came in so quickly. I don't remember seeing any fog from the balcony."

"Me neither. That could be a problem."

"How's that?"

"No one can rescue what they can't see."

"But I'm sure most ships have some sort of radar."

"Correct. They'll know we're here, but the rescue is going to be a visual, human-to-human thing."

Just as I gave that some thought, something lifted up our side of the lifeboat as it tore through the fiberglass two seats to my left. This big black thing continued to rip the boat in half. Our half wildly spun and repeatedly slammed against something.

Erica said, "A ship didn't see us and split us in half. When we stop spinning, our half will sink. It may even sink sooner. As soon as you feel water coming up your legs, unbuckle. Then we need to unbuckle as many of these other people as we can."

The violent spinning caused people to throw up. Stomach contents were strewn everywhere.

As we sunk, the spinning slowed down. I unbuckled myself and as many others as I could. The water got deeper and deeper. When it reached my chin, I took a deep breath and swam to the surface.

As soon as my head popped out of the water, I relaxed and looked for the ship that hit our lifeboat. I was concerned that vessel would suck me under and its huge propellers would rip me to shreds.

Fortunately, the ship was long gone. Debris and bodies floated all around me. I frantically looked for Erica. The fog made it difficult to see much of anything.

Someone suddenly grabbed the back of my life jacket and pulled me away from the debris. As soon as I could turn my head, I recognized Erica. I told her I could swim. She let go and suggested we swim as far away from all this commotion as we could.

I had no idea where we were headed or our prospects for rescue. About the time my arms and legs started cramping, Erica stopped swimming. The fog began to clear.

We could just make out the cruise ship in the distance. As we watched, the bow gently slipped under the water and the rest of the ship silently followed. Within seconds the entire vessel was gone. The scene was surreal—so gentle a motion and yet so violent an act.

Erica thought to pull the cord that activated her rescue beacon and flashing red light. I did the same. At that point, we didn't feel there was anything else we could do.

The life jackets kept our heads above water. Somehow, we were both able to fall asleep. We woke up with the sun. Our throats were so parched, we could hardly swallow.

Unbelievable. We were surrounded by water and had nothing to drink. Somewhere along the way we lost the water and snacks we'd taken from the cabin.

We repositioned ourselves with the backs of our heads facing the sun. That was about all we thought we could do. I must have dozed again because I woke up to Erica shaking my arm.

# Part Two

# Rescue

# Chapter Seven

A couple of hundred yards to our right, the ugliest, dirtiest ship I'd ever seen was dead in the water. A group of men lowered an inflatable over the side. As soon as it hit the water, three of them jumped in, started the motor, and chugged towards us.

As they got closer, I realized they were just as ugly and dirty as the boat they came from. They cut the engine just short of us and coasted the rest of the way.

The men yelled in some foreign language. I had no idea what it was.

Erica said, "Russian."

I asked, "Do you understand it?"

"Just a little. My great-grandmother was Russian and that was all she knew. I was a toddler when she died, but I can still remember some. They think I'm beautiful."

I wasn't surprised when they pulled Erica aboard first. To be honest, I didn't know if they intended to rescue me or not.

Erica yelled at them, in English, to pull me into the raft. She said she'd jump back in the water if they didn't get me as well. One of them must have understood. A minute later, I laid on my back in the raft.

I could tell the men talked about Erica on our short trip back to the ship. No big surprise. We climbed up a ladder on the side of the ship and as soon as our feet hit the deck, another man, just as ugly and dirty, hustled us to a storage locker at the rear of the deck.

He unlatched a padlock and opened the door. Two terrified faces stared back at us. The man pushed Erica and me through the door, slammed it shut and locked us in. Everything was pitch black. I couldn't even see the other faces, just inches from my own. The smell was a gut-wrenching combination of dirty ship and dirty Russian. I tried my best not to vomit.

Erica introduced us to the others. They said they were Angelina and Penelope, fellow survivors from our ship. They told us they'd been with their boyfriends in the water and the Russians had just left the men. Not a good sign as far as I was concerned.

I asked them if they'd been offered food or water. They said no. Another bad sign.

After what seemed like forever, the lock unlatched and the door flew open. Four bottles of water were thrown into the locker and the door slammed shut. The lock latched back immediately. We felt around the floor, found the bottles, sipped the water, and waited.

The women were in their early thirties and lived in Naples, Florida. Erica lived in New York City. I told them I lived in Nashville, Tennessee. We each said a little about ourselves. I passed on further conversation and listened for any activity on deck. Erica joined me after a few minutes. Neither woman spoke Russian, so Erica was our only hope of finding out what was happening.

I wasn't the best judge of ship speed, but knew we were moving right along. Erica told me she thought the ship was some sort of deep-sea fishing trawler and that they were probably anxious to deliver their catch.

I asked her for any ideas on likely ports. She suggested Havana or Caracas. Personally, I hoped for Havana. I knew a little Spanish, which would be helpful in either city, but Lilly and I had vacationed in Havana a number of times, so I was particularly familiar with that one.

For the next day and a half, there was no more water, no food, and no bathroom breaks. We all sweated profusely in the metal oven.

Mercifully, the ship finally came to a stop. We knew something was going to happen. None of us had a clue what that would be.

Without warning, the door to the locker flew open. Four men stood at the ready. Each man grabbed one of us and slammed our face against the outside of the locker. They then tied our hands behind our backs.

A few seconds later, a hose turned on and slammed us against the locker again. After a thorough rinse of our backs, we were flipped around for a similar cleansing of our fronts.

The three women were led off while I stood there. All of a sudden, Erica stopped and yelled, "I'm not going anywhere without that man."

One of the Russians ordered in broken English, "Shut up."

She walked up to the man that had spoken and kneed him as hard as she could in the balls. He collapsed to the deck.

Erica then said, "I can be extremely uncooperative."

With that, a compatriot helped the injured man to his feet, grabbed my arm, and threw me towards the group of women. We were led off the ship and down the dock. From what I could see, I thought we were definitely in Havana.

At the end of the dock, we were all shoved into the back of a van, which quickly sped off down a bumpy, curvy road. We flailed around from one side of the van to the other. As soon as I could, I braced myself with my legs. The ladies quickly followed suit.

I suggested we work with each other and try to untie our bindings. Within a few minutes, all our hands were free. The driver's swerves and sudden stops continued to make it difficult to keep our balance, but having our hands free helped cushion our falls.

I encouraged Erica to listen to what the men up front said. Hopefully, it would give us a clue to our fate and possibly help us identify an opportunity to escape. Even though the United States' relationship with Cuba was on the skids, I felt we stood a decent chance of surviving once we got away from these thugs.

# Chapter Eight

As best Erica could tell, we were being taken to some sort of auction. I suggested we would all probably be sold as sex slaves. That prospect helped further motivate our resolve to escape.

As we talked, Penelope managed to open the van's rear door. I took a peek out and saw nothing but trees and bushes. No buildings. We were on a dirt road and I suggested we jump while we could.

Penelope went first, immediately followed by Angelina, Erica, and myself. Fortunately, my Air Force parachute training came back to me. I tucked my body and rolled along the ground.

The truck sped off. No one was any worse for wear. I knew our captors would be back as soon as they realized we were gone.

We all jogged down the road, looking for a path off to the side. Within minutes, we found a driveway, turned, and hauled ass. I told the girls if we saw anyone, we needed to head into the woods.

A large house came into view. Several kids played soccer in front of it. I suggested we keep going. The girls asked why. I said I didn't want to put the kids at risk if our abductors showed up. Also, I didn't know if the occupants of the house would welcome us, arrest us, or shoot us.

I spotted a smaller path off to our left. We walked, took a short break, and walked some more. Each of us was dying of thirst.

Out of nowhere, someone yelled, "Stop." Both my hands shot up into the air. Was it the Russian thugs? The local militia? The police?

I turned my head to the side. All the girls were bent over in silent laughter.

As soon as they saw my face, they laughed out loud.

I lowered my hands and asked, "What's so funny?"

Erica replied, "You."

"Me? I thought someone spotted us."

The laughter died down. "Angelina wanted to show you something."

She stood next to a bush whose branches were heavily laden with berries.

Angelina explained, "I'm a nutritionist. These berries should help relieve our thirst and satisfy our hunger a bit."

We were on them like bees to honey. Soon, the branches were bare. The four of us, on the other hand, had grape-colored stains on our hands, mouths, and clothing.

We took a moment to relax and then resumed our trek. As the sun was setting, I caught a glimpse of water in the distance. I was relieved. Surely we'd find a fisherman willing to give us a ride back to Havana.

When we hit the shoreline, there was a beautiful beach but no sign of anyone. I suggested we continue along the water to put as much distance as we could between ourselves and our captors. No one objected and we slowly headed down the beach.

We walked, took breaks, and walked some more. When we finally decided to called it a day, we couldn't wait to cool off in the water.

Before we jumped in, I asked if anyone had a match or lighter. Between the four of us, we had two matchbooks and one lighter, which we carefully set on a large rock.

We then raced into the surf. After a refreshing swim, we meandered back to the beach.

Erica started picking up dry branches and twigs for a fire. We all joined in. I stacked the wood just so and struck a match. Nothing. Then another and another. The waterlogged matches weren't about to ignite. I grabbed the lighter but doubted it would work either.

A flame—good fortune finally blessed us. I was sure water had seeped into the fuel, but apparently that wasn't the case. Our fire started right up.

We spent the rest of the evening warming up and drying off. When the sun finally dropped below the horizon, I volunteered to be our lookout.

Within minutes, everyone scheduled turns until daybreak.

The girls fell asleep and I entertained myself stoking the fire. Around two, Erica relieved me. I don't think I've ever been so exhausted.

The morning sun breathed new life into us. We scanned the water for possible salvation and spotted teeny-tiny fishing boats far out to sea. That was a good sign, but we'd still have to walk and find some help. We extinguished our fire and trudged along the shore.

As the sun reached its highest point in the sky, we spotted a small shack just off another beach. A woman sat in a chair on the front porch. When she saw us, she said, "*Hola.*" We returned the greeting.

For a minute or two, I spoke with her in what little Spanish I could remember from eighth grade. She looked at me like I was crazy.

Finally, she motioned for me to stop. "*Son gringos?*"

We said, "*Sí.*"

"*Hablan Inglés?*"

"*Sí.*"

"Let's try that."

"Thank you. We were kidnapped by a group of Russian thugs who planned to sell us as sex slaves. We escaped on the way to the auction and are trying to get to Havana."

"I'm so sorry to hear about your troubles. My husband and son will be back later this afternoon and will be happy to take you to Havana. It's less than an hour away by boat.

"You all must be hungry and thirsty. Can I get you something to eat and drink?"

"We would be eternally grateful. Thank you so much."

We had a little pocket money between us and offered to pay for what we'd consumed. She said she'd have no part of that and went on to explain that in Cuba, neighbors helped neighbors. She said life here was difficult and they had to help each other just to get by. We could see that and thanked her profusely.

While we waited on the men to return, we talked with her about our best way to get home. She said without passports, we didn't have many options. She encouraged us to go to the embassy for assistance. We all agreed. What could be easier than that?

# Chapter Nine

Father and son came back midafternoon and unloaded their catch. Mama got to work preparing the fish for the trip to the local market. Papa wanted to leave immediately with us so he could get back before dark.

On the way, he told us the US embassy was on the Malecón, right on the Gulf of Mexico. He would drop us off at the rocks on the sea side of the road and we could climb up to the highway, cross it and enter the building. Sounded easy enough.

When we were close, we noticed a small pier and stairs up to the road. Even better. We docked and got out. The fisherman wouldn't accept payment. We offered our thanks and he immediately left for home.

The sun was setting as we approached a Marine guard at the embassy. We pleaded our case and he let us in. A woman at a reception desk welcomed us to the United States of America. I loved hearing those words after all our trials and tribulations.

The embassy had closed down for the day, but there were a few people on duty that could help us. I still had my billfold. The three women had no identification at all.

I looked the receptionist in the eyes. "My name is Jack Sparrow."

Everyone reacted to that. They immediately pictured Johnny Depp's character in *Pirates of the Caribbean*. My parents had named me long before those movies were made. Once the first one came out, I'd skyrocketed to one of the most popular kids in high school. Most people called me Pirate Jack. I had to admit, I liked it. Aye-aye, matey.

I pulled out my driver's license and handed it to the receptionist. She looked it over and then handed it back to me.

She said, "Passport, please."

I said, "That's why we're here. Our passports were lost at sea."

With that, she reevaluated the four of us. We definitely were a motley crew. She picked up her phone and called security. Four uniformed police officers quickly joined us.

She said to them, "Take these people to preliminary intake and make them comfortable." Then she had an afterthought and turned to us. "Are you thirsty, hungry?"

We all responded yes.

She told the officers, "Take them to the cafeteria first. I'll need to round up the processing crew anyway. When they're done eating and drinking, take them to intake."

We were accompanied to the cafeteria, which was mostly shut down for the evening. They still had a decent selection of drinks as well as pizza, burgers, and the basics.

Even though we'd eaten at the shack by the sea, we were still a little hungry and thirsty. The cafeteria food and drink took care of that. When we were done, the officers escorted us to a small conference room.

A man and a woman stood up as soon as we walked in. They introduced themselves and asked us to make ourselves comfortable.

The woman asked, "Are you all United States citizens?"

We all said we were.

"I'll need you to fill these out with your names, current addresses, birth dates, birthplaces and Social Security numbers."

She gave each of us a pen and a blank form. When we were done, the woman gathered the completed paperwork and left the room.

The man explained what was going to happen. "Our process is straightforward and shouldn't take more than a couple of days. You will be provided accommodations, meals and clothing. We will verify your identities and then begin making each of you a new passport. Your old passports will be canceled as we don't want them getting into the wrong hands and used fraudulently.

"Once you have your new passports, we will transport you to the airport where you will catch a commercial flight back to Washington, D.C. The FBI wants to question you regarding your kidnapping. After that, you'll be free to go wherever you want."

I asked, "Can we check out Havana or are we prisoners here?"

"You are absolutely not prisoners. You're free to leave at any time. However, you will not have a valid passport, and if the Cuban authorities detain you, we won't be able to help. Any other questions?"

There were none. We were shown to our rooms, showered and went to sleep. I woke up sometime the next day, showered again—I didn't know how long it would take to cleanse the filth from my body—then dressed and went to the cafeteria for breakfast.

When I got there, the girls were all at a table drinking coffee. I grabbed a cup and joined them.

I asked, "How is everyone?"

Penelope replied, "Gucci."

I had no idea what that meant and said, "Looks like we're stuck here for the duration."

They agreed. We talked about some of the recreational activities available and planned our day. Erica and I would try to get a tennis court for the afternoon.

By one fifteen, we had our court, rackets and balls. I'd always been a decent player. Erica was probably a little better. We played to a draw after an untold number of games. I felt lucky to get off with that.

# Chapter Ten

On the way back into the embassy building, I walked up to the reception desk and asked if I could make a call back to the States. The gal sitting behind the desk said sure and put the phone on the counter.

Rob answered. "Hello?"

"Hi, Rob, it's Dad."

He dropped the phone and yelled and screamed for Anna. I couldn't make out exactly what he was saying, but I could tell he was excited to hear from me.

Soon, Anna joined him on the phone. She said excitedly, "Dad, you're alive! Oh my God, you're alive! We were so worried about you. When we didn't hear from you right away, we both thought the worst. Where are you?"

"I'm at the embassy in Havana, Cuba."

"That's crazy. I can't imagine how you got there. Put Mom on the line."

This was afraid of that. I replied, "Mom isn't with me. We were separated before we abandoned ship, and I haven't seen her since."

"She's alright, isn't she?"

"I don't know. Have you heard anything from the cruise line?"

"Not recently. Initially, they said you were both missing. I'm so excited you're alive. Rob and I have been worried sick."

"I can imagine. I've been just as worried about Mom."

I didn't want the kids to have to suffer through this alone. "Rob, would you mind calling Aunt Caroline and inviting her to Nashville for a few days?"

Rob agreed to do that. Caroline, who lived in Sarasota, was Lilly's only sister. I felt she needed to be with us. I knew the kids would feel much better with her there as well.

The woman at the reception desk drew a line across her throat. She wanted me to hang up.

"Kids, I have to go. I'll call you when I'm back in the States. I love you both."

In unison, they said, "We love you, Dad."

Reluctantly, I hung up, thanked the lady for the phone, and headed back to my room.

I cleaned up for dinner and enjoyed a romantic meal (only kidding) with the girls in the embassy cafeteria. After that, Erica and I relaxed on the outdoor patio, where we checked out the sights and sounds of Havana.

For me, the Malecón was the lifeblood of the city. Every night, the seaside of the shoreline road was packed with people—talking, playing music, dancing—doing whatever they wanted to do. We were tempted to join them but knew our momentary pleasure could end in long-term disaster.

So, we just kicked back and relaxed. We had purchased a couple of bottles of wine at the embassy commissary and enjoyed savoring that sweet refreshment.

Erica stood up and walked to the railing. I followed and put my arm around her. She rested her head on my shoulder.

After a couple of minutes, she said, "I like it here."

"Me too. Do you think we should stay?"

"Not hardly, but I wouldn't mind experiencing a little of Havana's nightlife."

"Me neither. But we have three problems."

"Which are?"

"One—no passport; two—no visa; and three, no CUCs."

"What are CUCs?"

"That's the Cuban convertible currency. Most places are banned from accepting US dollars. You need to exchange them for CUCs to pay for pretty much anything."

"Where can you do that?"

"Lilly and I always did it at the cruise terminal, but I think you can also do it at banks and hotels."

"No problem, then."

"Just the first two."

"I think I've figured a way to sneak out of here."

"I'm not sure I even want to hear."

"Come on. Jack Sparrow would never shy from any such adventure."

"Jack Sparrow shies from the Cuban justice system, which typically involves no justice at all."

"Think of the stories you could tell your kids."

"Only if we make it out of there, which is doubtful."

# Chapter Eleven

Erica grabbed the bottle of wine we'd opened and headed for the tennis complex. I thought this was a terrible idea but didn't want her to go off by herself, so I followed right behind.

Her escape succeeded and in no time, we strolled along the Malecón. We stopped to enjoy a group playing music and dancing. Erica gracefully moved to the rhythm and I joined her.

We drank, we danced, we laughed and we walked. We ended up at a club at the Hotel Nacional. The band was playing Cuban jazz, the drinks were cold and they took our money.

Once the sun peeked over the horizon, we got one of the '50s cars to take us back to the embassy. I had just enough cash left to cover the short trip. When we walked up to the Marine guards, I'm sure they could tell we were both drunk from a night of imbibing and partying. Thankfully, they let us in anyway.

We were met by the same man that had briefed us the night before last. He was getting off his shift and was pissed.

"I thought you two idiots would find your way back here. Do you have any idea how lucky you both were? You could just as easily be in a Cuban jail right now."

Neither one of us said a word. Our minds were dulled by the alcohol. Plus, what could we say? We were a couple of idiots.

"We have your passports. The van leaves in two hours. Try to clean yourselves up as best you can."

With that, he slapped a passport in each of our hands, turned and left. We put our arms around each other and stumbled to our rooms. The shower helped a little, the coffee a little more. By the time we left for the airport, we were both a little less drunk but figured we'd recover on the flight to D.C. My plan was to sleep all the way. I was sure Erica had similar thoughts.

Penelope and Angelina didn't seem to want to have much to do with us, and I couldn't blame them. We kept to ourselves, boarded the plane, got situated in our seats, and dozed to D.C.

We woke up over Virginia and managed to keep down a light meal. Coca-Cola helped. Erica and I were sitting beside each other, but we probably didn't say two words the entire flight.

When we landed, we were met by FBI agents. They escorted us to our rooms at the Willard and said they would pick us up at eight forty-five the next morning for our debriefing at FBI headquarters.

Erica and I felt much better that night and enjoyed a fabulous meal in the hotel dining room. We spared no expense. I figured the FBI was picking up the tab in exchange for all the valuable information we would be providing them the next day.

We both got up early in the morning, worked out in the hotel gym, cleaned up, and enjoyed a big breakfast with as much coffee as we had time to consume. The car picked us up at eight forty-five, and by nine, we were sitting at a conference table in the Hoover Building.

Agents Jeffries and Henry entered the room. Jeffries explained, "You will all be sworn in and then taken to individual rooms for questioning."

The interrogation room contained coffee, water, juice and breakfast treats. This wasn't nearly as bad as I'd thought it would be. Of course, the questioning hadn't actually begun.

Agent Jeffries interrogated me. "When and where did you meet each of the other women?"

I told him the two stories.

Then he asked, "What is your relationship with Erica Richards?"

We both realized there were few heterosexual men on the planet that would not want to sample her sexual pleasures.

"We're friends."

Jeffries had a hard time believing Erica and I were just friends.

I elaborated, "I'm married and I love my wife. Ever since the collision, I've been devastated. I've always believed Lilly is alive and pray every day she is safe and recovering somewhere. I realize the chances of her survival are slim, but I've never given up hope."

"I apologize for not having any updates on your wife. That said, I have a couple of more questions about you and Erica."

I was pissed. "My relationship with Erica is none of your damned business." I took a minute to regain my composure. "I understood we were here to talk about the kidnapping."

With that, he got down to the meat of the matter—our abduction and ultimate escape. What I thought would take an hour or two lasted all day. We were driven back to the hotel individually as we finished our questioning. I got back about eight p.m. and had a lovely dinner by myself. By then, all I wanted to do was go home, be with my kids and find out about Lilly.

Erica came through the door and joined me about the time I was done. She asked me to stay while she ate. Sure, what the hell did I have to do anyway?

Between bites, she said, "They asked me a lot about you."

"As they did me about you. I'm sure they thought we were having an affair and had possibly done something to Lilly."

"That's the same impression I got."

"I think after a couple of hours, they believed me when I said we were just friends."

"Friends, really?"

"I don't know. We haven't discussed our feelings towards each other."

"That's right. But I feel we've gotten incredibly close over the last few days."

"I agree."

"Right now, there's no one I'd rather be with than you."

I replied, "I appreciate that, but right now, I have a responsibility to take care of my family."

"I understand. I'd be happy to help you anyway I can."

"Thanks, but this one is on me. If you ever need to get in touch, here's all my contact information." I handed her my waterlogged business card.

She read my information and smiled. "Inspirational speaker, impressive. Can I have another card?"

She wrote something on the back of the second card and handed it back. I looked at it and smiled as big as she had. "Supermodel, can't say I'm surprised."

We gave each other a long hug and went our separate ways. I planned on staying in D.C. and seeing what information I could get on Lilly.

When I'd called the kids from Cuba, we weren't able to talk as long as I would have liked. I called them again from my room.

Caroline answered and put me on speaker. They first thing the kids wanted to know was whether I was alright. I said I was fine.

Then Rob asked, "There were pictures of you with three women on the internet. Who were they?"

"They were fellow passengers on the cruise. The four of us were snatched from the sea by a Russian trawler and held prisoner."

Anna said, "We really haven't heard much of your story. All we get are bits and pieces from the press."

I said, "I know. I'll fill you in on everything when I get home. Caroline, do you have any new information on Lilly?"

Caroline answered, "Not really. The cruise line published a list of survivors. Neither you nor Lilly were on it, so we really can't go by that."

"I agree. Any information on the bodies they've recovered?"

Anna broke down in tears. I realized that was an insensitive question, so I quickly said, "Never mind. I'm going to stay in D.C. a day or two and see if I can find out more here. Please call me if you hear anything. I love you guys and will be home soon. Thanks so much, Caroline, for everything you've done. Will you be alright staying another couple of days?"

"No problem. Take care of yourself."

I thought that went as well as could be expected. I'd need to watch what I said in front of the kids. Even though they were both adults, when we talked about their mother, they were still kids.

# Part Three

# Grief

# Chapter Twelve

The next morning, I contacted the cruise line and the Coast Guard. They had a list of bodies that had been recovered and identified. Lilly was not on it.

I asked if there were any unidentified bodies. They said no. Between the cruise line and the State Department, they felt they had everything they needed for preliminary identifications. If they thought they'd found Lilly, they'd be in touch.

I left that afternoon and flew down to Miami so I could be closer to the area of operations. I checked into the Fontainebleau Hotel in Miami Beach.

The next morning, I contacted the Coast Guard again. They told me they recovered a body that could be Lilly and wanted me to go to the Miami morgue first thing the next day.

I was heartbroken. Granted, I knew she probably didn't survive, but I always held on to the slim possibility that she might have. There were a lot of people looking for her the night of the disaster.

And then, the ship had been evacuated and many more boats were in the water, also looking for survivors. I'd always held out hope she survived. Now, for the first time, I was afraid she hadn't. I lay down on my bed and cried. I'm sure I didn't sleep at all that night.

The next morning, I caught a cab to the morgue. There was a lot of activity there. At last count, one hundred and fifty-six passengers died and twenty-one were still unaccounted for. That's a lot of bodies and a lot of anxious and grieving relatives.

They took my name and told me to have a seat. I patiently waited my turn.

About two hours later, someone called for Sparrow. When I stood up and looked around, a young girl was waving at me. She couldn't have been much older than my daughter.

The thought of Anna's mom and my wife on a steel slab was terrifying. I prayed I was man enough to handle it.

The girl told me the procedures and exactly what I could expect. She said normally the bodies would be on gurneys, but due to limited floor space and sheer numbers, the bodies were in storage lockers against the walls.

She said all she needed was a nod when she pulled the sheet back. My legs started to give way. As we walked, tears cascaded down my cheeks. Before she opened the door to the morgue itself, she asked if I was going to be alright. I said I didn't know. She called over an orderly to join us.

I'd never been in a morgue. As soon as she opened the door, I was almost blown over by the burst of cold air. I'd worried about the smell, but there wasn't any. Stainless steel lockers covered the walls from floor to ceiling. Apparently, the locker I was going to view was on the top row. The three of us got on a small lift. The girl was at the controls and we quickly went up so high we all had to duck to avoid hitting the ceiling.

The girl rolled out the top tray. I could see a body covered by a white sheet. I grabbed hold of the railing on the lift. The girl asked again if I was going to be alright. Apparently, I didn't look too well. The orderly grabbed my arm.

She gently took hold of the top of the sheet and slowly pulled it back. I saw the hair first, red. Then, I saw the eyebrows, also red. I jumped when I saw the blue eyes wide open and staring into nothingness. I knew right then—this was Lilly.

I jerked my head and came to. The orderly was holding smelling salts below my nose. I must have passed out. Apparently, he carried me to a chair outside the doors to the morgue.

The girl was extremely considerate and gave me several minutes to recover. Finally, she asked, "Was the body you saw your wife, Lilly Sparrow?"

I answered, "Yes," and almost passed out a second time. Back came the smelling salts to rescue me before I totally lost consciousness.

After a while, I was helped from the facility into a cab. A representative from the cruise line rode back with me and got me safely into my room. I greatly appreciated their consideration. I knew I had to call Caroline and the kids, but I fell asleep before I was fully functioning again.

# Chapter Thirteen

The next morning, I had breakfast and coffee and thought about how I'd tell the kids. I suddenly realized this was something I could only do in person. I hustled back to my room, packed, checked out, and got a cab to the airport. I made the airline reservation from the taxi.

My flight was scheduled to leave in two hours. While I was waiting, I called Erica to tell her about Lilly. She sounded almost as devastated as I felt. I was surprised. I had expected her sympathy, but her grief went way beyond that. Just then, they announced my flight was boarding. I quickly said goodbye and headed to the gate.

The flight home went by faster than expected. I was in no hurry to tell the kids their mom died. When the cab pulled up to my house, I still didn't know exactly what I'd say.

Everyone was as overjoyed to see me as I was to see them. After hugs and kisses all around, we settled down in the living room.

My eyes traveled from Caroline to Anna to Rob and back again. Suddenly, the weight of Lilly's death overpowered me. I totally broke down and tears flooded my face.

At that point, everyone realized the truth and we became a chorus of crying and sighs. We stood up and hugged, trying to console each other. After about twenty minutes, everyone regained a small amount of composure and we sat back down.

I told the kids and Caroline everything that had happened on the cruise. The only things I left out were the parts with Erica and Daphne. I figured they had enough to deal with already.

I then told them about the evacuation, the collision, my survival, the Russian fishing trawler, our abduction, and eventual escape. Then, the trip from Cuba to Washington, and finally I got to Miami. This was the part I feared the most. I gave everyone an overview of what happened there.

When I described identifying the body, we all broke down again. I took a deep breath—I knew we somehow needed to get through all this together.

Once the crying turned to whimpers, we continued our conversation. Rob and Anna wanted to know what was going to happen. I said Caroline and I would make the funeral arrangements, that Lilly and I had purchased two cemetery plots, and she would be buried in one and eventually they could put me to rest in the other.

I was so thankful to have this much behind me. I knew it wasn't going to be easy, but it was even more difficult than I feared. I planned to call our minister the next morning and get his recommendation on funeral homes.

The next day, Reverend Fischer gave me a name and I arranged to have the body transported. That sounds way too impersonal. This was Lilly, not some inanimate object. This was an amazing person—that I loved, that I'd shared my life with, that had given birth to our two beautiful children.

I arranged to transport Lilly—not a body, but a real, beautiful person. I was determined to insist that everyone refer to her by name. Anything else would be unforgivable in my opinion.

An airplane was taking Lilly to Nashville. I flew back to Miami and was determined to be on that plane. I rode in the hearse from the airport to the funeral home. I made sure everyone gave Lilly the respect and consideration she deserved.

When I got home, I told Caroline she could go home if she wanted. She insisted on staying. Together, we planned the funeral and the internment. She called all the other relatives and our close friends.

I didn't think I could handle all those people right now. Hopefully, I'd be more comfortable when we all were face-to-face in a few days.

I talked with the kids and we decided to suggest donations to the Legal Aid Society in lieu of flowers. We all knew that's what Lilly would have wanted.

The society provided us with a list of donors. I was surprised to see a $10,000 gift from Erica Richards. I texted her a personal thank you. She replied she was overwhelmed with sadness when she read of Lilly's passing online.

Online? I'd called her. Now that I thought about that conversation, the woman that answered her phone knew Lilly but didn't sound like Erica. How could that possibly be?

Caroline represented the family at the viewing. And then, the day of the services arrived. Reverend Fischer would be officiating and I'd also be speaking.

Funny, I spoke for a living—often in front of hundreds of people—and I never thought anything about it. But today, I was shaking in my boots. I knew it was all emotion but was afraid I wouldn't be able to speak at all.

We were seated in the front pew. The pallbearers escorted Lilly down the aisle. I bowed my head and said a short prayer that the Lord would give me the strength I needed to praise Lilly's incredible life.

Reverend Fischer's eulogy touched my heart. He'd known us for almost twenty years. He christened both the children when they were infants. He renewed our vows, in this very church, one short year ago. And then, my world turned upside down.

# Chapter Fourteen

Reverend Fischer finished and motioned for me to come to the pulpit. I felt like I was glued to the pew. He sensed my problem, walked over to me, and helped me up. I was alright after that.

Standing behind the pulpit was an entirely new experience for me. I was surprised how many people were here. I recognized relatives and friends from as far away as Alaska.

I found the words. "Thank you all so much for showing your love and support for Lilly."

I paused for a minute and looked at the large stained-glass window above the choir balcony. The sun illuminated every colorful pane. Jesus was sitting there with his hands out, palms up.

Head down, I added, "Thank you, Jesus, for the love and strength you've given my family in this most trying time."

I looked up into the eyes of the anxious mourners. "Lilly and I met in law school at the University of Michigan. I remember it like it was yesterday. We both lived in the quaint Law Quad. Lilly loved the law.

"She practiced law her entire life. As most of you know, she focused on the downtrodden and disadvantaged. People she thought society had all but forgotten.

"There were no enormous financial settlements; no highly acclaimed court appearances. She did it for the people. Their struggles, and the extent to which she could help, warmed her heart. That was all the reward she needed.

"I got my degree but never sat for the bar. I sought to help people in an entirely different way. I don't know where Lilly got the time or the energy, but she was always there when I needed her. When I had self-doubts, when failure seemed much more likely than success, she supported and encouraged me until I could make it on my own.

"And her life was about so much more. She was so excited to bring Robert and Anna into the world. No mother ever gave more thought to the values she taught her children, to the principles she instilled in them, and to their relationships with others and with our Lord, Jesus Christ.

"We are all so thankful for the many years we shared with Lilly. She blessed and elevated our lives. Thank you, beautiful."

I felt like collapsing on the spot but somehow stumbled back to the pew. Reverend Fischer caught me before I fell down.

The kids spoke. Caroline and Lilly's brother spoke. Her best friend, Silvia, had many kind words to say. This was truly a heartwarming celebration.

I knew the internment would be the most difficult part of the day. For me, this was joy, that was grief. This was celebrating a glorious life, that was saying goodbye.

Before I knew it, we were standing at the grave site. Only family and Lilly's closest friends were here. The minister recited the "Twenty-Third Psalm" and gave us all words of comfort. Flowers were placed on the casket, and each and every person told us how sorry they were for our loss.

Except for one. She was standing on the other side of the casket. Her body was shaking. She was crying and wailing.

Rob asked me, "Who is that?"

I replied, "I don't know but I'm going to find out. I'll meet you in the limo in a few minutes."

I walked around the casket and gently took the woman's elbow. I said, "Thank you for coming. I'm Jack Sparrow, Lilly's husband."

She had blond hair up in a bun with a small black hat, a veil across her face, and wore a stylish black dress. She also had sunglasses on. She took a deep breath and held out her hand. "I'm Daphne Erwin."

I thought my head was going to explode. "Daphne, from the ship? What the hell are you doing here?"

She said, "Calm down, you're making a scene."

"Don't begin to think you can tell me what to do. I should have you arrested."

"For what, loving Lilly?"

"Love? What the hell are you talking about?"

"I loved Lilly and Lilly loved me."

"That's ridiculous. Lilly said you raped her."

"We made love. Many times. I'd never met anyone like Lilly."

"You need to leave right now and I never want to see you again. You better never mention Lilly's name or I will have you arrested. Now get the hell out of here."

With that, I gave her a little push. She lost her footing and fell to the ground.

I took a deep breath, turned, walked back to the limo, and told the driver to get out of here as quickly as he could. He gunned it.

Rob asked, "What was that all about, Dad?"

"Nothing."

"I don't think 'nothing' is going to hack it. Who was she?"

"A woman from the cruise."

"She looks quite beautiful."

"She's an evil monster."

"What happened, Dad?"

"I don't care to talk about it now. If you'll give me some time, I'll try to fill you in on all the details. Until then, I don't want to even think about it."

"Fair enough. New subject. Do you remember that picture of you and the three women from the cruise? One of those women looked like Erica Richards."

"She was. How do you know her?"

"I don't, but Erica Richards is one of the most famous supermodels in the world. She's been in the *Sports Illustrated* Swimsuit Edition three times. She was even on the cover once."

"She did look good in a bikini, but I don't want to talk about her now either."

"Fair enough. Maybe later."

"Maybe."

# Chapter Fifteen

A couple of days passed. Caroline went home. Rob and Anna needed to get back to college. I offered to fly them the next day. I had an old six-passenger Cessna I'd been flying since my speaking business required too much travel for commercial aviation to work—I'd say for about twelve years. Rob had his pilot license as well.

We planned to drop Anna off first at Brown University in Providence, Rhode Island. Rob and I would then fly to Duke in Durham, North Carolina. Once we reached cruise altitude and engaged the autopilot, Rob felt the time was right.

He said, "We all miss Mom and it will take years for us to come to terms with her loss. I understand and accept that. However, as soon as I get back to campus, I know I'm going to be bombarded with questions about you and Erica Richards. I'm surprised the press hasn't been hounding you already. To say she's a hot number would be a gross understatement."

"I agree, but there's not much to tell."

Rob rolled his eyes.

I ignored him and continued, "Erica was the captain's girlfriend. As such, she hung out in the bar a lot by herself. I started talking with her. That's what we were doing when the ship swerved to miss the rocks. The turn was violent and everyone fell to the ground. I rushed off to see if Mom was alright. Erica followed me. I have no idea why. She helped me look for Mom.

"We evacuated the ship together and were rescued together. I'm sure she's back with the captain and hasn't given me another thought. End of story."

Rob had more questions, but eventually he let the issue go.

I was relieved. I didn't feel I could tell him the truth. Erica hadn't called since we'd parted ways in D.C. I had no idea where our relationship stood but knew I'd talk with her eventually.

I had a hard time telling Rob goodbye. I stayed in Durham a couple of days and we ate at most of his favorite restaurants.

The local hamburger place served the best burger ever. The owner was a little quirky and wouldn't let you put ketchup on the burger. Ketchup on fries was allowed. He also wanted you to eat the burger just like he made it. If you didn't want one item on the burger, he'd give you a hard time. At the end of the day, the burger was worth the hassle. Over time, the owner became one of the things I liked best about the place. We made a point to eat there every time I was in town.

The flight back to Nashville was quiet. Even though I knew Lilly was gone, much of the time it felt like she was still with me. She was my biggest fan and an integral part of my success. We'd built my business together, as a team.

I offered two basic workshops—one on goal setting and the other on time management. Each was essential to the other. Sometimes I'd do a motivational talk at a sales conference or to other business groups.

I practiced what I preached and applied all the principles I espoused to my own life. They gave me a constant direction, a singular purpose. Now more than ever, that was what I needed.

There were no other women in my life. The only woman I could think about was Lilly. She was never far from my thoughts. She gave me a great deal of comfort and made my daily activities much easier.

I had no idea what it was like for other widowers, but I felt I was handling my loss as well as I could. Life went on and I went on as well. Sure, some would say I immersed myself in my work, and maybe I did. But I never thought that was a bad thing.

After a few months, it was time to pick up the kids for the summer. This trip, I planned to land at Durham first and get Rob. My plane was large enough to accommodate as much stuff as he cared to bring home.

Rob picked me up, we grabbed a burger at our special place, and headed back to the airfield. As we loaded the plane, Rob said, "I've got something for you," and handed me a copy of *Maxim* magazine.

I gave it back to him. "No, thanks. I'm doing fine without the thought of alluring women."

"Not that, Dad. You need to read the interview."

"Sorry, son. I'm just not that interested. I'd rather focus on positive, inspiring things."

He said, "Okay," and headed towards a trash can.

I had second thoughts and asked, "Who's being interviewed?"

"Oh, no one special—just Erica Richards."

"Hold on a second, Rob. Bring that back. What does she have to say?"

"You know, just the usual—abandoning the ship, collision at sea, survival—pretty routine stuff."

"I'd like to read that."

"I thought you would. This issue is the first of a three-part interview with Erica."

I sat down on the airplane steps and read. She mentioned she was with a man she called John. She then described in intimate detail everything that happened to us, including her thoughts. Of course, at the time, I didn't know what she was thinking.

I was surprised she made it seem more like I'd saved her rather than the truth—that she rescued me. I was sure that was a minor concession to *Maxim*'s readership—feeding their own male superhero, macho-man image.

This portion of the interview ended when we both floated by ourselves in the vast Caribbean. We would be forlorn until next month's issue. I quickly checked the date on the cover—this month and year. I'd have to wait at least a couple of weeks for the next installment. I handed the magazine back to Rob.

He said, "That was you, Dad. Right?"

"It was me, but things didn't happen exactly as she portrays."

"What really happened? You've never told me."

"Fair enough. Let's close up the plane and get in the air for Providence. I can tell you on the way."

# Chapter Sixteen

Once we reached cruise altitude and I set the autopilot, I turned to Rob. "The basic sequence of events is accurate. The only thing that isn't quite true is that she saved me rather than me saving her. She told me what to do every step of the way. Since it was all new to me, I followed her instructions exactly."

"Wasn't this new to her as well?"

"Probably, but she sounded like she knew what she was talking about. And everything worked out as well as could be expected."

"The *Maxim* version makes you sound like the hero."

"I don't mind that. I'm surprised she was so generous with her praise."

"Maybe she has feelings for you and is trying to make you sound like the kind of man she'd fall in love with."

"I doubt that." *But, it could be possible.*

"I'm sure it wasn't all her."

"I hate to shatter your image of me, but it was."

"Can I tell my friends that John is you?"

"Why not? I'm sure word will get out before the next issue hits the newsstands anyway."

"Cool."

"Right, cool."

I asked Rob if he wanted to take the landing and he quickly agreed. I gave him control of the aircraft.

Over the last six months, I'd seldom thought about Erica. She hadn't called or made any effort to get in touch with me. I thought I never really had a chance with her. I was sure thousands, maybe millions, of guys were interested in Erica Richards. I couldn't imagine what she'd see in me.

Rob took the landing in Providence, we picked up Anna and her stuff, and departed for Nashville. As soon as we leveled off, Rob handed her the magazine.

Anna said, "No, thanks. That trash is more for losers like you."

"Thanks, sis. I'm glad you hold me in such high regard. Maybe you can overlook the cover, the articles, and the photos and bring yourself to read the interview."

"Why would I want to do that?"

"Oh, I don't know. Maybe because the interview is with Erica Richards describing her ordeal at sea. The man she calls John is Dad."

"Give me that."

Anna didn't say another word for twenty minutes. Her expressions said it all. When she was done reading, she handed it back to Rob.

She looked at me. "Dad, you're a hero."

I replied, "Not hardly. Erica was the hero. But it makes a better story the way she presented it."

"Why would she do that?"

"I don't know. Could be modesty, chivalry, believability—who knows?"

"This should help your business."

"I don't know about that. I'll definitely have my fifteen minutes of fame and will need to allow some time for the press. I don't know if it's going to help my business that much—we'll just have to see."

"What about you and Erica?"

"There is no me and Erica. I haven't talked with her since we said goodbye in D.C. over six months ago."

"I'm sorry to tell you, Dad, but after reading the interview, I've got to say there's definitely a you and Erica."

"We'll see about that." And we certainly did.

# Chapter Seventeen

The rest of the flight back to Nashville was uneventful; the drive home, routine. But as soon as we turned onto our street, we saw the satellite trucks and horde of reporters in our front yard.

I decided to drive by and get a couple of hotel rooms until I could figure this whole thing out. My company had used a public relations firm in the past, and I thought I'd contact them for some guidance. That was the best call I ever made.

Emily Ashford, their media representative, was already at the hotel when we arrived. She suggested we all talk in the hotel dining room. The kids and I were hungry anyway, so that would work out great.

We all ordered a late dinner, Emily had coffee. She asked me to fill her in on the situation. I was still talking when dessert arrived. I wrapped up as my coffee was set down on the table.

Emily took a copy of *Maxim* out of her bag and set it on the table. She began, "The key with this type of revelation is to get ahead of it. Do you have any idea where all this is going?"

"Clueless."

"*Maxim*'s objective is to sell magazines. Erica wants positive media coverage. What do you want?"

"That's easy. I'd have to say positive media coverage as well."

"Since you and Erica seem to have the same objective, I think the best response would be a joint press conference, probably in New York City. Are you able to get in touch with her?"

"I think so. Let me see if I still have her information."

I knew right where it was in my billfold. I'd been carrying it everywhere I went for the last six months. I'm not sure why, but it was always there if I needed it. I handed the card to Emily.

She looked at it and handed it back. "Would you text or call her and get the name of her media representative for me? I'd like to coordinate the press conference directly with him or her."

"Sure."

I thought for a minute—text or call? Texting was a fairly impersonal way to get information. A call would open us up to much more conversation. Although that wouldn't necessarily be a bad thing, now was definitely not the right time.

I texted and told her how much I'd enjoyed the first installment of her interview. I went on to mention my press challenges and that I'd hired a media rep. I said she'd like to meet with her media rep and coordinate a joint press conference. I asked for her media rep's contact info and ended by saying I was looking forward to talking with her soon."

As quickly as I sent the message, my phone rang. It was Erica.

She said, "How's this for soon?"

"Great. How have you been?"

"Busy, and you?"

"Same."

"I scanned your text—it was way too long. You need to get Rob or Anna to teach you textspeak."

"What's that?"

"Just ask them. In the meantime, we need to figure how best to deal with the press. I'll have my media rep, Patsy Herrington, text you her contact info and you can give it to your rep. Can't wait to get together. Bye."

She hung up before I could say goodbye. She really was busy. Seconds later I got a text with Patsy's contact info. I showed it to Emily and she gave Patsy a call.

They scheduled a joint press conference for ten a.m. the day after tomorrow at the Plaza Hotel in New York City. Emily suggested I fly up there with the kids in the morning. She'd drive by the house and update the press.

Tomorrow, she'd fly to New York as well. I told her we had lots of room on our plane and invited her to travel with us. She was hesitant at first but ultimately consented. We agreed to meet at the airport the next morning at eleven. I called to have the plane refueled and ready to go.

Before we left, I asked Anna to teach me textspeak. I was a quick learner and was totally ready for Erica's text the next morning.

*when do u land*
*late aft*
*dinner @ my place*
*have the kids + Emily*
*4*
*y*
*i'll invite Patsy—bus mtg—lol*
*big group*
*chef can handle*
*dinner @ 7*
*8*
*k—address*

Erica had a penthouse on Central Park. Sounded amazing. I let everyone know about dinner. A cheer went up. The kids could hardly wait.

# Chapter Eighteen

Erica sent a car to pick us up at the hotel. The top floors of her building disappeared into the clouds. The doorman led us to her private elevator, which took us directly to her penthouse. She greeted us as the elevator doors opened.

Erica and I hugged like two long lost lovers. She took my breath away. After I recovered, I introduced Emily and the kids and she introduced Patsy. A grand tour of his high-rise palace followed. When we got back to the living room, she offered us drinks.

Rob asked, "Do you have the entire floor?"

Erica replied, "No, just the half facing the park. I love all the trees, gardens and beautiful lawns. It reminds me of home."

I asked, "And where's that?"

"I'm surprised you don't know—Brunswick, Maine."

"Former home of the P-3."

"And Erica Richards."

The media ladies huddled, Erica and I talked, and the kids took in the grandeur of the place. After dinner, Erica suggested the two of us go out on the balcony. The ladies went to the living room to continue planning for the press conference. The chef took the kids into the kitchen for a cooking demonstration.

Once we were alone, Erica asked, "How are you doing?"

"I can't say it's been easy, but I think I'm doing as well as could be expected."

"I've missed you."

I almost dropped my cognac over the railing. "Really?"

"Yes, really. Why are you so surprised?"

"I imagined you'd be fending off guys right and left. I didn't think you'd have the time or inclination to think about me."

"Well, I did. You need to remember that under the glamour and glitz, I'm just a girl."

"I felt that when we met and during our crazy struggle to survive. We were as close as two people could ever be. But since then, it's almost like we're on different planets."

"I wanted to call, but I knew you needed time to heal."

"Thank you. I'm happy we're here now."

Erica smiled, set down her cognac and put her arms around me. Our lips met and she kissed me like no one has ever kissed me before. I'm not sure how long we stayed lip-locked, but after a while, someone knocked on the sliding glass door and we both straightened up.

Emily said, "We need to discuss strategy for tomorrow's press conference."

We both went back inside. This time, we held hands when we walked. We sat down on the sofa right next to each other.

Emily gave me copies of the next two installments of the *Maxim* interview. "Read this prior to the press conference. Patsy and I have agreed you should stick to the story exactly as Erica has told it."

I replied, "I'm fine with that, being the hero after all."

Emily continued, "We need to know about you and Erica's relationship."

By this time, the kids had rejoined us and they were as curious as everyone else.

Erica took that one. "During our ordeal, we had developed a strong personal connection. Jack and I haven't spoken since then. Jack's wife had passed and I felt he needed time to come to terms with his loss. We were reunited for the first time at dinner last night. That's the extent of our relationship."

Patsy asked, "You're not going to budge from that response?"

"No. What do you think, Jack?"

"I'm comfortable with that."

We talked a few more minutes and called it a night. The kids were all questions when we got in the car to go back to the Plaza.

"Do you love her?" "Are we moving to New York?" "Does she love you?" And on and on and on.

I said, "The answer to all your questions is no."

Anna pointed out, "But you kissed her."

Rob added, "For a very long time."

"No comment."

Rob persisted, "Come on, Dad. Level with us."

"You sound excited."

"I am. She's unbelievable."

"I know. We'll just have to see what happens as time goes on."

Anna said, "Dad, we both think it's time."

"For what?"

"For you to move on. For you to live your life. For you to date."

"Thanks, kids. I'm glad I have your permission."

Rob said, "You have our encouragement. Good luck, old man."

"Who are you calling 'old man'?"

"Seriously?"

And with that, we all laughed and put the subject behind us. I knew it wouldn't stay there for long, but I also couldn't imagine I had a chance with Erica. Time would tell.

Once we got back to the hotel and Emily went to her room, Rob had a question. We all sat down in our parlor.

He said, "We talked with Chef Louie, spelled L-o-u-i-s, tonight."

I asked, "Who's that?"

"Erica's chef."

"And?"

"He mentioned a name I was familiar with but couldn't place. I thought you might know."

"What's the name?"

"Daphne Erwin."

"Oh God, that was the psycho at your mom's funeral."

"Right. I remember now."

"What did he say about her?"

"He said he also cooked for her when she hosted dinner parties."

"She must live in New York, then."

"I'd say so."

There wasn't much more to say. Daphne was a terrifying memory and I hoped we'd never run into her again. As I soon found out, that was not to be.

# Chapter Nineteen

The press conference was a much larger event than I expected. We had it in the ballroom at the Plaza. Two chairs with microphones were set up on a small platform at the front. Hundreds of chairs faced them. More microphones were scattered throughout the hall. Cameramen and photographers each had their separate sections so they wouldn't interfere with one another.

*Maxim* would definitely get some mileage out of this publicity. They undoubtedly printed extra copies of their two upcoming issues. Erica had told me she would be on the cover of the next issue. I thought, *As long as she keeps her clothes on, I'm happy for her.*

The *Maxim* CEO opened by saying what an important part of his magazine the interviews had always been. He talked about some of the most well-known interviews over the years. Then he got to Erica's story. He found it gripping, exciting, spell-binding and fascinating to read. I was thinking, *You should have lived it. The story is nothing compared to the actual experience.*

And with that came the flood of questions. Some asked about what had happened, but most wanted to know about our relationship, then and now. I relived the events of Lilly going overboard, the search, the recovery, and eventual funeral. I left out the part about Daphne Erwin.

I emphasized that Erica and I hadn't talked since we'd parted in D.C. until the day before yesterday. To be honest, most reporters were much more interested in what Erica had to say. She pretty well took over the press conference at that point.

The questioning lasted two hours before Patsy put an end to it. Erica invited me and the kids over to her place for a late lunch. She figured it would be our best chance to escape the press and we agreed.

Our lunch was much more relaxed than our dinner the evening before. After our meal, Chef Louis wanted the kids to help him prepare for tonight's dinner. That gave me and Erica a chance to continue our conversation from the night before.

As soon as the kitchen door shut, she put her wine on the coffee table and scooted next to me. She then put her hands on my face and kissed me. Fine by me, although I had my doubts this was going anywhere.

The kissing went on a lot longer than I had expected. Much more and we'd need to head to the bedroom. When she was done, she said, "I hope this isn't the last time we see each other."

"I feel the same way. Maybe, we can hook up while I'm traveling."

"That's a great idea. Plus, you know you've always got a place to stay in the city."

"As do you in Franklin, Tennessee." I couldn't imagine what she'd think about my place in Franklin. It wasn't much compared to her digs here.

"Where is Franklin?"

"About thirty minutes south of Nashville. That's where I live. My office is in Nashville."

"I'd love to spend some time there but mostly I just want to be with you."

"Your welcome any time. By the way, you won't believe who was at Lilly's funeral."

"Who?"

"Daphne Erwin."

"How did she even know about the services?"

"I have no idea. I didn't realize she was there until everyone else left."

"What did she say?"

"That she loved Lilly and that Lilly loved her."

"That's disturbing."

"I agree. To top it off, she was overcome with grief."

"She meant it, then?"

"I believe she did in her own twisted mind."

"What did you tell her?"

"I told her I never wanted to see her again."

"That could be a problem."

"How so?"

"The other penthouse on this floor, the one facing the city, belongs to Daphne Erwin."

I was so shocked I couldn't speak. Finally, I managed to say the obvious, "Are you kidding me?"

"No. She moved in a couple of months ago. I wouldn't have even known it was her, except Chef Louie helps her out with some of her dinner parties."

"Has she ever invited you?"

"No. And I doubt she ever will."

"Are these units connected?"

"Not as such, but we do share two emergency stairways. One door is at the east end of my unit and the other is at the west end."

"That's so odd she moved here. Do you think she'd ever do anything to harm you?"

"She'd better never try. Over the years, I've learned a number of personal defense techniques. You wouldn't believe the number of creeps who tried to take advantage of me."

"I'm not surprised, but I'm sorry to hear that."

"Don't be. Now, where were we?"

She grabbed my shoulders and kissed me again. I know I've said this already, but this woman could kiss like no one I'd ever known. I didn't think I'd ever get tired of it.

Just as Erica was untucking my shirt, the kids came back out. Rob cleared his throat. We straightened up, but I'm sure we were both a mess. My shirt, our hair, Erica's makeup—oh well, Rob and Anna were adults now. They shouldn't have been too shocked.

The next day, we flew home. I got back into the routine of my business and the kids enjoyed a little time off.

# Part Four

# Love

# Chapter Twenty

The summer flew by. The occasional reporter called—generally right after a new issue of *Maxim* hit the newsstand. I'd already read the last two installments of the interview, so there was nothing surprising to me. Rob and Anna had a number of questions for me as well, which I answered as well as I could.

I hadn't heard a word from Erica. I shouldn't be too surprised, I hadn't called her either.

Rob left early for the fall semester at Duke. Before his freshman year, he participated in a community service program. This year, he was going to be a youth leader for that same program. I encouraged him to do it, but I also knew his real motivation—he wanted to check out the freshman babes before the rest of the upperclassmen arrived. I couldn't say I blamed him. I was sure I would have done the same thing at his age.

Anna wanted to go with some girlfriends to New York City for a few days before her school started. I asked Caroline to go along as a chaperone and she was as excited as the girls. I thought to call Erica and see if she had any recommendations on things they might enjoy doing.

I was surprised she was home and recognized my voice.

She said, "I was wondering when you'd get around to calling me."

"I think about you all the time, but I also know how busy you are and didn't want to burden you with a lot of phone calls."

"Come on."

"Right. I may be just a little shy around you."

"That I can believe. I've missed you."

"And I've missed you. How have you been?"

"A little lonely."

"Let's see what we can do to change that."

"I'm up for anything."

*Am I the luckiest guy on the planet or what?* "What's your schedule look like next week?"

"I'm leaving for Cuba in the morning."

"Okay. What about the week after that?"

"I've got a better idea. Why don't you come to Cuba with me?"

"I didn't think Americans could generally go there."

"They can't. This is under a special agreement between the State Department and the Cuban government. I'll be down there ten days for a photo shoot."

"Let me look at my schedule," I said as I pulled up my calendar on the phone. "I could go for six days starting this Saturday. Would that work?"

"I can't think of anything that would make me happier."

"Great. What do I need to do?"

"Just pack. I'll have my assistant take care of everything else. Is that alright?"

It was amazing. I loved Cuba and I really liked Erica. What more could I ask for? "Works for me."

"Can't wait. I'll meet you at the airport in Havana Saturday. This is going to be so much fun. Thanks for making me the happiest girl in the world."

"You'll be with the happiest guy, so we should have a blast."

"Great. Start packing."

"Oh, I almost forgot."

"What's that?"

"Anna is coming to the city tomorrow with Caroline and two friends for a few days. Any recommendations on shows they should see or things they should do?"

"I'm sorry I'll miss her. How about this? Anna, her aunt, and friends can stay in my condo. Chef Louie should be here, as will the maid and butler. She'll love it."

"That's kind of you, but we couldn't impose like that."

"Hey, you're almost family. There's no imposition with family. I'll email you a list of shows and activities and you can pass it on if you don't mind."

"Not at all. You're the best, Erica."

"Thanks. I can't wait until Saturday."

"Me neither. Take care."

Caroline, Anna, and her two girlfriends were not going to believe this. I couldn't wait to tell them. Caroline was already here. She and Anna were out picking up last-minute supplies for their trip. The girls' flight left first thing in the morning.

As soon as they got home, I told them, "You're going to have to cancel your hotel reservations for New York."

Anna protested. "What? Are you serious?"

I quickly answered, "No—well, yes, but it's good news."

"How could this be good news?"

"Because I talked with Erica. She said she's sorry she'll be out of town while you're there. That being said, she insists you all stay at her place."

Anna had been there, so she knew exactly how big a deal this was. She screamed. Caroline smiled. Anna immediately told Caroline how luxurious and large this penthouse was. At that point, I didn't know who was more excited. When I told them the chef, maid, and butler were included, their jubilation went through the roof. You'd have thought they were both teenagers.

I also let them know I was going with Erica to Cuba for a few days. No excitement there at all. I knew Rob would react differently. The next morning, the girls were off and I got everything in order for my trip.

Erica left for Cuba about the same time the girls left for New York. Her friends were overjoyed when Anna told them about staying at Erica's. They all knew who Erica was and were blown away by the thought of staying at her place.

Their flight was uneventful. The girls grabbed two Ubers from La Guardia and arrived at Erica's building within an hour. The doorman welcomed them and held the massive front door open so they could enter the spacious lobby.

Erica's butler, Oliver, had come down for their bags and told them to go on ahead. Chef Louis would greet them upstairs.

When the elevator doors opened to the penthouse, the opulence blew them away. After the initial oohs and ahhs, Anna gave everyone a quick tour. Altogether, there were four of them for three bedrooms. Since two bedrooms had two beds, the accommodations would work out fine.

Chief Louis announced he would be working next door tonight, preparing a large meal for a dinner party there. Oliver would bring meals over for the girls. Everyone was pleased, especially since they were all a little tired from the trip.

That evening, they all chose their seats at the exquisite dining room table. Oliver poured the wine and served the appetizers. Caroline said the girls could drink the wine but put a two-glass limit on each of them.

The main course rivaled dinner at the most exclusive New York restaurant. Dessert was just as sumptuous. Oliver opened the connecting doors to the other condo to facilitate retrieving the serving and dinner pieces.

# Chapter Twenty-One

The girls could hear the laughter and the jazz ensemble from the party. Oliver noted their interest and said, "You all are invited to join the party next door if you like."

They screamed with excitement and charged into their rooms to change into something more appropriate. Caroline had specific instructions for all the girls—no drinking alcohol and no leaving with any men. Everyone agreed to those terms.

Oliver led them through the two doors. This condo was as exquisite as Erica's. The only difference was the city view as opposed to the park view. Anna preferred the city lights herself, but the park was nice during the day.

She ordered a ginger ale and sat down to enjoy the music. She was surprised there were so many women here and so few men. Oh well, she was more interested in the jazz quartet anyway.

Caroline was hitting the bottle pretty heavily, ignoring her advice to the girls. After an hour or so, Caroline was getting a little out of control. The two other girls were a little bored, so they volunteered to take her back to Erica's. Anna wanted to stay a while longer. She was loving the jazz rhymes.

A woman sat down next to her and the two laughed and talked. Anna's glass was almost empty and the woman volunteered to get her something a little stronger. Anna agreed and minutes later was sipping a piña colada. She could hardly taste the alcohol.

The more she talked with her new friend, the closer the women got. Eventually, the other woman put her hand on the back of Anna's head and gave her a kiss. Anna was surprised, but had to admit, she enjoyed the woman's affection.

The room was starting to spin a little and Anna wanted to lie down for a minute. Much to her surprise, the other woman joined her in bed. The kissing continued with a little more passion and progressed to more intimate touching. Anna couldn't believe how good it all felt.

She'd never been with a woman and had limited experience with men, but this was definitely well within her comfort zone. The tender kisses and gentle caresses aroused the most intense sexual pleasure imaginable. She ended up spending the night and woke up early the next morning.

Anna knew she'd have to get back to Erica's apartment as quickly as she could. When she walked in, everyone was still asleep. She got undressed and fell asleep as soon as her head hit the pillow. Her evening had been exhausting.

She dreamt about the woman next door and hoped she hadn't squealed in her sleep. The next day, she joined the girls as they went from one exclusive store to another with a midday respite at a fashionable midtown restaurant.

Anna's mind, though, was elsewhere. All she could think about was her night of extreme sexual pleasure. She'd never been so aroused, so satisfied. She couldn't wait to be with the woman again.

That night, after everyone was asleep, she snuck out of the condo to go next door. The woman greeted her wearing a sheer gown. Anna didn't need any enticement—she was more than ready to pick up where they'd left off the night before.

The woman offered her a pill that would increase her sexual satisfaction. She said she'd already taken one herself. Anna quickly washed it down with a piña colada. The night was more pleasurable than the previous one. Anna's expectations made every kiss, every touch, every caress more satisfying than the last.

After a couple of hours of intense rapture, Anna made it clear she couldn't spend the night. As they kissed goodnight at the door, the woman told Anna she would be out of town for several days, but she wanted to get back together with her after she returned to college. Anna was more than happy to give her all her contact information. When she asked the woman her name, she replied, "Just call me Dee—it's a nickname I had as a child." She couldn't tell Anna her real name or their affair would be over before it started. Daphne might have been a little foolish, but she wasn't dumb.

The attraction they had for each other was undeniable but Anna couldn't tell a soul. In fact, when she thought about people finding out, she felt a little uncomfortable, but not enough to stop seeing Dee. She couldn't resist her.

Anna was still interested in guys. In fact, she had no interest in women, besides Dee. Maybe, in time, it would all make some sense to her. For now, all she could think about was Dee.

# Chapter Twenty-Two

Saturday came quickly. The girls were having a great time in New York and I was on my way to Havana. I was amazed to have a Cuban visa and my trip approved by the State Department and the Cuban government.

Erica had told me a little about her assignment. About five years ago, tourism became Cuba's number one industry. Almost all of that was in Havana. With this campaign, the Cubans wanted to expand tourism all across their island paradise.

During this week, they would produce a number of video and print pieces to further promote their beautiful country to the rest of the world. Who better to star in these pieces than the most beautiful girl in the world—Erica Richards? I couldn't imagine who'd they'd find to be the guy with her in the promos. Quite honestly, I couldn't picture her with any man, even me.

Erica met me at the airport. She was in a newer Mercedes limo with a young Cuban girl behind the wheel. After passionate hugs and kisses, Erica introduced her driver, Carmen.

Once we were on our way, Erica's mood darkened. "We've got a problem."

I could imagine any number of things that could be, but I didn't want to speculate. "What's that?"

"The male model I'm supposed to work with wasn't allowed into the country—both governments had problems with his military background."

"Surely they can find someone else."

"You'd think so, but so far no luck. They've also thought about writing out the male character and just using me to tell their story."

76

"That would certainly work for all the guys, but I don't see it doing much for the female audience."

"That's what they decided."

"What are they going to do?"

"Well, I had one, last desperate idea."

"What was that?"

"You could do the promos with me."

I must have been in shock. In an instant, my mouth went dry, a cold chill ran across my body and my mind went blank.

Erica smiled and gave me an expectant look. I hated to disappoint her, but I'd never done any modeling or acting. Truth be told, I wasn't even a fan of having my picture taken. She couldn't have asked a more unlikely person.

But then, there was my relationship with Erica. God, she was so beautiful and I felt so good when I was with her. I thought this trip would be our chance to finally bond and possibly fall in love. I didn't think me saying no to the modeling would be a good start.

She could tell I had doubts and tried to help me along. "What attracted you to me the first time you saw me?"

"Your incredible beauty."

"The same thing attracted me to you."

"My incredible beauty?"

Erica chuckled. "In a sense, yes. You're one of the best-looking men I've ever seen. You'd definitely fit the mold of tall, dark and handsome. How tall are you—six one?"

"Six one and a half."

She laughed. "Can you begin to see why you'd be perfect for the campaign? Not to mention how much fun it would be for both of us."

"When you put it that way, there's nothing I'd rather do."

She hugged me. "This is going to be great. Let's go back to the room and work on our chemistry."

I wasn't sure what that meant, but it sounded to me like she wanted to take me to her room and have sex. Whatever she had in mind, I was up for it.

Turns out my thought was correct. We enjoyed an entire night of the most passionate sex I could have ever imagined. After a while, I wondered how much I could handle. She was extremely sensual.

Erica could tell I was fading and suggested we get some rest. Before she could even turn off the light, I was sound asleep.

The next morning, I realized my bags were still in the car. I looked at the other side of the bed and no one was there. Erica was singing in the kitchen as she cooked breakfast.

I walked in there, gave her a hug and kiss, and asked about my bags. She said they were in the other bedroom of her suite. She thought I might like my own bathroom and closet. I liked her thinking.

I showered, shaved and got dressed for the day, having no idea what to expect. Erica told me to relax and enjoy myself. I felt I'd done that most of the night. This woman was one in a million, maybe a billion.

Our first location was on the beach in front of the resort. The sand was a fine white powder and the water, a sparkling green. The palm trees and flowering plants complimented the tropical feel. I was blown away by the incredible natural beauty. We could have been anywhere in the Caribbean.

I would have never thought we were in Communist Cuba. In all my trips to Cuba, I'd never been to one of their beaches. They were always on the US no-go list.

Erica walked onto the beach in a bright blue bikini. I knew I needed to change. The government had set up tents for us to use. I walked into my tent and was surprised to see a young woman inside. I asked her what she was doing there. She said she was my personal masseuse and assistant. She had my clothes laid out and asked if I wanted help changing. I declined and asked her to turn around. She seemed amused.

The director laid out the scene for us. Today, we did still photograph. He tried to set the mood that would evoke the feelings he sought. I thought he was quite good, but I wasn't sure he could help a rookie like me.

Erica was a natural. This was her bread and butter. I thought being with her would pretty much evoke the emotions the director wanted from me.

Of course, it wasn't near that easy. He told me to relax and act natural. I tried my best. After ten to fifteen failed shots, he finally got what he was looking for.

The rest of the morning went much better. Working with Erica wasn't work at all.

That afternoon, we did yoga on the beach. This was another new experience for me. Somehow, I'd missed the whole yoga thing. With a great deal of instruction and practice, I finally got the hang of it. Erica was amused. She laughed and laughed and laughed. I loved the sound of her laughter, but after a while, it got a little old.

The next shot was a sunset dinner on a balcony overlooking the sea. We had both cleaned up and changed. The director situated us just so at the table. The food looked amazing. I asked Erica if we could eat it. Another laugh.

She said the food was inedible—simply a prop. I asked about the glass of wine and she said after the shoot.

Later, I'd lost interest and we both headed up to our room. Once we were alone, Erica took off all her clothes. "Do you want to go eat or have some fun?"

I was hungry but answered, "Have some fun."

Later that night, we ordered room service. The next day was more of the same. We did photographs for the first couple of days and then shot videos. I was surprised how quickly I'd gotten the hang of it all.

After a long day's shooting, Erica teased me, "You're a natural. Modeling could be your next career."

I didn't know about that, but I was curious. "How much is this gig paying?"

"Not much. You'll get $250,000 US and I'll make $500,000 US."

I was shocked. "That's a ton of money."

"I've gotten used to it. Usually, I get significantly more. Does the money tempt you to make a career change?"

"Not really but it's still a lot of money."

I can see why modelling was such an attractive career, but I was happy with my current occupation.

I continued, "This is just a lark for me."

"We'll see about that."

I wondered what she meant but guessed I'd just have to wait and see.

# Chapter Twenty-Three

Halfway through the shoot, we were told we'd need to take a break—a hurricane was headed our way. I suggested we fly back to Nashville to wait it out. Erica was game. She'd never experienced "Music City."

She wanted to stay in a suite at the Opryland Hotel. I was all for it. She loved the traditionally appointed rooms, the atriums, the gardens, the river cruise and all the amenities. By now, I realized I was starting to fall in love with her.

We checked out the Bluebird Café, Grand Ole Opry, Ryman Auditorium, and the clubs on lower Broadway. We even managed to take in a Titans game. A friend of Erica's recommended a number of restaurants, and we dined at each one.

After a few days, we got word the destruction in Cuba from the hurricane was significant and that we would need to reschedule the balance of the shootings after everything returned to normal. We were both disappointed but happy to move on with our lives.

Erica had several jobs in the eastern half of the US, and I scheduled one workshop after another in the same general area. Everything was perfect. We'd been able to get together once or twice a week. Our lovemaking reached the legendary level.

About a month in, we met in Key West. I loved the city and Erica had never been. I showed her the sights, the galleries, the bars, and the restaurants. We stayed in a little bungalow off Mallory Square. The first night, we participated in the nightly sunset celebration.

The weather was perfect. We opened our windows in the evening and enjoyed the breeze. After yet another night of passion, I was lying in bed with a stupid smile on my face, looking at Erica.

"What?" she said a little impatiently.

I hugged her and gave her a kiss. She said, "Again?"

I said, "You know the last few weeks have been magical for me."

"For me as well."

"I don't think I've ever been happier or more at peace with the world."

"I feel the same way."

"Erica, I never thought I'd say this to another woman but, then again, I've never met a woman like you."

She smiled, put her arms around me and gave me a gentle hug.

I pulled away slightly, so we could look into each other eyes. "I've been attracted to you since the first night we met. I felt a special bond throughout our struggles to survive our disaster at sea. The last few weeks have been beyond anything I could have ever imagined. I can't picture my world without you. Erica, I love you to the moon and back."

She elevated herself slightly and gave me a tender kiss. "Jack, my life has been a dream. I would have never imagined I would do all the things I've done. The fact that I've made a ton of money makes it that much better. But there's always been something missing—an emptiness in my heart, until I met you. From that first night, all I could think about was being with you.

"One of the saddest days I've had in a long time is when I flew back to New York alone. I understood that you needed to come to terms with your loss and I was happy to give you space to do that. Once we finally got back together, I hoped I'd never have to say goodbye again. Jack, I love you more than you can imagine and I see an amazing future ahead of us."

My God. I was so happy I thought I'd burst. She loves me. I was elated. We were perfect. Or so I thought.

# Chapter Twenty-Four

About a month later, Erica got an assignment in Iceland. She wanted to see me before she left. I rearranged my schedule and flew to New York. We only had a couple of nights, and tonight was her last night in the city. We wanted to make the most of our time together, and I believe we did.

The next morning, I saw Erica off and had a full day of meetings with clients and prospects. Erica had insisted I stay at her place, and I couldn't see any reason not to.

I went to bed around ten and tossed and turned. I should have slept soundly. My day was unusually productive. Chef Louis prepared a superb dinner. Erica left an outstanding selection of wines, whiskey, and liquors. Sure, I missed her, but that was no reason not to get a good night's sleep.

The clock read three-fifteen. As I rolled over, I sensed there was someone else in the room. Disturbing. Scary. Unlikely. Everyone had left for the night. All the doors were locked. The elevator was parked at the lobby level. It was literally impossible for anyone else to be here.

I peeked out one eye. Maybe there was a shadow in the chair next to the door. Some sort of form. Or maybe not. I'd imagined dark figures in the dead of night before. Generally, I'd ignored them because I knew they weren't real.

For some reason, I couldn't get this shadow out of my mind. I rose up on one elbow and opened both eyes.

"How have you been, Jack?"

Jesus Christ. I thought I was going to jump out of my skin. My breathing quickened to the point I couldn't speak.

"Take a minute to settle down, Jack. We've got the rest of the night."

I tried taking some deep breaths. Who could this be? Definitely a woman, but who? Someone I knew? A stranger? How had they gotten in? Why were they here at all?

A hundred questions twirled around my head. I asked just one. "Who are you?"

"Daphne Erwin."

Holy crap. "What are you doing here?"

"I came to see you, Jack."

"Why?"

"I thought we needed to talk."

"You're a crazy bitch, what would we possibly have to talk about?"

"Your daughter, Anna."

"You don't even know her. Now get out."

"Oh, but I do. I know her intimately."

"That's disgusting. What's the matter with you?"

"Nothing. I'm great. You seem to be the one that's upset. What's the matter with you, Jack?"

"I need you out of this condo and out of my life. Right now!"

"I don't see that happening."

I jumped out of bed and made a move towards Daphne. She fired a shot over my head.

I froze. "Why do you have a gun?"

"I was hoping we could talk like two adults. But if you want to get rough, I can handle that as well."

I sat back down. "I don't believe you'll shoot me. If you do, you will no longer be able to torment me."

"Au contraire. I wouldn't hesitate for a second to put a bullet in you, but I'd prefer not to. I'd hate you to miss all the fun. Face it, Jack—you're mine."

"In your dreams."

"Anna is the one in my dreams, not you."

"What do you want?"

"I want to make your life as miserable as you've made mine."

"How have I made your life miserable?"

"You took Lilly from me."

"Lilly's death was an accident."

"You always stood between Lilly and me. You probably thought her death would end that. But you were wrong."

"You're a crazy bitch. That makes no sense."

"It makes sense to me and that's all that matters."

"Let me try this one more time. What do you want?"

"I want you to leave me alone. Anna and I are in love. You don't need to get between us."

"Anna is a child."

"Anna is an independent adult woman. Accept that. You also need to accept she loves me."

"Not in a million years."

I then heard a hissing noise. Before I could identify the source, I passed out.

When I woke up, the maid was knocking at the door. "Hello, Mr. Sparrow, are you alright?"

My mouth was parched. I stumbled to the door and tried to open it. It didn't budge. The lock wasn't engaged, so it must have been jammed shut.

"I'm fine. The door is jammed. Do you see a pencil or other small object wedged between the door and the jamb?" We used to pencil guys into their dorm rooms all the time when I was a college freshman.

"Yes, I do."

"I need you to remove it."

"Alright, give me a minute to get something."

Five minutes later, the pencil was gone and the door opened. I charged out of the room, across the living room, and through the door to the emergency stairs.

I pounded on Daphne's door. "Open this door, you crazy bitch."

The maid was looking at me like I was nuts. Daphne didn't respond. I called the police.

I explained as best I could to the 911 operator what happened to me. She said they would send out a detective. My schedule was full, with one appointment after another. I gave her my cell number. She said she would have him call me so we could schedule a time and place to meet.

I didn't hear from the detective until five forty-five that afternoon. He apologized and said he'd had a busy day. I could only imagine the seedy side of life he dealt with. I told him my experience wouldn't be nearly as unpleasant as most of the others he faced. We agreed to meet the next morning at a local donut shop.

# Chapter Twenty-Five

Thankfully, last night was uneventful. I'd gotten up early this morning and left to meet the detective. He was reading the paper when I walked in. Of course, I'd never seen him before, but the guy drinking coffee and reading the paper looked exactly what I pictured an NYPD detective would look like.

I walked up to him. "Are you Detective Hannity?"

He looked up. "No. I'm the tooth fairy. Sit down."

Hannity jumped right into it. "What's up with you and this Erwin broad?"

"Nothing. For some unknown reason, she wants to wreak havoc in my life."

"Lucky you. What exactly happened the night before last?"

I went through the events in great detail. After a couple of minutes, Hannity picked up his donut and took a couple of bites. Then he picked up his coffee and drank some.

I abruptly stopped my narrative. "Don't you want to write this down?"

"My hand would have already been cramping. I'll dictate a summary into my recorder when we're done."

Hannity continued. "Did this Erwin broad have a key to the condo?"

"I don't know, but I can find out."

"Who lives in the condo you were in?"

"Erica Richards."

"What were you doing there?"

"We're dating."

He gave me the once-over. "You're dating that babe?"

"Yes, I am." I was afraid I was starting to sound like a prick.

"Is Erwin a friend of hers?"

"No, I don't think so."

"I need Erica's number so I can get some answers from her. What is it?"

"I'll need to ask her if I can give it to you."

"Are you serious? Do you want me to investigate this or not? Give me the dammed number or I'm going to close this complaint."

I gave him Erica's phone number.

Hannity scribbled it down. "Now, that wasn't so hard, was it? Have you talked to her since this all happened?"

"No, I haven't."

"Good. Give me time to call her before you do."

"No problem."

"I'm going to send someone up to the condo to check for any evidence of a firearm discharge. That's the only possible crime that could have happened there."

"What about the threats? My daughter?"

"Those are your problems. Here's my card, call me if you have any questions."

With that, he grabbed his newspaper and left. I had another busy day ahead of me. I decided I'd try to get in touch with Erica after lunch. I also needed to call Anna.

I had lunch with a prospective client. That lasted right up till my next appointment. I finally had a break around three and called Erica.

She answered on the first ring. "I'm glad you're alright. The detective called and told me what happened. I can't imagine Daphne would do anything like that. She's never been a problem in the past."

I fired away with my questions. "Have you ever met Daphne?"

"No."

"Does she have a key to the condo?"

"Maybe—I'm not sure. All our communications are through Chef Louie or notes we've exchanged under our doors."

"From what you're saying, you hardly know her at all."

"Exactly."

"I don't know what to make of her appearance the other night."

"Sounds to me like she was worried you'd interfere in her relationship with Anna."

"Could be. I'm going to call Anna when we're done talking."

"I'd encourage you to choose your words carefully when you talk with her. Affairs of the heart can be delicate. I don't think she'd welcome your intrusion."

"I may have to give some more thought to how I handle that."

"Probably time well spent. Listen, I've got to leave for dinner. Call me again as soon as you can. I miss you. Love you. Bye."

She hung up before I could say "Love you" or even "Bye." Oh well, I knew she was an extremely busy person. I didn't expect her to caution me about talking with Anna, but I appreciated her perspective.

As I wound up my last appointment of the day, my phone rang. "Hello?"

"Is this Captain Jack Sparrow?"

My inclination was to hang up, but I thought the voice sounded a little like Hannity.

"Is this Detective Hannity?"

"Good guess. Maybe you should be the detective."

"What can I do for you?"

"My partner, Detective Clinton, and a couple of friends would like to come by your place tonight for drinks."

This was strange, but I knew I was talking with a strange fellow.

"Sure, what time."

"How about five?"

"That's ten minutes from now. Are you close?"

"We're standing out front."

"I'll be right there."

# Chapter Twenty-Six

Fortunately, I was nearby and arrived a little past five. Hannity was there with three women. I led them to the express elevator to Erica's penthouse.

Hannity commented, "This is nice."

I said, "You haven't seen anything yet."

The elevator doors opened and all my guests gasped at the lavishness.

Hannity whistled. "Being one of the world's top models must pay pretty well."

We all sat down in the living room. The butler took our coats and asked if anyone would like anything to drink. Hannity ordered a double scotch on the rocks, and the girls each wanted a gin fizz—whatever that was. I requested a beer.

Hannity introduced the girls. "This is my partner, Detective Clinton; Amber, a ballistics technician; and, Rachael, our fingerprint expert."

I showed Amber and Rachael to the bedroom where the incident occurred. They both went to work.

I sat back down with the two detectives and said, "Detective Clinton, I'm surprised you weren't at our meeting yesterday morning."

Hannity said, "Yeah, she got a mani-pedi."

With that, Clinton swatted Hannity on his ear. He recoiled a little. "Ouch, that hurt, Hillary."

Hillary Clinton, no shit.

I said, "I'm surprised you're drinking on duty."

Hannity shot back, "We're not on duty, limp dick, we're off the clock.

This is a little bonus we're providing for a valued guest of the city."

"Thank you. What do you think is happening here?"

Clinton replied, "More than meets the eye. We did some checking. Did you know Erica owns the penthouse next door as well?"

*You've got to be kidding me. That makes no sense.*

I hesitated a moment and then asked, "Daphne's a tenant, then?"

"Not as far as we could tell. All our records would indicate Daphne Erwin is a ghost."

"No record of her anywhere?"

"No. Nothing. No birth certificate, no Social Security card, no driver's license, no tax returns, nothing."

"That's crazy. I know she's real because I've seen and talked to her twice. My wife, God rest her soul, also told me about an encounter with her."

Hannity asked, "Could you fill us in on the details?"

I told both of them what Lilly told me had happened on the ship as well as the exchange Daphne and I had had at the funeral.

Clinton took notes. About that time, Amber and Rachael sat down and finished their drinks.

Hannity asked if I could describe Daphne. I said, "She's about five foot eleven, great figure, pretty face, blond with blue eyes. Every time I've seen her she's had her hair in a bun and wore glasses."

Hannity said, "Except for the bun and the glasses that could describe Erica."

"I'd never thought of that. Now that you mention it, there is a resemblance between the two women."

"Has Erica ever mentioned any family relationship?"

"No."

I had a thought. Chef Louis knew Daphne as well. I asked the detectives to hold on a second and got him.

"This is Chef Louie. He's Erica's chef and does some work for Daphne as well. Maybe he knows something that could help."

Hannity told Louis to have a seat, remove his chef's hat, and tell them about Daphne.

The chef asked, "What do you want to know?"

"Does she have a key to this condo?"

"Yes."

"Why is that?"

"She uses me for dinner parties and needs to coordinate the menus and other arrangements."

"You don't use her kitchen?"

"Occasionally, but I find this one much more convenient."

"Tell me about these dinner parties."

"They're quite different from Erica's get-togethers."

"How's that?"

"Erica generally has an equal amount of men and women attend. Daphne primarily invites women. Sure, there's always a few men, but they're greatly outnumbered. Jack's daughter, Anna, and her friends even attended a dinner there. When I left, about two in the morning, Anna still hadn't come back."

What the hell! I had no idea. Why couldn't this woman leave my family alone? I was really pissed and could feel my face turning red.

Hannity noticed and asked, "Jack, are you alright?"

"Fine. Continue, Louie."

"That's about all I know."

Hannity had one more question. "How does Daphne pay you?"

"She doesn't. I work for Erica and she pays for everything."

That was interesting. Daphne didn't pay for food, didn't pay rent, and pretty much didn't exist. A true phantom. Erica covered all her expenses but claimed not even to know her. Odd.

Hannity thanked Louis. As he was about to leave, Louis asked how many there would be for dinner. I invited Hannity and his friends. They all readily accepted. I told Louis dinner for five. He took that information in stride and got to work.

After another couple of drinks, the night became all laughter and fun. Each of my guests was from a different borough of the city. Hillary grew up in the Harlem neighborhood of Manhattan; Amber, the Bronx; Rachael, Queens; and Hannity, Brooklyn. They all had the strong New York accent, except for

Hannity, who was pure Brooklyn. I've got to admit, I had a good time.

Before she left, Amber told me she located the bullet, took some pictures, figured a trajectory, and removed the shell from the wall. I was cleared to fix the hole.

Rachael said, "I only found three sets of fingerprints in the bedroom. I need you and the maid to come by the police station so we can get your prints."

I asked, "Who do you think the three sets of print belong to?"

"You, Erica and the maid."

"What about Daphne?"

"Could you tell if she was wearing gloves?"

"Possibly, but it was difficult to see in the dark."

Hannity stood. "We'll be back in touch soon."

"Do I need to stay in the city?"

"No. You can leave any time after you've been fingerprinted at the station."

Once the detectives left, I reviewed my schedule for the next couple of weeks. I was surprised at the number of people I needed to contact in the New England area. I also had nearby workshops to put on.

I called Erica to see if I could stay a few extra days in her condo. She didn't answer, so I left her a message.

# Chapter Twenty-Seven

Unbeknownst to me, Daphne called Anna. She told her she planned to spend a few days in the Providence area and wanted to get together. Anna was thrilled and quickly agreed to dinner the next evening.

When Anna arrived at the dark, cozy Italian restaurant, Daphne was already seated in a booth, drinking a glass of wine. She stood up and the women hugged and kissed.

Anna said, "You're actually here! I'm thrilled."

"Me, too. How are you doing?"

"Getting along but you're always on my mind and I've really missed you."

"Same here."

Daphne filled Anna's wineglass and both women perused the menu. They each ordered a light dinner. The wine flowed freely. After dinner, Anna suggested a nearby jazz club for a few drinks. Daphne was all in.

The girls became one with the music as they drank and danced. By the time they got back to Daphne's room, they'd consumed more liquor than either woman realized.

Daphne had arranged a ton of candles around the bed. She gave Anna a sheer gown and asked her to light the candles while she excused herself. About fifteen minutes later, Anna had changed into the gossamer gown, lit the candles, turned off the lights, and laid down on the bed.

The soft, melodic music from Daphne's phone caused Anna to stir. She slowly sat up and smiled when she saw Daphne wearing a similar gown. Daphne handed Anna a pill and swallowed one herself. The candles, the music, the gowns, the pills—everything was perfect.

Daphne said, "You look utterly delicious."

Anna replied, "I feel like I'm going to melt."

"I fully expect you will."

The kissing began gently, as did their caresses. As passions rose, they both became wilder and more aroused. Within minutes, the two women were out of control.

They woke up well into the next day. After some good morning affection, they dressed and had brunch at a place Daphne found online. They drank mimosas with their meals.

Anna then showed Daphne some of the things she loved most about Providence. High on that list were the local artists and galleries. Providence began as a manufacturing and industrial center and grew to become the largest town and capital of Rhode Island. The main influences in the area today were the seven college campuses and the art community. That, combined with its classic New England charm, made it hard for visitors not to enjoy.

That night, the girls chose Japanese fare. They both enjoyed the sake as much as the deliciousness they ate. The night was pretty much a repeat of the previous night's pleasures. Anna had never been happier or more in love. Daphne shared both feelings.

The next day, Anna got a call from her dad. He was in New York and wanted to fly over and share some important information. She said she looked forward to seeing him.

Daphne said she would be leaving for Europe. Anna wanted to go with her but knew she needed to stay. The women shared a romantic goodbye and Anna returned to her dorm room.

# Chapter Twenty-Eight

I flew to Providence that afternoon to talk with Anna about Daphne. I still didn't know how I should broach the subject. If I asked Anna about any new relationships or friends, she'd probably tell me it was none of my business and she'd be right.

I knew Anna liked and possibly loved (ugh) this woman, so I'd have to be extremely careful. She was my daughter after all and I always loved her regardless of the stupid things she did.

We met around four that afternoon. Anna was thrilled to see me. I suggested we go to a local coffee shop. Once we had our lattes, I began, "Something terrible happened the other night. Daphne was involved."

Anna was shocked. "Oh, no. Is she alright?"

"I'm sure she's fine."

I covered the entire incident in as much detail as I could remember. When I came to the part where Daphne fired the gun at me, Anna explained, "Oh my God, that must have been terrifying."

"I tried to keep my cool. I didn't know what kind of person I was dealing with."

"Are you sure the woman was Daphne?"

"One hundred percent."

"I don't understand why she would do something like that. It seems to me that entire conversation was unnecessary."

"I'm worried about you."

"I'm fine. You shouldn't be concerned."

"What about Daphne?"

She shrugged it off—no big deal. I suspected she wasn't being honest with me, unless Daphne lied and just wanted to get my goat.

I asked her point-blank, "Are you and Daphne Erwin in love?"

Anna hesitated and gave her response some thought. She wasn't ready to tell her dad that she and Daphne were head over heels in love.

Instead, she said, "Right now, we just enjoy each other's company. She has these pills…"

"Pills? Are you serious? She gave your mom pills as well."

"That's disgusting. I can't imagine her with Mom."

"You heard Daphne at the funeral, right?"

"Not so much. You two walked off and faced the other direction when you talked."

"Let me fill you in, then. Daphne was uncontrollably upset because she and Mom were madly in love and she felt I took Mom from her."

"That's crazy. Mom fell overboard, right? You were in the bar with Erica. While we're talking about it, let me say for the record, that was not your finest hour. Rob and I both think you should have been with Mom."

"Mom asked me to get her a Coca-Cola with crushed ice. She didn't feel well. Granted, I spent more time than I should have with Erica, but I went to the bar for your mom's Coke, not to see Erica."

"If you say so. Just remember, we both realize Erica is drop-dead gorgeous."

"True. But we're talking about Daphne. She hates me."

"Why would she?"

"She blames me for Mom's death and believes I'm going to get in the way of her love for you. Now that I think about it, Daphne seems to focus all her wrath towards me. There's no telling what she's capable of. I've got to admit, I feel she's nothing but evil."

"When we're together, she's anything but evil."

"Maybe wicked would be a better word."

"Possibly, but I was thinking naughty. That's probably something you'd just as soon not hear about."

"You've got that right. What do you want to do for dinner?"

We didn't waste another word on Daphne. Anna and I had a phenomenal meal and evening. I left early the next morning for Nashville.

As soon as I got back to town, I looked over my calendar. I had only three types of activities—workshops, motivational conferences, and business development. I had a fair share of all three well into the future. My time in Cuba and New York had caused me to reschedule a number of things. I'd have to work especially hard for the next couple of months to catch up.

Erica and I talked on the phone about every other day. Her work in Iceland was going well. She said the island nation was one of the most beautiful places on Earth and that we needed to spend some time there. I was up for anything as long as it involved Erica. All I needed to do was find the time.

Daphne had apparently gone dormant. Anna never mentioned her. And I rarely thought about her—until Detective Hannity called one afternoon.

"Hey, Captain, I forgot to thank you for the drinks and dinner at Erica's. We're all still talking about what a great time we had."

"I enjoyed the company as well."

No one said anything for probably thirty seconds. Finally, I said, "Hello?"

"Hello to you. I was reviewing the file on Daphne Erwin. I called to bring you up-to-date. Hold on a second."

Another long period of silence.

"Here it is. The maid finally made it in so we could get her fingerprints. I think she might have thought we intended to deport her, but Louie finally coaxed her in."

"Good."

"Yeah, good. Anyway, apparently Daphne wore gloves or she's actually one of the three of you."

That made no sense. "I'd say she wore gloves."

"Probably so, because we couldn't find another print on anything she might have touched in Erica's place."

"That's frustrating."

"No kidding. And then, there's the bullet. It's a .45-caliber. Of course, since Daphne basically doesn't exist, she doesn't have any guns registered in her name either. But here's the kicker—Erica has a Colt 1911 registered in her name."

"I'm sorry. I'm not that familiar with guns. Is that a .45-caliber?"

"Right. We'd like to test-fire it and see if it's the gun Daphne used."

"You've got Erica's number, call her and ask."

"Will do. If you talk to her first, I'd appreciate it if you could tell her we need the gun."

"No problem."

"Thanks, Captain."

Hannity was the only person I knew who called me "Captain." You'd think it would annoy me, but for some reason I liked it. Oh, well.

I asked Erica about the gun the next time we spoke. She said it was in her nightstand drawer. I could see Daphne sneaking the gun out before I woke up and replacing it after she'd gassed me. Erica agreed that was probably what happened. Regardless, she'd let the maid know Hannity would be by to pick it up.

I sent him a text to that effect. He replied the ballistics specialist, Amber, would pick up the gun and have it tested. I passed her name on to Erica.

# Chapter Twenty-Nine

Spring break time. Erica was back in New York, but I'd promised Rob I'd take him fly-fishing in Colorado.

Anna was going to Cancun with friends. I wasn't thrilled by that prospect, but at some point, I just had to let go. At least she wasn't going to be spending the time with Daphne.

Rob and I were fishing the headwaters of the Colorado River in Blue River, Colorado. I'd bought a complete package from Mac's Fish Camp almost a year ago. That was prior to the disastrous cruise and the many other events of the last year.

I called Anna before she left Providence and asked her to text me contact information for her friends. I didn't know if I'd get anything, but it didn't hurt to ask.

The fish camp couldn't have been any better. Rustic two-bedroom cabins surrounded a massive log lodge. Wood stoves heated the cabins and contributed greatly to the ambiance.

We took all our meals and had our morning briefings in the lodge. That building also offered pool tables, fishing gear, and a bar that only served Yeti Imperial Stout, a popular local brew.

Rob and I quickly adjusted to our fishing and beer drinking routines. We really enjoyed life's simple pleasures. Our phones were fairly unreliable as the cell service was pretty sketchy.

After three of the greatest days of our lives, I finally had a signal. I called Anna and the call went to voicemail. I left a brief message. Then I called Erica and the call went to voicemail. I left another brief message.

I'd never gotten Anna's list of the friends she was vacationing with. I asked Rob if he knew any of the girls Anna hung out with. Not surprisingly, he had the phone numbers of a couple. I started calling and finally got Tami on the line. She said Anna didn't come with them. I asked if she had any idea where Anna went. She said no, but she thought Anna may have gone away with her "special friend".

I got a hollow feeling in my gut. Anna and Daphne were together and I had no idea where they were. I didn't feel Daphne would hurt her—at least no more than the emotional turmoil she was currently putting her through—but I still worried about her.

I couldn't understand why I wasn't able to reach Erica. She almost always answered her phone or returned calls quickly. She hadn't said anything to me about a job or any travels. I was probably as worried about her as I was about Anna.

I called Detective Hannity to see if he had discovered anything from test firing the gun. He never answered any of my calls but always got back with me eventually.

To my surprise, Hannity picked up on the sixth ring. "Hey, Cap, what's up?"

"I wanted to see if you've made any progress with the ballistics tests and finding Daphne."

"Erica's gun was definitely the weapon Daphne used. The bullets were a perfect match. The only fingerprints on it belonged to Erica."

No big surprise. Once again, nothing decisive. I wondered if we'd ever get to the bottom of things.

Hannity continued, "Locating Daphne has been a challenge. We can't seem to get any leads on her whereabouts."

"I think she may be with my daughter."

"Whoa, whoa, whoa. Back up a little, Cap. Why would she be with your daughter?"

"They've been spending a fair amount of time together ever since the night Daphne took a shot at me."

"You should have let us know. Maybe, your daughter could have given us some leads on Daphne's whereabouts."

"Lately, I think they've been getting together out-of-state."

"Maybe, we could get the FBI involved. How old is your daughter?"

"She just turned nineteen."

"That's a shame. I hoped she was a minor."

"Thanks, but that doesn't make me feel any better. She's still a child to me."

"Whatever you say, Cap."

"I've also lost touch with Erica."

"Sorry to hear that. She's definitely a once-in-a-lifetime kind of gal."

"I don't mean we've broken up, I just don't know where she is or what's she's doing."

"Can't help you there."

"Maybe you can. Would you do me a favor and go by her place and talk to the doorman? He may know where both women are."

"You know, if I do you a favor, you're going to have to do me a favor. No questions asked. No hesitation. Would you be willing to do that?"

"Maybe."

"Not good enough."

"Yes, yes, I will."

"Great, I'll let you know what I find out. Got to run. Bye."

Rob had fallen asleep while I talked to Hannity. When I woke up the next morning, he'd already left for breakfast. I cleaned up quickly and joined him.

"Hey, Dad. I know where Anna is."

I was surprised. "Really? Did she call?"

"No, but I'd forgotten we both have this *Find Your Friends* app on our phones that tells us where each other's phone is located."

"Where is she?"

"West Virginia."

"I would have never guessed. Why in the world would she be in West Virginia?"

Rob shrugged.

"Do you have a town?"

"Sure, just outside of White Sulphur Springs."

"Any idea what's there?"

"The Greenbrier Resort?"

"That makes some sense. I'll just have to assume she's alright."

"Why don't you ask Erica to install this app on her phone? That way you'd always know where she was."

"I don't think she'd go for it. Everyone needs a little privacy now and again. You know, it's part of our DNA."

"You mean like Anna?"

"Right. I'll just have to accept the fact she and Daphne are together."

"Good move, Dad."

Hannity called again before we left to go fishing the next morning.

"Hey, Cap, I've got some news."

"Great. Go ahead."

"According to the doorman, Daphne left a couple of days ago and he hadn't seen Erica at all. I checked with Chef Louie and he said he confirmed they were both gone."

"Thanks, Hannity, I owe you one."

"You better believe it. Bye."

Rob asked, "What was that all about?"

"Nothing. Let's go fishing and forget about everything else."

The fishing was like nothing I'd ever experienced before—the rippling water, the majestic mountains, the cool breeze, the graceful casts, all contributed to one perfect day after another. I put the drama of Daphne behind me. This week was all about Rob and me, and we had a great time.

After our amazing week, I flew Rob back to Duke. I was tempted to go to New York from there, but since I still hadn't heard from Erica, I flew back to Nashville.

# Chapter Thirty

Erica finally called me several days later. "I've been really busy, but I've missed talking with you. How was your trip with Rob?"

"We had the time of our lives. The fishing was incredible."

"I didn't realize you were such an outdoorsman."

"I love the outdoors—enjoying nature and playing sports. How about you?"

"The same but almost all our fun has been between the sheets."

"Maybe, we can change that."

"I don't want to change it too much. In fact, I'm ready for a little intense sheet time right now. Let's get together this weekend."

"Can't wait. I'll fly up Thursday to avoid the weekend crush."

"I'll be counting the days. Love you. Bye."

The next day, Anna finally called. After I unleashed my emotions, she said, "Why are you so upset? I called and left you a message that I changed my plans and decided to spend spring break with Daphne."

"I never got your message and have been worried sick."

"You worry too much. I'm a grown woman after all. You need to keep that in mind when I tell you what I'm going to do."

I wasn't so sure about that. I told her, "We'll see."

She charged on. "Daphne and I had such an amazing time at the Greenbrier that I decided to drop out of college and move in with her."

Surely she couldn't be serious. What an unbelievably foolish thing to do. I calmed down as much as I could and said, "That is so wrong on so many levels. Your education is vital if you intend to compete for jobs in the twenty-first century. Equally important is the socialization aspect of campus life. You need to learn how to get along with other people who have mature viewpoints and attitudes. Plus, the students at Brown represent many of the movers and shakers of the next generation. Friendships developed there could be crucial to your future success."

Anna had a one-word response. "Bullshit."

As I thought about what I'd just said, maybe she was right. But moving in with Daphne was still all wrong.

I pointed out, "Daphne travels a lot and would be gone much of the time."

"That's fine. I want to pursue my passion for writing and plan to take courses at NYU."

I couldn't argue with that.

Finally, I gave up. "It's your life and you can ruin it anyway you want."

Maybe that was a little strong, but I was so mad, I actually thought about saying something much worse.

She responded with, "I love you. Got to go."

I couldn't begin to express how upset this made me. All I could think to do was to bury myself in my work and put it out of my mind.

Thursday afternoon, I flew to New York. I hated to leave early but wanted to avoid the weekend gridlock at La Guardia and in the city.

Erica was thrilled to see me. I couldn't have been happier. At that moment, all I could think about was the incredible woman standing in front of me. We had drinks, a Chef Louis gourmet meal and spent hours and hours making up for lost time in each other's arms. The next morning, we got up around ten.

Erica and I both took some work calls on Friday. Once the real weekend started, we ignored our phones. Erica wanted to go to a show and I hadn't been to one in forever. Our tickets were a couple of rows back in the center section. All in all, we enjoyed an unforgettable weekend.

When I left on Sunday, I was ready for a rest. As we were saying goodbye, she said, "I almost forgot."

"What?"

"My agent called and said the Cubans are ready to complete the photo shoot."

"I'm pretty busy right now."

"I know, but they're flexible. Look at your schedule and see what would work for you. We'll need a maximum of ten days."

"I'll try."

"It's important. I want to get paid, and it would be good money for you as well."

"You're right. I'll try harder."

More kisses, more hugs, and finally, I was off to the airport.

I called Anna as soon as I got home.

She answered, "Are you in a better mood?"

"I was fine the last time we spoke. You can't blame me for being upset, considering your antics over spring break."

"If you call spending meaningful time with the person you love 'antics,' how were your antics this weekend?"

"How did you know I was in New York?"

"Daphne told me."

"She's spying on me now?"

"No, she just heard all the lovemaking squeals and shouts from Erica's place."

"That's ridiculous. There's no way she heard anything from her condo."

"You're right. She was in Erica's living room at the time."

"Are you serious? That's just plain creepy. What was she doing there?"

"She was going through Erica's mail."

"Isn't that a little personal?"

"Not really. They get each other's mail all the time. The postman is an idiot."

"That still gives me a chill to think of that crazy bitch in the living room while we're in the bedroom."

"I wish you wouldn't call her that. She's one of the most kind and loving people I've ever known."

"Are you still planning on moving?"

"Yes, I've let the school know and rented a U-Haul for next weekend."

"I hope you know what you're doing."

"Of course, Dad. I'm nineteen years old, after all."

"That's what concerns me."

"Bye, Dad."

I then checked in with Rob, unpacked my bag, and went to bed.

The next couple of weeks were some of my busiest ever. The hero status I'd achieved as a result of Erica's *Maxim* interview was a shot in the arm for my business. Erica and I talked often. She wanted to come to Nashville over the next weekend and we also agreed on a date to head to Cuba.

When I picked her up at the Nashville Airport, a handsome young man was carrying her bag as the two of them walked down the corridor. I stepped right up to her, gave her a kiss and told Prince Charming I had the bag. With that, we both turned and walked away.

For the first time in our relationship, Erica wanted to stay at my house. Granted, my place wasn't shabby, but it couldn't begin to approach the luxury she was accustom to. She was kind, though, and complimented me on one thing after another.

I suggested we fly to the Smokies the next day and get a cabin in the mountains. She was all for it.

The mountain air was crisp and clean. We built a roaring fire in the fireplace. The log cabin we stayed in seemed right at home in the wilderness surrounding it.

I told Erica to watch out for bears. She thought I was joking until a noise woke us up Sunday morning. Sure enough, a huge black bear was digging through our trash. I guessed I hadn't properly secured the lid last night. Once she was certain the bear was long gone, we drove back to the local airfield.

She asked, "Do you mind flying me to New York?"

"I'd be happy to. Can I spend the night before I return to Nashville?"

"I was counting on it."

I had no idea how long this would last but God I loved it while it did. Erica was everything I'd ever wanted in a woman. In addition to all the obvious qualities, she was charming and caring and had a great sense of humor. Sometimes I think we laughed as much as we did anything else.

# Chapter Thirty-One

Before long, it was time to go to Cuba. We'd be staying in Old Havana and had our choice of the best hotels. We decided to stay at the scene of our crime the first time we were there and chose Hotel Nacional.

This time, we were legit and could freely explore any area of the city that interested us. I told Erica about many spots I'd enjoyed on previous trips and she said she was up for anything.

One of the great things about staying at the Hotel Nacional was its proximity to the Malecón. We strolled the sidewalks there many a night.

Our shooting schedule featured one major attraction after another. After the photographer got all the pictures and videos he wanted, we were usually free to enjoy wherever we were.

We spent two nights at the Cabaret Tropicana—the huge outdoor floor show. There were hundreds of dancers and singers and the entire spectacle was something to behold. The shooting took two nights because they didn't want our activity to distract from the guests' enjoyment of the performance. After we finished working each night, we were treated like all the paying customers and even got our free fifth of Havana Club rum. By the end of each evening, we felt no pain.

During the day between, we went to the San Juan Markets—another great tourist stop. The quality and variety of souvenirs and handicrafts surprised Erica.

The government selected three vendors for us to be photographed and videotaped with. When we were done, we spent another couple of hours checking everything out. We ran out of time. The artwork alone would take the better part of a day to thoroughly peruse.

A couple of days later, we got married at the Catedral de San Cristóbal in Old Havana. Construction on this cathedral began in 1748 and was completed in 1777. Christopher Columbus's remains were kept in the cathedral from 1796 to 1898, when they were relocated to the Seville Cathedral in Spain.

Erica was the most beautiful bride I'd ever seen. I guess I was handsome enough. In addition to the two of us, there was a Roman Catholic priest in the scene.

They shot Erica walking down the aisle, magically filled with bright red rose petals. They filmed us holding hands and gazing lovingly into one another's eyes. We exchanged rings, kissed, greeted the empty cathedral, and strolled down the aisle, hand in hand. Our smiles shone brightly. What a glorious day.

After we changed and were relaxing in one of the pews, Erica whispered, "I really enjoyed that."

I gave her a kiss and whispered back, "So did I."

"Do you think we should do it for real?"

I looked at her and smiled. As I was about to respond, the director yelled that we needed to clear out so they could lock up the cathedral for the day.

As we walked out, Erica said, "Saved by the bell. We can talk over dinner."

The Cuban government ran everything in Havana. They owned all the gift shops, stores, and restaurants. Surprisingly, they did allow a limited amount of private enterprise under their direct supervision.

One such class of businesses was the small family restaurants called *paladares*. We tended to seek those out when we weren't dining with our government employers.

Tonight was just such an evening. We chose to dine at *Le Chansonnier*. We were having a lovely evening until Erica brought up the wedding—in this case, our wedding.

She asked, "Where do you see our relationship going?"

I didn't want to leave any doubt in her mind. "Erica, I'm head over heels in love with you and nothing would make me happier than to be your husband."

"Wow. That's not what I expected you to say at all after your hesitation this afternoon."

"I know. I wasn't expecting you to bring up marriage. The whole wedding thing is really emotional."

"For sure. Unfortunately, I can think of seventeen reasons we shouldn't get married. I made a list." And she pulled a sheet of hotel stationery out of her purse.

"I had no idea you were so analytical."

"You have a lot to learn about me."

"I do but I'm not sure I'm ready for your list."

Erica responded, "Here's how I look at it. We solve these seventeen concerns and it's full speed ahead."

"I've got an idea."

"What's that?"

"Picture this—a hurdler running a race. He has seventeen hurdles to clear between the start and the finish line."

"I like that. Much more positive. Rather than an obstacle, these are more like steps to accomplish a goal." She thought for a moment. "You know you're good. Maybe you should do this for a living?"

"I do. I help people create word pictures of how they can achieve their goals."

"I know. Just kidding."

"Can I make one more suggestion?"

"Certainly."

"Seventeen is a lot of hurdles. How about twelve? Twelve seems like it's much more doable. What do you think?"

"I understand. Twelve is good. I may have been a little too nitpicky with this list anyway."

"Twelve it is. Why don't we start with the first hurdle and resolve that before we move on to the second one?"

"Works for me."

# Chapter Thirty-Two

Erica charged ahead. "Here's the first hurdle—I'm concerned about your negative obsession with Daphne Erwin."

I had to admit—that one hit home. I did have a negative obsession with Daphne. I thought of her as pure evil and would have loved nothing better than to see her absolute demise. This was going to be a tough one.

I said, "Let's just talk about that one now. We may not be able to check it off tonight, but at least we'll know where each other is coming from and we'll be in a better position to ultimately resolve it. I know you have a different view of Daphne."

"I do, and I don't feel I need to justify my feelings."

"Of course not. I'm not asking you to. I just need you to elaborate a little."

"As you know, I've never met Daphne. I do know two people that know her fairly well—Chef Louie and Anna. They've both told me quite a bit about her."

"You've talked with Anna?"

"Of course. We're friends. Is that a problem?"

"No. Not at all. Go on."

I wasn't sure I was being totally honest here. When people talked behind my back and I didn't know what they talked about, I tended to worry.

"Anna loves and respects Daphne. She's shared many of Daphne's better qualities with me. I believe Daphne is a good person and truly loves your daughter. Maybe you should try talking with Anna about that."

"I've had two contacts with Daphne—at Lilly's funeral and in your bedroom. She totally took me by surprise at the funeral. From what the ship security fellow told me, she was a criminal rapist. At the funeral, she seemed overly distraught. We were all upset, but none of us to Daphne's extreme."

"Some people show their emotions more than others."

"True. But I thought I needed to call the cops the entire time."

"I remember the incident on the ship. I, too, had a different opinion of Daphne then."

"The second time I saw her was in your bedroom, threatening me with a gun."

"I can understand how you felt. But you need to realize Daphne may have thought she was threatened by you."

"Are you serious?"

"Yes. She may have feared you would try to undermine her relationship with Anna. She did what she felt was necessary to keep that from happening."

"I'm sorry, but those two incidents resulted in my negative obsession with Daphne."

"Here's an idea—talk with Anna. Try to keep an open mind. That may cause you to look differently at the two events that are causing your negative feelings towards Daphne."

"Alright, I can do that. I'm not saying I'll feel any differently, but I'll try to put everything that has happened out of my mind while we're having that conversation."

"Hurdle number two is closely related. Do you want me to mention that now?"

"Why not."

"The second hurdle is your attitude about same-sex relationships. That has affected both your relationship with Anna and your feelings toward Daphne. I'd like you to think how you really feel about those types of relationships."

"Fair enough. I think that's plenty for one night."

"I agree. How about a stroll down the Malecón?"

"Now you're talking."

By the time we got back to our hotel, the challenging discussions of earlier this evening were distant memories. I knew I couldn't avoid them forever, but

I hoped we could put them off to a better time. For now, all I wanted to do was enjoy Cuba and Erica.

We only had a couple more days of shooting and then some time on our own. There were a number of places I still wanted to share with Erica.

Tonight, we experienced the Buena Vista Social Club. I'd made the reservation last week and even arranged for a classic car to pick us up.

A pink 1953 Cadillac arrived a little after eight. The club looked like it hadn't changed in fifty years. Our seats were close to the stage. The dinner was delicious Cuban cuisine. Three drinks were included—mojitos, the tourist drink of Cuba.

The real highlight of the evening was the entertainment. We enjoyed the Cuban music on the Malecón, but this took it to an entirely new level. The performers used every ounce of energy they could muster. Musicians and singers alike were some of the best we'd ever heard.

The original club started in the '30s as a black fraternal organization. Similar groups popped up in New Orleans. The ones here disbanded with the Cuban Revolution but were revived in 1996. Since then, they'd made recordings and films. Among their honors were two Grammy Awards.

Late into the program, the two of us, along with many of the other guests, were led onstage to join the fun. Erica was in her groove. I tried my best to keep up. All in all, another memorable evening in this amazing town.

For the next couple of days, we wandered the streets of Old Havana. We discovered the tiny House of Chocolate. It was one of the few air-conditioned stores we'd been in. We bought churros from a street vendor dressed all in white with a red strip of cloth tied around his waist.

One day, we did a Hemingway tour. We saw the home where he'd written *For Whom the Bell Tolls* and *The Old Man and the Sea*. We stood in room 511 at the Hotel Ambos Mundos, where he'd lived for seven years and finished *Death in the Afternoon* and started both the *Green Hills of Africa* and *To Have and Have Not*. We ended the day at one of Hemingway's favorite bars, El Floridita, where we drank Hemingway daiquiris well into the night.

We paid for the daiquiris the next morning. The hangovers were devasting. Around noon, we finally began feeling human again. Our flights home left at three. Erica flew to New York and I headed to Nashville.

# Chapter Thirty-Three

We talked on the phone more frequently than ever. I found myself swamped with work, but Erica had several months before her next assignment.

The phone rang and, as usual, it was Erica. I was busy but always took time for her. I loved to listen to her voice. Her tone was soft, tender and seductive.

After the usual small talk, she got down to business. "I need to be with you. Can I come down to Tennessee this weekend?"

What could I say? "Of course, but I'll need to do some work."

"That's alright. I'll bring a book."

"I can't wait."

"I hope you know you're in for the time of your life."

Sometimes, Erica just took my breath away. I turned off my computer and called it a night.

A couple of days later, I picked up Erica at the airport. We decided to hang out at my humble abode. After a tasty BBQ dinner, we relaxed on the patio. The view was typical Tennessee countryside. I lived in an exclusive subdivision and there were no homes behind me. Instead a small lake, rolling hills and huge trees set the mood for a relaxing evening.

After a few minutes, Erica spoiled it. "Is now a good time to discuss the hurdles? I'd like to get through them."

"As good a time as any. Let's start with number two—same-sex relationships."

"Great. What have you got?"

"I have many friends in same-sex relationships. I don't look at them any differently than male-female couples. To me, it's simply a choice they make.

I have to be honest, though, I don't ever see myself having a similar preference. But that's me. I'm fine with others having same-sex relationships."

"Glad to hear that. But, how about Anna and Daphne?"

"Yeah, I have a little problem with that one. Same-sex may be part of it, but the age difference concerns me as well."

"That's interesting. The age difference between Daphne and Anna is eleven years. The age difference between you and me is eight years—pretty much the same thing, I'd say. Are you concerned about our age difference?"

"No. Not in the least."

"You're concerned about two things in Daphne and Anna's relationship that appear not to concern you in anyone else's relationship. Does that strike you as a little odd?"

"Maybe there are other issues."

"Now we're getting somewhere. What could those issues be?"

"My negative obsession with Daphne?"

"Duh."

"So, we can cross off the second hurdle."

"Right, and also the eleventh hurdle, which is our age difference."

"I feel we're making good progress."

"We've still got the first hurdle and nine more."

"I think we're on a roll. What's number three?"

"Okay. You probably noticed you and I have a lot of sex."

"I love that."

"I know. I do as well, but that can't be our only source of pleasure. I feel we need to enjoy other activities together as well."

"We like music and going to shows."

"All that's good, but I'm thinking more outdoor pursuits—like sports. We could ski, snowboard, ice skate, tennis, golf, run—there's a million things we could enjoy together."

"I understand. Let's choose two or three and do them. I'd enjoy snowboarding and tennis, but I'm more than open to what you'd like to do."

"Believe it or not, snowboarding is at the top of my list. Let's find a place we can go next weekend."

"That's an easy hurdle—let's cross it off our list."

"Fair enough. Hurdle number four—except for your kids, we don't know anything about each other's families. Before the wedding, would be a great time to meet everyone."

"I agree. Let's ask our parents to put together a meet-and-greet with the entire extended family."

"Good. Hurdle number five—money. I realize you don't know how wealthy I am, but I'm concerned once you know you'll want to spend my money like it's nothing."

"I'm not like that and I don't think I ever would be. Money doesn't mean much to me. I don't think about wealth or even the creature comforts money can buy. I'm thankful for what I earn and try to do the best job I can with the money I have."

"But what about when you have access to my money? Would you like to buy a hundred-and-ten-foot yacht with a full-time crew or maybe a small jet to fly around? How about a winter home in Aspen? All these things would be well within our means."

"I see what you're saying. A person could easily get carried away."

"True. And it's a concern. Any thoughts?"

"Just what I've already told you. I don't care about money, I care about you and our life together."

"I think that's beautiful, but you may want to keep what I said in the back of your mind. I'm sure it's bound to come up."

# Chapter Thirty-Four

I thought we were making good progress and wanted to continue. "Fair enough. Next?"

"Number six is where we would live."

"I'm flexible. I could run my business anywhere I have the internet—which is just about everywhere now. How about you?"

"New York works well for me. A lot of my business is right there. New York also offers flight connections to almost anywhere in the world, greatly facilitating international travel."

"New York works for me. How would you feel about finding a new home?"

"That makes sense. Nothing ties me to the penthouse."

"What about Daphne?"

"What about her?"

"You own her condo as well."

"I do?"

"Yes. Detective Hannity did some checking and he said you purchased the entire floor of the building."

"I don't remember that. Why was Detective Hannity investigating me?"

"He wasn't. He was investigating Daphne."

"Well, I can check with Daphne on that. I can either transfer ownership to her or sell it and she can find a new place to live as well."

"Why would you let Daphne live there for free?"

"I didn't realize I owned it. But either way, I don't believe that's any of your concern. That's the type of thing I'm worried about. If you truly respect me controlling my money, you shouldn't question how I spend it."

"Fair enough."

*But extremely odd.* I realized Erica was rich beyond belief, but why give something that valuable to someone you hadn't even met? As time went on, I had more and more questions about Daphne and her relationship with Erica. Hopefully time would provide the answers I needed.

I offered, "I understand your concern about money, but you're just going to have to accept the fact that I don't intend to have any say in what you do with it. What about number seven?"

"This one is going to be easy—children."

"We'll already have two—Rob and Anna."

"What about more?"

"More?"

"As much as I love Rob and Anna, maybe I'd like to have some of our own."

"Some?"

"Say ten or twelve."

I'd have chuckled, but I wasn't sure she was kidding. Rob was never been a problem growing up, but Anna was nothing but trouble once she turned thirteen. I'd never thought about having more children.

Cautiously, I retorted, "I'd say I'd be more comfortable with single digits."

"Like eight or nine?"

"More towards the lower end."

"One or two?"

"I was an only child, so not one."

"Two or three?"

"Sure. I'd enjoy that."

"Me too. That was easy. You've already experienced number eight. We've actually had it pretty easy, but the press, paparazzi, and the tabloids can be brutal. Do you think you're ready for that?"

"I understand it comes with the territory. For you, I'd endure even greater challenges."

"How noble. Number nine may be a little more difficult. We'll probably be apart quite a bit. Both our jobs require us to work away from home. For me, there'll be a lot of men that I work for and with. For you, a lot of women. I trust you, so I won't worry. If you do decide to stray, we're done—it's as simple as that. How do you feel about me?"

"I'll have no choice but to trust you."

"Correct, but I've had relationships with men that start out fine but before I know it they're jealous of every man I so much as look at. That's a no-go for me."

"That's harsh."

"Maybe, but I want you to know what you're getting into. Shall I continue?"

"Yes."

"I make all my own decisions. So far, so good. How do you see that changing?"

"I know that all the decisions you currently make, you'll continue to make. However, I feel we should both have input into decisions that affect our lives together or our children."

"We've already discussed the one about the difference in our ages. The last and final hurdle involves Rob and Anna."

"Really? In what way?"

"How will I fit into their lives? I don't want to be the wicked stepmother, but I do want to be able to speak up when I disagree with something they say or do."

"I understand. I don't see that as a problem. If something does come up, I'm sure we'll discuss it."

"That's exactly what I'm talking about."

She lost me on that one. "What?"

"I want you to trust me enough to know if I correct the kids it's something that needs to be done. No discussion between us beforehand. If I feel the need to say something, you'll stand behind me. No hesitation. We speak as one."

"You want to speak to the kids just like you're their mom?"

"Which I will be."

"You're right. There's no other way to effectively parent. I know you, I love you, and I always trust you to do what's right and appropriate."

"Great. We managed to successfully navigate all twelve hurtles. When do you want to get married?"

I wasn't quite ready to set a date. "From what we've talked about, I still think we have some things we need to do before the big day. Like go snowboarding, meet the family, and so on. Let's defer setting the date until we've done everything on your list. How does that sound?"

"Fine. Don't wait too long. I may lose interest."

"Really?"

"Just kidding, but the biological clock is ticking."

"Right."

# Chapter Thirty-Five

The next weekend, we snowboarded in Winter Park, Colorado. This was the end of the season and the slopes were packed. But, we both were experienced snowboarders, so we still had a ton of fun.

We planned to fly to Lake Geneva, Wisconsin, and introduce Erica to my family, the weekend after next. Much to her surprise, a last-minute overseas assignment required Erica to leave for Copenhagen the day we got back.

Rob called to touch base and I asked if he could hold on while I conferenced in Anna. Fortunately, she was available.

I asked Anna, "Is Daphne there?"

She replied, "Why, did you want to conference her in as well?"

"Not hardly. I have something private I need to tell you and Rob. I wish I could do it in person, but I don't see that happening."

Anna asked, "Is everything alright, Dad?"

"Yes. This is good news."

Rob said, "Fire away!"

"I've got a life changing event to share with you both."

Anna was concerned. "That sounds like bad news."

"Not hardly. This is one of the biggest decisions I've ever made."

Rob injected. "Just get on with it, Dad. We can tell this is something you don't take lightly."

"That's for sure. Erica and I have spent a good deal of time together over the last couple of months. We've really explored our relationship and deepened the love we have for each other."

Anna, the sensitive one, said, "Oh my God, Dad. You're getting married!"

Rob asked, "Are you serious? You're marrying Erica Richards—one of the most beautiful and sought-after women in the world? Is that it, Dad?"

"Yes. Erica and I are getting married."

Cheers went up. Rob pounded something—his desk or the bar—he could have easily been at either place. Anna seemed overjoyed as well. I sighed in relief.

I said, "I'm ecstatic. But before we tell anyone else, I wanted you both to know."

Rob tried to calm down. "Dad, I'm so excited for you. This has got to be one of the most thrilling moments of your life. As for me—Erica Richards is going to be my stepmom. Can you imagine what a chic magnet that's going to make me? To top it off, she's one of the kindest and most caring people I've ever known. I'll be the luckiest stepson in the world.

"I have the same feeling myself."

"You feel like a lucky stepson?"

"Of course not. I feel I'm one of the luckiest men in the world."

Rob shouted, "Yippee ki yay—look at us—two guys at the top of their game."

Anna thought this had gone on long enough. "Don't forget about me, boys."

I replied, "We would never do that, honey. How do you feel about me marrying Erica?"

"I love her. She's already like a second mom to me. I couldn't be any more excited."

"More excited than Rob?"

Anna said, "He's totally over the top. My excitement is a more mature reaction."

Rob couldn't let that pass. "More mature? I'll be drinking legally in a little over a year. How's that for mature?"

"Exactly. Case closed."

With that, the sibling rivalry ran its course. I'm glad they were so happy about Erica and me getting married—even if it is for totally different reasons.

I had an afterthought. "One more thing. We're going to Lake Geneva to introduce Erica to the family in two weeks and then, two week after that, we're going to meet Erica's family. You kids are a big part of both outings and I need to make sure you're available to attend."

Rob responded first, "Can't wait."

Anna added, "You can always count on me."

A couple of days later, Anna called and said Daphne wanted to meet with me before Rob got out of school. I agreed and said I'd fly up to New York the next weekend. Erica was still in Copenhagen and happy to have me stay in her condo.

Daphne and Anna hosted a dinner party the night I arrived in the city. Against my better judgment, I attended. I was surprised how beautifully Daphne's condo was decorated. If I didn't know better, I would have thought I was in Erica's. Maybe, she helped with the decorating.

There were only two other males in attendance and they came as a couple. All the women also appeared to be couples. Daphne and Anna hung all over each other.

Tonight was going to be a challenge. I loved Anna and I would have to learn to love Daphne as well. This would be hard but shouldn't be impossible. I'd start tonight by giving everyone I met hugs, even Daphne. I tried to show her the same love I showed Anna. God, this was difficult.

I could see Daphne relaxing her guard as she gave me the same care and affection I showed her. Maybe this could work.

Anna told me she wanted to bring Daphne to meet her grandparents. I knew that would be a total disaster. As accommodating as I could be, my parents were just the opposite. They viewed same-sex relationships as a sin, as an abomination before God. Daphne showing up would be the match that lit the powder keg.

I knew I shouldn't, but I said yes, that would be fine. Two steps forward, one step back. The girls were both thrilled. I doubted Daphne would make it, but I was open to the possibility. I enjoyed a good fireworks show as much as the next guy.

A few days later, Erica finished her overseas assignment and returned to

New York. I'd been working there since Daphne's party. We were able to enjoy some unexpected together time before we took off for Lake Geneva. The plan was for Daphne and Anna to join us, we'd all fly down to Durham to pick up Rob, and then on to Wisconsin.

I looked forward to seeing my parents. My mother had no filter. Whatever she thought, she said. At least half her remarks were either inappropriate or downright rude. I didn't think she'd have much of a problem with Erica, but Daphne was a whole 'nother story.

At the last minute, Daphne backed out—no big surprise. The flight up was quieter than I'd been expecting. I imagined the kids thought about what Grandma Sparrow would have to say.

We arrived before the aunts, uncles, and cousins and that helped. With Erica's notoriety, I knew the group would include many distant relatives I didn't know I even had.

Mom fixed lemonades for everyone and we all sat out on the back patio. Mom and Dad were enthralled with Erica—especially Dad, the lust-filled old man that he was.

They both knew about our rescue at sea and thanked Erica for everything she'd done. They probably didn't read it in *Maxim*.

Rob told them he switched his major at Duke from engineering to history. Grandma was concerned a history degree wouldn't be that useful. He explained he planned to go to law school. She became an instant fan. Growing up, she constantly told me I should be a lawyer. When I finally decided to go to law school, she was thrilled to death.

Anna said, "I can't wait to tell you both about my new relationship. I have a girlfriend."

Grandma didn't catch Anna's drift. "That's nice, honey. Girls need as many friends as they can have."

"No, not that kind of girlfriend. What I mean is girlfriend as in lover."

With that, Grandma's eyes opened wide, immediately followed by her mouth. Dad quickly raised his hand to deflect her next words as he helped her out of her chair. He took her into the house without saying a thing.

Anna asked, "What's the matter with Grandma?"

I said, "Nothing, sweetie. Grandpa just needed to have a word with her."

Even though Dad shut the door, we still heard the yelling and screaming but couldn't make out exactly what they said. Without Dad's intervention, I knew Anna would have been devastated and I was sure Erica would have been a little shocked as well. Rob had seen it all before, so it wouldn't have been a big deal to him. Anna was just a babe in the woods at this point.

When Anna and I were alone, we talked about her telling the other relatives about her new sexual orientation. I suggested kids her age would be supportive. Some would think it was cool. I thought their parents could go either way. And those kids' grandparents would tend to be more like Grandma. That said, I encouraged her to do whatever she wanted but to be prepared for any adverse reaction.

Erica heard about my childhood, which I'd have to say was pretty average. Most people thought I would have been spoiled as an only child, but I honestly didn't think I had it all that easy.

Erica was particularly interested in the pictures of me as a kid. Maybe she thought that would be an indication of what our kids would look like. I'd always thought I was a pretty cute child.

The next day, all my other relatives arrived. Anna got some frank reactions to her new sexual orientation, but she took them better than I would have thought. All in all, it was a good get-together and I could hardly wait to leave after church on Sunday.

Somehow, we'd made it through the weekend. The flight back was much livelier than the flight out. We couldn't stop talking about our weekend experiences.

Erica grew up in Brunswick, Maine. We would be going there in two weeks. I was glad we had some down time prior to the next parents' weekend.

# Chapter Thirty-Six

The next couple of weeks flew by. I worked ten-hour days, seven days a week. Erica had another overseas assignment. Rob started a summer seminar in banking program with Bancshares International in Nashville and Anna was living with Daphne, taking writing courses at NYU.

Erica got back to New York the day before we were scheduled to leave for her mother's home in Maine. I asked her if we were still on and she replied, "Of course."

I left early Friday morning with Rob. The plan was to pick up Erica and Anna in New York and fly to Maine. All went well.

Before we knew it, Rob and I were studying the approach to Brunswick Field. The airfield was a former naval air station, so the runways were wide and extralong. Based on prevailing winds, we expected to land on runway 19L.

Our landing instructions confirmed that was the active runway. We requested and got a VFR approach. I took the landing, and the airplane gently kissed the runway.

We taxied, parked, and arranged for overnight hangar facilities. Erica handled the car rental and we were on our way. She mentioned she was raised by a single mom, Harriett, and had an older sister, Kathleen. Her sister lived in rural Vermont.

Apparently, her mom still lived in the small cottage where she raised her girls. Erica told us she offered numerous times to buy a more substantial place for her mom to live, but she felt comfortable there and had no desire to move.

Anna and I reserved rooms at a local inn. Her mom's home was way too small to accommodate many guests, and we didn't want to burden her.

When we arrived at the house, Erica's mom, Harriett, was sweeping the front porch. How quaint. She called into the living room and on command Erica's sister, Kathleen, popped through the front door.

Erica gave her mom and sister hugs. We tried to shake hands, but neither woman would have anything to do with that and gave us all big family-style embraces. Her mom ushered us all inside.

The house had a traditional feel to it. We all sat down and Harriett brought us unsweetened iced tea. That would take some getting used to. Sweet tea had always been my brew of choice.

After a few minutes of chitchat, Erica broke the big news. "Mom, Kathleen, I wanted you to meet Jack and his children. I know you've heard me talk about them. Rob is a junior at Duke University and plans to study law. Anna is currently taking writing courses at NYU and plans on going into journalism. Jack and I are engaged."

I guess that all flowed, but I felt she'd attached a whopper to the end of pretty much routine information. I could tell from Kathleen and Harriett's stunned looks they felt the same way.

Kathleen reacted first. "Erica, this comes as quite a surprise. I know you've known Jack awhile and you two have been through some trying times together, but marriage?"

Erica confidently replied, "Yes, marriage. You're right on both counts. Jack are I are deeply in love and we've had a number of heart-to-heart discussions. Neither one of us takes marriage lightly, and we wouldn't get married if we had any reservations whatsoever."

That pretty much said it all. Harriett and Kathleen's concerns were silenced. They congratulated all four of us and told us how thrilled they were to hear the big news.

Erica's mom insisted on fixing dinner. There wasn't much we could say. I'd never seen Erica cook anything besides breakfast, but her mom's culinary skills were over the top. Dinner was a feast to behold. We all devoured dessert as well.

Table conversation was light. We were all tired and around nine, the kids and I excused ourselves. Erica wanted to stay with her sister and Mom and gave me the car keys. We drove back to the inn, checked into our rooms and quickly fell asleep.

The next morning, the three of us grabbed the complimentary breakfast and headed back to the house. When we got there, Erica said she wanted to show us the town she'd grown up in. We all thought that would be fun.

Brunswick was basically a Navy town. Most everyone had some sort of connection to the former naval air station. Erica never mentioned her dad to me but told us this morning he'd been a Navy P-3 pilot. Rob and I both thought that was pretty cool.

She also mentioned a younger sister who along with her dad were killed by a drunk driver. Anna commented to Erica that that loss must have been difficult for the entire family. Erica replied that she'd been devastated. We let that subject drop without any further discussion.

# Chapter Thirty-Seven

A few minutes later, Erica was in tour guide mode. She showed us the schools she attended, the parks she frequented and all the famous local hangouts and landmarks. Brunswick got its start as a fishing village, and the area featured a number of sea captains' houses. The home I found most interesting, though, was the one where Harriet Beecher Stowe wrote *Uncle Tom's Cabin* between 1850 and 1852. As a promising writer herself, Anna found that equally intriguing.

For lunch, we enjoyed fresh lobster at a bustling waterfront restaurant. Erica worked there as a teenager and most of the people she worked with were still on the job. They greeted her like returning royalty. I'm sure it was great fun for her. She had real affection for everyone. I was glad to see that.

By the time we got back to her house, I was ready to take it easy for a while. Apparently, that wasn't in the cards. Kathleen's husband, Hank, and their three kids, ages five to nine, joined us for the afternoon festivities.

The change in the activity level was pronounced. The men, including Hank's two boys, threw the football in the front yard. The women and Kathleen's daughter were inside, sitting on the sofa, looking through old photo albums.

When I came back in from football, I noticed a number of family photos on the hallway wall. Erica's mom saw I was studying them as she walked by. She stopped and joined me.

The one I was looking at was an eight-by-ten of Kathleen, Erica, her little sister, Harriett and her dad. Harriett got a little choked up on that one. She took it down from the wall and ran her hand across all five people. She wiped a tear from her eye.

I put my arm around her and she leaned her shoulder against my chest. After a couple of minutes, she hung the photo back up and asked me to follow her to the kitchen. She said she needed a hand with the drinks.

As she was pouring, she stopped and looked at me. "Did Erica tell you about her younger sister and father?"

"She did. It sounded terrible."

"Oh, you don't know the half of it."

I guessed I didn't. We both sat down at the little table in the kitchen and Harriett began, "Erica was five when her baby sister was born. She doted on her and would feed her, change her diapers, and rock her, even though she wasn't much older herself. I don't know what I would have done without Erica's help.

"As the baby got older, Erica was the first person to serve her solid food. She taught her how to use the potty and was pretty much her second mom. Erica loved that little girl more than anyone in the world."

I could see what was coming and reached across the table to put my hand on top of Harriett's. She appreciated that.

She continued, "One afternoon, Erica's dad took our youngest to the local market for a couple of things I needed for dinner. As they walked from the car to the store, a drunk driver hit and killed them both.

"We were all devastated. Erica was uncontrollable. I've never seen anyone as upset as she was over the death of her baby sister. That little girl was almost Erica's entire world. She refused to believe she was gone. We put her in counseling, and continued that for many years. Eventually, Erica recovered enough to function again.

"She and I have talked about our loss a number of times. She remembers almost nothing from the first couple of years after her sister died. The doctor told us that wasn't unusual.

"Erica experienced severe trauma. I felt so sorry for her, but besides counseling, there wasn't much I could do. Eventually, she came around. For the last ten years, I'd say she's mostly recovered."

I ventured, "I don't know what to say. That's so awful. Poor Erica—the whole family for that matter. I'm so glad you all somehow made it through that."

"As am I. I wouldn't tell this to anyone except you. Since the two of you are getting married, I thought you should know all her history."

"I don't think it's anything I'd ever bring up, but I appreciate you telling me. By the way, what was her little sister's name?"

"Daphne."

*What? No. Not possible. No way. Unh-uh.*

Trembling, I managed, "And your husband's name?"

"Well, we both grew up on farms. Back then, a whole different set of names was popular—thus my name, Harriett."

Enough. "And your husband's name?"

"His name was Erwin."

I couldn't breathe. Everything around me blurred. My heart loudly pounded in my head. I couldn't speak. I didn't know what was happening.

Oh my God. Daphne Erwin—Erica's baby sister and dad. I didn't know what to do. And poor Harriett. How would she take the news? I wasn't about to say anything until I could calm down and get an idea how to deal with this absolute shitstorm.

I tried my best to put this out of my mind, but it was much easier said than done. I helped carry the drinks and snacks into the living room. I talked as much as I could with Kathleen, Hank, and their kids. I'm sure Erica noticed I avoided her, but I wasn't ready to face her. I had no idea what I would say.

Finally, she'd had about as much as she could stand and took me aside. She asked, "Is something the matter?"

I lied, "I'm not feeling well. I need to go back to the room. Would that be alright?"

Hesitantly, she said, "Fine. Are you able to drive?"

"Yes. Thanks."

# Chapter Thirty-Eight

Once I got back to the inn, I knew I'd have to stage some sort of fake emergency that would allow us to make a quick exit and return to Tennessee. *I've got it.* I'd tell everyone Caroline had a bad accident and we needed to fly to Florida as soon as possible. Rob and Anna would be upset and have a million questions. I'd have to field them as best I could.

I called Erica. "I just got a call. Aunt Caroline has been in a terrible accident and they don't know if she's going to live. The kids and I need to leave this afternoon and fly down to Florida. Could you please give everyone our apologies? I'll pack things up here and be by to pick the kids up in twenty minutes. Thanks."

Erica bought that. She asked if she needed to join us. I said thanks but thought we could better handle this on our own. She understood.

I packed up everything, checked out, and drove to Erica's. We all said our goodbyes and took off for the airport. I'd called ahead so our plane could be pulled out of the hangar and refueled.

I'd told Rob and Anna it was too late to fly all the way to Florida so I planned to only fly as far as Nashville tonight. They both seemed fine with that.

As soon as we leveled off, I set the autopilot, and asked them if they could hear me. They both replied in the affirmative.

I began, "Aunt Caroline is fine. There was no accident."

The protests were instantaneous. "How could you upset us like that, Dad?" "We were both heartbroken." "You know how we feel about Aunt Caroline."

"I'm sorry. But I discovered Erica has a serious mental illness and didn't know how to deal with it. I thought the best thing would be to leave and take

131

some time to figure things out. I hope you both understand."

Rob asked, "What kind of mental illness does Erica have?"

"I don't feel comfortable discussing that until I have more facts. Anna, I'm hoping you can stay in Nashville for a little while and help me do some research. I could really use your support."

"Of course, Dad. You know you can always count on me."

Rob objected, "What about me? I'm a year older with one more year of college—shouldn't I be helping you with the research?"

"You're right, Rob, but you need to get back to your job with Bancshares. You can report for work first thing in the morning."

"Fine, but I want to know all the details as soon as you put everything together."

"Will do."

"Does Erica know?"

"No."

"Her mom, her sister?"

"No and no."

"That's odd. So, her fiancé knows something about her mental health that neither she nor anyone in her family knows."

"Correct."

"That's so strange."

"I'll tell you as soon as we figure it out. Believe me, you'll be the first to know."

"I guess that will have to do."

"I love you both more than words can express."

Anna replied, "Thanks, Dad. We love you and we're going to help you through this. You can always count on the two of us."

"I know. I'm so thankful to have the two best kids in the world."

"Boy, Dad, this has really changed your perspective."

"Totally." And I left it at that.

We landed at Nashville, picked up the car, and drove home. We arrived a little before midnight. I told the kids goodnight and called Erica to let her know we'd made the first leg of the trip just fine.

# Chapter Thirty-Nine

I got up around eight and made breakfast. Rob had already left for his internship in downtown Nashville. As soon as Anna came into the kitchen, I served her bacon, eggs, and toast, and joined her at the table.

When she was almost done, I said, "You know I mentioned Erica's mental illness."

"Yes."

"I'm afraid to say it affects Daphne as well."

With that, she let her fork drop to her plate and gave me her undivided attention.

I continued, "When we were at Erica's house, I looked at some of the family photos on the hallway wall. A picture that included Harriett, a man I guessed to be the dad, and three little girls, caught my eye. Her mom walked by and stopped to tell me about the baby.

"She said the little girl was Erica's pride and joy. She was like her favorite doll that had come to life. Erica was like a second mom. That little girl was almost her entire world. And then, the unthinkable happened."

"I felt so sorry for Erica when she told us."

"Well, you don't know the half of it. Erica was devastated. She couldn't sleep, couldn't eat. Her world collapsed around her. Neither her mom nor her older sister could console her. She felt like she'd lost everything.

"After a couple of months, her mom put her in therapy. Her progress was unbearably slow. She refused to accept her sister was gone. She would tell the therapist the little girl still lived with them. Her mom didn't know what to do."

I paused. Anna said, "That's one of the most disturbing stories I've ever heard. I'm surprised she ever recovered from that trauma."

"She seems normal now, but I'm not sure she ever has recovered."

"Why do you say that, Dad?"

"Her sister's name was Daphne."

I could see a look of confusion in Anna's eyes. She asked, "How could that be?"

I ignored her question. "Her dad's name was Erwin."

Anna burst into tears and held her head in her hands. She cried uncontrollably and was so upset she had difficulty catching her breath. I tried to comfort her, but it was useless, so I just let her cry it out. We both knew the truth. Accepting it was a whole 'nother thing.

I wanted to give Anna some time to calm down and poured us some coffee. Her crying tapered off.

After about thirty minutes, she said, "What are we going to do?"

"I don't know. I'd thought we'd start by talking to a psychiatrist and getting all the facts we can. When I was a kid, I saw a movie called *The Three Faces of Eve*. Eve had two additional personalities. One of them was scary as hell."

"You think Erica and Daphne are the same person?"

"I do."

"Do you have any proof?"

"No. But I do have four things that make me think that. The first is the name—Daphne Erwin—her deceased sister and father. That's way too much of a coincidence.

"Second, when Daphne fired the gun at me in Erica's bedroom, I reported the incident to the police. They checked everything out. They recovered the bullet in the wall. The gun was back in the nightstand and they test-fired it. The two bullets matched. Then they dusted the room and the gun for fingerprints. All they found was the maid's, mine, and Erica's. Granted, Daphne could have worn gloves, but it's mighty suspicious.

"Third, I've never seen the two together at the same time.

"Fourth, the two women resemble each other. The glasses and the hair bun are a relatively simple disguise."

Anna took exception to that. "The glasses are for real. Daphne is as blind as a bat without them. I've looked through them myself and all I saw were blurs."

"Well, we'll need to research that as well."

"I still don't believe they're the same person."

"I'm not one hundred percent sure either."

"What if Daphne calls?"

"Put her off. Say your dad needs help in Nashville for a while and then you'll be returning to New York."

Just then, my cell phone rang. It was Erica. I knew I had to answer.

She said, "I'd thought you'd be on your way to Florida by now."

"We would be, but we got a call from Caroline's husband and he said the injuries weren't nearly as serious as they first thought."

"I'm relieved to hear that. Are you still going?"

"Maybe in a few days. I need to take care of some unexpected business here first."

"I was so worried about Caroline that I went online to see if I could get some information on the accident, but I couldn't find a thing."

"That's odd, but I know Caroline's driver's license is still in her maiden name."

"What's that?"

"Krzyzanowski."

"How do you spell it?"

"I used to know but I can't remember. I haven't thought about it for years."

"That's alright. Please give her my best wishes."

"Will do."

"I'm actually leaving for Poland in the morning. I've got a photo shoot in Ganske. If you remember how to spell the name, text it to me and I'll do some research."

"You got it. Safe travels. Love you."

Once again, she hung up without reciprocating the "Love you" or saying goodbye.

Anna reacted, "That was a little dicey."

"Right. I hope she bought it."

"Sounds like she did. I hope Daphne doesn't call anytime soon."

"Why don't you send her a text outlining your plans?"

"Good idea."

# Chapter Forty

Anna and I both did some research on multiple personalities. Turns out, the disorder wasn't called that anymore. Now it was known as Dissociative Identity Disorder. I read that there was no cure, but long-term treatment could help. I also discovered that people with the disorder could experience a number of other psychiatric problems. Those ran the gamut of mental illnesses.

I felt we needed to talk with a professional and called Vanderbilt University. The receptionist directed my call to Dr. Ernst Leonhard, chief of staff of the psychiatric hospital and a specialist in treating psychotic disorders. I made an appointment for Anna and me to meet with him the following afternoon.

The next morning, we made a list of our questions. We were interrupted by a call from Daphne. Anna took it in the other room.

She came back about an hour later and I asked her how it had gone.

She replied, "Probably as well as could be expected. I'm really not comfortable lying to Daphne. She's such an honest and sincere person. I did the best I could under the circumstances."

"You do realize Daphne and Erica are probably the same person?"

"They may be physically the same, but psychologically they're two different people. I'm in love with one and you're in love with the other."

"I never thought of it in that way, but you're right."

With that in mind, I jotted down a couple of additional questions for Dr. Leonhard.

After lunch, we reviewed our questions. Anna and I took a few minutes to identify and refine the most important ones. We decided to save the rest for another day.

The drive to Vanderbilt took less than thirty minutes. Dr. Leonhard's offices were in the psychiatric hospital on Twenty-Third Street South—the southern edge of the campus. As a result, it was easy to locate and parking was readily available.

Dr. Leonhard graciously welcomed us. I'd told him a couple of things over the phone the day before.

He began, "You both know different personalities that you believe belong to the same woman."

We answered simultaneously. "Correct."

"Can you tell me a little more about those two people?"

I replied, "We can, but we're pretty sure we're talking about one person."

"What gives us our individuality if not our personalities? I want to learn about each person, each personality."

We told him. I spoke about Erica and Anna spoke about Daphne.

After about twenty minutes, he said, "I think that's enough information. Obviously, you both care deeply about the personality you experience. Now, please tell me why you believe these two personalities belong to the same person."

I relayed our trip to Erica's house and what the mom told me about Daphne and Erwin. The professor looked like he had that same aha moment both Anna and I experienced.

When we were done, he said, "You know I can't make a diagnosis without personally talking with one or preferably both of these women."

I said, "Yes, we know that. We're not here for a diagnosis, but we'd like to learn a little bit more about this disorder and possible treatments."

"Those are two things I can definitely help you with. What are your questions?"

"Our main concern is could one of these women become violent and be a threat to either one of us?"

"Most people with DID are not violent, contrary to what the movies depict. That said, you never know with this disorder. Really, anything could happen."

"We both know we can't continue our relationships. What's the safest way to break them off?"

"I honestly don't know. Anything you say or do could trigger an unexpected and possibly violent reaction."

"That sounds both scary and potentially dangerous."

"Maybe so, maybe not. You never know. Have you ever seen either woman exhibit violent or threatening behavior?"

I replied, "Yes."

"Well, there you go."

"Is there any way we could help these women recover from this disorder?"

"No. Now that you suspect it, your best route would be to steer clear of both of them. The only thing you could possibly do is to get them some professional help."

"Will they ever recover?"

"In all honesty, they probably won't."

"Do you have any idea what could have caused this?"

"Usually a traumatic childhood event like the one Erica experienced."

"One of the women needs glasses and the other doesn't. Is that possible?"

"Yes. That's been documented in several cases." Dr. Leonhard looked at his watch. "I'm sorry, but I've got another appointment. I'd be happy to talk with you further if you'd like to schedule another time to do that."

We thanked him and left. Anna and I had both hoped for some answers. We'd gotten a couple, but the big question—what should we do?—was still up in the air. We'd have to figure that out on our own.

# Part Five

# Murder

# Chapter Forty-One

A couple of weeks later, I got an unexpected call from Detective Hannity. I couldn't imagine why he was calling.

I answered the phone with, "You're probably the last person in the world I expected to hear from."

"Yeah, good to hear your voice as well."

"I'm sorry. How can I help you?"

"I need you to fly to Brunswick, Maine, and I'll meet you there."

"Can you tell me a little more about what's going on?"

"Nope. And I need you not to say a word to anyone, especially Erica Richards."

"Alright. I can be there tomorrow afternoon."

"Great. Hillary and I will meet you at the airport."

Anna was in the living room with me when I took the call.

She asked, "What was all that about?"

"I'm not supposed to say and really I don't have any idea."

"Okay—that's weird."

"I know. I need to fly to Brunswick, Maine, tomorrow."

"Can I come?"

"Sure. I don't see why not. I can't tell you anything, which is easy because I know nothing."

"That's so strange, Dad. Who was on the phone?"

"Detective Hannity with the New York Police Department."

"I can't imagine why he'd be in Brunswick, Maine."

"Me neither. We'll just have to wait and see."

We got up bright and early the next morning and took off for Maine. We had an unexpected tailwind and made great time. We landed just after lunch. I'd called Hannity on the satellite phone when we were over New York. He told us to get a room at the inn and he'd meet us there.

Hannity and Clinton arrived around three thirty that afternoon. The four of us sat at one of the tables the innkeeper used for breakfast.

Hannity began, "I've got some sad news."

I grabbed ahold of Anna's hand and asked him what that was.

He said, "Erica's mother has been murdered."

Anna and I both gasped. We were shocked. She was such a kind, gentle person. Who would ever want to hurt her?

I asked, "Do you have any leads?"

"Just a couple so far."

"What are they?"

"Harriett was shot at close range and the bullet went clean through her body. Forensics dug the slug out of the wall. The caliber is .45.

"We believe the lab will establish that bullet was fired from Erica's 1911 Colt revolver."

"How could that be? I can't imagine Erica would ever hurt her mother. She thought the world of her."

"We don't think she did it."

"Who do you suspect?"

"Daphne Erwin."

"I don't believe Daphne even knows the woman much less where she lives. Why in the world would you suspect Daphne?"

"Harriett Richards didn't die immediately. Whoever shot her left her for dead. Before she breathed her last breath, she was able to write 'Dap' on the kitchen floor in her own blood."

# Chapter Forty-Two

Anna raced for the bathroom and threw up. I understood how she felt. My stomach turned somersaults as well.

I asked, "How can I help?"

Hannity replied, "We'd like you to come with us to the house and fill in some blanks."

"What about Anna?"

"I think she should stay at the inn. I can have Hillary stay with her if that would help."

"That would be great. Thanks, Hillary."

Hillary replied, "Don't mention it."

When Anna came back into the room, we told her what Hannity and I were going to do. She seemed relieved that Hillary would be staying with her.

We met a local detective, Henry Sparks, at the house. The three of us went in through the front door.

I asked, "Was there any sign of a forced entry?"

Sparks replied, "None at all. The perpetrator either had a key or knew Harriett."

We walked down the hall. Three pictures were missing from the wall.

"Did you take down some of the pictures?"

"We didn't. That was one of the things we wanted to ask you about."

"Well, when we were here, there were three more pictures on the wall."

"Can you remember anything about the pictures that are missing?"

"Let me study the wall a minute." After several minutes, I said, "Two of those pictures included Erica's deceased younger sister, Daphne."

"Bingo."

"And the third?"

"Her father, Erwin."

"Double bingo. Daphne Erwin—our number one suspect."

"What could her motive have been?"

"We're not sure Daphne Erwin is a real person."

"Anna would steadfastly object to that statement. She's in love with Daphne."

"That may well be, but from all the facts, Daphne and Erica are the same person."

"They seem like different people to me. One I'm in love with. The other I can't stand."

"Different personalities, same person."

"Why do you say that?"

"Only one set of prints between them. Daphne has no basis to exist. Except for the fact that several people know her, she has none of the attributes of a living, breathing human being."

"I ask again, what could her motive have been?"

"We'll need to talk more with our psychiatrist, but on the surface, we think she may have felt threatened by Erica's mom. She may have feared the mom would reveal her as a fraud."

"The mom didn't even know her."

"True. But the mom knew Daphne and the mom knew Erwin and she would be most skeptical of a woman that lived next door to Erica with the name Daphne Erwin."

"How are you going to handle this?"

"We're working on that."

"What about Erica? She's going to be devastated by this news. Who's going to tell her?"

Hannity volunteered. "You are."

"No way."

"Way. You remember that favor you owe me."

"Uh-huh."

"Well, this is it. You're going to tell Erica."

"Okay, but I'm going to need some support."

"Don't worry about that. I'm going with you and I'll bring a department psychiatrist."

"Maybe Anna should come as well."

"Either way. That's up to you."

"Are you going to arrest her?"

"Probably not. We may take her for psychiatric care."

"A mental hospital?"

"A facility. For her own protection and so we can better work through this whole issue."

That made sense. Really, it might have been the best solution for everyone.

# Chapter Forty-Three

That night, I called Erica's public relations person.

"Hi, Patsy, Jack Sparrow."

"Hi, Jack. I wasn't expecting you to call."

"I wouldn't but Erica is desperately going to need your help tomorrow. I'll be heading up a group that will be meeting with her."

"Of course, Jack. I'm happy to help Erica any way I can. But I'm a little curious—why didn't she call?"

"She doesn't know about the meeting."

"That's a little odd."

"You have no idea."

"I appreciate your help, Jack, but I work for Erica. I'll need to talk with her before I do anything."

"What happens tomorrow will come as a total shock to Erica. All I can tell you is it's a police matter. Anything you say to her before then would make her situation that much more difficult.

"Patsy, we've known each other for some time and you're just going to have to trust me. Erica needs you. Are you alright with that?"

"Jack, I think the world of you and realize you're the best thing to ever happen to Erica. I'm really not comfortable with this, but I'm willing to go along—just this one time."

"Thank you, Patsy. We're all going to meet in Erica's lobby at ten tomorrow morning. Will that work for you?"

"No problem. I'll keep my mouth shut and see you then. Bye."

I told Hannity about Patsy and he seemed pleased she was coming. His exact words were "the more the merrier."

The next morning, we all met in the lobby of Erica's building. I'd called the doorman beforehand and asked him not to announce our presence to Erica. He reluctantly agreed.

As soon as everyone was there, I called Erica and told her I was in the lobby and needed to meet with her urgently. She said fine and sent the elevator down. Our group shuffled inside and took off for the penthouse.

The doors opened. I stood in front. Erica was surprised to see the crowd of people behind me. We hugged. Erica and Anna hugged. Erica asked Patsy what she was doing here. She replied that I had asked her to come.

She had never met Detective Hannity, so I introduced them. He introduced his partner, Detective Hillary Clinton, and the department psychiatrist, Dr. Farley Hammond. Erica shook hands with each of them. She invited us all to sit in the living room.

I sat next to Erica and took both of her hands in mine. "Erica, I have some heartbreaking news. I wish I could tell you by myself, but that's not possible. It concerns your mom."

I could see the panic in her eyes. She started to squirm away. "No, not Mom. I don't want to hear it."

"You need to know"—I grabbed her hands again—"your mom has passed away."

"No, no, no. That's not possible. We talked this weekend and she was great. No complaints. No problems. She's got to be alright."

"I'm so sorry, but she's not. She was murdered."

"Murdered? How could that be?"

"Someone killed her."

"No, no, no. That can't be. She is too nice a person. No one would ever do that."

Right then, Erica realized what had happened. I felt so sorry for her. We both cried. We hugged. I patted her back. Suddenly, I felt her whole demeanor change. She threw me back and violently stood up.

Daphne viciously looked at us. "That bitch didn't deserve to live. She threatened to destroy me. I had no choice."

With that she pulled a gun from her purse and pointed it at us. All of a sudden, she noticed Anna, and lowered the gun. "I'm so sorry you have to be here, love. I'm not like this. I really don't understand what's happening."

With that, Hannity lunged for the gun. As he fell on top of Daphne, there was a loud bang. We all jumped for cover. I wasn't sure where the shot went. Hannity was lying on top of Daphne on the sofa. In a minute, he stood up and took the handcuffs off his belt. He turned Daphne over and handcuffed her. I could see blood on the sofa.

Hannity picked up his radio and requested an ambulance. He asked me to notify the doorman and send down the elevator.

Minutes later, the medics arrived, treated Daphne, and put her on a stretcher. Anna and Hillary went with her to the hospital. I stayed with Patsy.

She looked confused. "What just happened?"

I understood how she felt. It was nothing anyone could possibly be prepared to deal with. Hannity tried his best to review the facts with her. All Patsy could say was, "I'm so confused. I don't understand."

I comforted her as best I could. Hannity explained he had to return to the police station to file his report.

I asked him, "What's going to happen?"

"I don't know. This is an unusual case. Erica's notoriety and mental illness make it much harder to see how things are going to play out."

"Where will they take her?"

"To Mount Sinai Hospital to treat the gunshot wound. After that, she'll be going to the prison ward at Elmhurst Hospital in Queens, where she'll receive psychiatric care."

"Can I see her?"

"Yes, any day between nine a.m. and six p.m."

"Thank you, Detective Hannity."

"For what? I arrested your girlfriend."

"When she pulled the gun, you could have pulled yours and shot her. She's alive because of your restraint."

Hannity smiled. "I didn't want to shoot the wrong woman."

Patsy collected herself and asked Hannity, "Do you have any idea how the district attorney will deal with this?"

"None whatsoever. I can't wait to lay everything in his lap."

Hannity excused himself, and Patsy and I sat at the dining room table.

I explained the situation to her one more time, and asked, "What can we do to protect Erica?"

"I don't know. I'm not familiar with the whole multiple personality thing. I think we need to get a psychiatrist and Erica's lawyer up here as soon as possible."

# Chapter Forty-Four

I agreed and Patsy made the calls. Within an hour, we assembled a complete psychiatric and legal team. They asked me to briefly describe what had happened with enough background for them to understand it.

I did my best. "Erica and I were making plans to get married. She took me to her mother's house to meet with her, her sister, and a number of other relatives. The mom told me about Erica's younger sister, Daphne, and father, Erwin, who were both killed by a drunk driver. Daphne was more than a sister to Erica. She thought of Daphne as her baby. Needless to say, Daphne's death devastated Erica.

"The woman that occupies the other half of this penthouse floor is Daphne Erwin. She resembles Erica but looks different enough to be her own person. Daphne has a violent side and threatened me once with a gun.

"Apparently, Daphne killed Erica's mother. The mom, just before she died, was able to write the letters 'Dap' on the kitchen floor in her own blood. Daphne Erwin. The detective asked me to break the news to Erica about her mom. As soon as I told her, she became enraged and assumed her Daphne personality. She immediately pulled a gun on us. The detective wrestled with her and the gun went off. Daphne was wounded and taken to Elmhurst Hospital. How's that?"

The lead attorney responded, "Unbelievable."

"Exactly. But we desperately need to help Erica. I feel she's in terrible danger both from other prisoners and herself. We need to come up with a plan right now to get her released from custody and placed into the best possible care we can find. Any ideas?"

I surveyed the group. The psychiatrist responded first. "I would need to talk with Erica to be sure, but from what you've said she seems to be suffering from Dissociative Identity Disorder and probably a number of other psychoses. As such, the best treatment program I'm aware of is near Geneva, Switzerland, at the Château de Flavienne."

I started a list of actions. "Number one, psychiatric evaluation."

The criminal attorney said, "We need to prepare an argument for releasing Erica to the custody of the Swiss clinic."

I added, "Two. Legal argument to release Erica to clinic."

The attorney continued, "Jack, I propose we offer the court a sweetener—a deal so good they'd never even think about turning us down."

"What do you have in mind?"

"I think we should offer to pay all the expenses of Erica's transport to the clinic and the cost of care while she's there. Knowing how tight prisons budgets are in New York, I can't imagine the court not accepting."

A consensus developed between the attorneys. I agreed to do what I could to make that happen and added it as number three on my list.

Another attorney chimed in, "I doubt they'll even charge her until her psychological condition is resolved. That can be to our advantage. I'm going to file a request for her transfer to the clinic immediately."

"So ultimately, do you feel she could be charged with murder?"

"That's so far down the road it's not worth considering. Doctor, is this disease curable?"

The psychiatrist answered, "Generally, no."

"There you go."

I asked Patsy, "Do you see Erica's career as over?"

"Definitely. I don't think she'll ever model again. Fortunately, she's already made more than enough money to take care of herself for the rest of her life."

"We need to do everything we can to assure Erica continues to be endeared by the public. She'll need their love and support now more than ever. Do you think you could put together a public relations plan?"

"Absolutely. I'll get right on it."

Everyone knew what they needed to do, so I asked each to proceed along those lines.

Once I gave the situation a little more thought, I realized I was going to have to call Erica's sister, Kathleen. She would be the one to coordinate Erica's legal battle and psychiatrist treatment. I got her on the phone and asked if I could fly up to Vermont and meet with her as soon as possible.

She already knew about her mother's murder but hadn't heard anything from Erica. I told her I would fill her in when I got there. I called the airport to ready my plane and the car service to pick me up. While I waited, I called Anna to check on Erica.

She began, "The prison ward is pretty gruesome. Many of the patients are yelling and screaming at the top of their lungs. Most want drugs.

"Erica is confused. Daphne understands everything that's happening. Erica is experiencing an ongoing switch between personalities. One minute she's Erica, the next she's Daphne. It's almost more than I can handle."

Anna took a breath and I interjected, "Anything else?"

"Daphne has requested her glasses and told me where you can find them." She relayed the instructions.

"I'm flying to Vermont tonight to meet with Kathleen. The psychiatrist should be leaving momentarily to meet with Erica. I'll give him the glasses for Daphne and then I'm off to the airport."

Anna was close to reaching her limit. "I don't know how much more of this I can take."

"Please stay until the psychiatrist arrives, and tell Erica I'll be there as soon as I can."

"I'll do my best."

Kathleen lived just outside Stowe, Vermont. I landed at the local airport a little after eight that evening, rented a car, and drove to her small farm. She and Hank had just put the kids to bed.

I quickly determined how much they already knew. I wanted to fill in the blanks the best I could. I told them about Erica's mental illness, about Daphne Erwin and what happened earlier today in New York. Kathleen and Hank both looked at me in disbelief.

I went on, "Kathleen, as Erica's closest relative, you will need to manage her finances, her legal situation, and her care."

Kathleen thought for a minute. "No way."

"Excuse me?"

"There's no possible way I could do all that. I have my hands full helping Hank on the farm, taking care of the kids, and handling my mom's affairs. Jack, you're the one person who knows and understands everything that's happening. Erica trusts you. You need to take control of all her affairs and do what's best for her."

"Thank you. But I'm just a fiancé. I have no legal relationship with Erica."

"That's what attorneys are for. I understand she has a shitload of them. Put them to work. Send me whatever I need to sign. I trust you. Erica is fortunate to have you."

"Alright, I can do that. You realize there's a significant amount of money involved."

"I do. All that money is Erica's. As long as she's alive, it needs to benefit her. I have no claim to it whatsoever."

"Neither do I."

"Of course not, but you will need to live while you're working on Erica's behalf."

"As her sister, you'll always have the ultimate say in everything that happens."

"I'm fine with that. I just desperately need your help. I can take care of Mom's stuff, but you're going to have to take control of Erica's affairs."

"I understand. I'll talk with the attorneys and keep you informed of everything that's happening. You'll also need to approve any payments to me."

"Fair enough. I can do that."

"Please let me know when you've made arrangements for your mom. I want to be sure to be there. I'll try to see if there's any way Erica can come as well."

"That's fine as long as Daphne doesn't show up."

"That could be tricky. I'd have to coordinate everything with the courts and the psychiatrist. Maybe a video feed would be the best solution."

"That's a much better idea, Jack. I feel so good that you're going to coordinate Erica's care."

"I'll do the best I can."

"I know you will. Thank you."

# Chapter Forty-Five

Kathleen invited me to spend the night at the farm. I told her I needed to get to the hospital as soon as possible. While I was pulling out of the driveway, I called Anna.

She answered, "Oh my God, Dad. This place is a madhouse."

"What's happening?"

"Well, first of all we have the alternating appearances of Erica and Daphne. When Daphne appears, she immediately makes her presence known. Then we have Erica's team of psychiatrists, and then the city team of specialists. It's exhausting."

"I should be there in a couple of hours. Please hang on. I know Erica and Daphne both love you, and right now they're both depending on your support."

"You're right, but I'm so tired I can hardly keep my eyes open. I can't wait to see you. Please hurry."

Before I took off, I located the airfield closest to the hospital. I filed an IFR flight plan since I'd be flying on instruments.

Once I leveled off and set the autopilot, I called Erica's lead attorney. He said he was waiting on a preliminary evaluation from the psychiatrist. He'd also been in touch with the clinic in Switzerland and was arranging for Erica's admission to that facility. I felt things moved forward as quickly as they could.

I knew the key would be to get New York to release Erica to the clinic. I doubted the city wanted to bear the cost of her care and treatment. Also, I didn't see how the legal system could possibly treat Daphne and Erica both fairly.

My hope was that the clinic could cure Erica and that Daphne would disappear. I knew that was a long shot, but I also knew how important it was to have a goal. I preached that to my groups day in and day out. I had my goal. Now, all I'd need to do was figure out how to achieve it.

The flight and landing were uneventful. By now, it was well after midnight. I took a cab to Elmhurst. Hannity met me at the hospital and asked me if I had a minute. I figured it would be time well spent. We talked in the cafeteria over coffee.

Hannity began, "Lots has happened. I thought you'd want an update."

"Thanks."

"You bet. Both city and private psychiatrists completed their preliminary psychological evaluations. They're in total agreement and are currently presenting a joint report to the night court judge. Both attorneys are recommending a transfer to the Swiss clinic for Erica's care and treatment. Erica has offered to cover the entire cost. I think the court is going to accept her offer.

"The court will require an evaluation of the clinic's security and a plan as to how the clinic will ensure Erica doesn't leave the facility without proper authorization. That shouldn't take long to prepare and review. In addition, the clinic will have to provide monthly reports to the court and district attorney on Erica's treatment and current evaluation.

"What about the murder charges in Brunswick, Maine?"

"We haven't received an extradition order on those. In the meantime, Erica's been charged with menacing a police officer in New York City, which is a Class D felony with a minimum sentence of two years and a maximum of seven. The DA has offered to defer prosecution on that charge if Erica voluntarily agrees to psychiatric treatment and covers all the costs."

"That's a lot of moving parts."

"You're telling me. Meanwhile, after the psychiatrists completed their work, Erica was heavily medicated. I sent Anna to a hotel and suggest you join her there."

"When can I see Erica?"

"You can schedule a time to come by tomorrow and the doctors will manage her medication accordingly. Here's a name and number for you to call to do that." Hannity handed me a piece of paper.

"I can't thank you enough for all you've done. You're a real jewel."

"Yeah, that's what all the girls say. Now, go to the hotel and get some rest. We'll talk again tomorrow."

I grabbed a cab to the hotel where Anna was staying. She had a room with two beds and was knocked out on one of them. I quickly crashed in the other.

We both woke up around ten the next morning. I called the hospital first thing and scheduled an appointment for three that afternoon. They said they'd try to wean Erica off the medication between now and then.

Anna and I had a delicious breakfast in the hotel dining room. I couldn't remember the last time I'd eaten and was famished. Anna wasn't far behind.

I asked her, "How are you doing?"

"Much better now. Yesterday afternoon and last night were a nightmare."

"I'm sorry, but I felt it was important for you to be there."

"I suppose so. Both women appreciated that I was there. I, on the other hand, had a tough time dealing with them as they went back and forth from one personality to the other. Add to that the mayhem of the psych ward and I thought I was the one losing my mind."

"I'm sure you did a great job."

Then I filled her in on my trip to Kathleen's and what Hannity told me last night.

She replied, "That all sounds good, but for now all I want to do is go home to Franklin and try my best to regain my sanity."

I understood and made her a flight reservation. I then said, "I'm going to stay with Erica for now."

She wished me luck.

# Chapter Forty-Six

After I dropped Anna off at LaGuardia, I called Erica's lead attorney, Harmon Stanus, for an update.

He got right to the point. "The court approved Erica's transfer to the Swiss clinic."

I was surprised. "How did you get them to do that?"

"Erica's offer to cover all the costs did the trick. The city looked to save hundreds of thousands of dollars and readily accepted her offer.

"The actual transfer process has a number of security provisions that require a great deal of coordination between our team and the US Marshals. The marshals will be providing all the security for transporting her to the clinic. We need to assure that every aspect of the court order is strictly adhered to.

"At Kathleen's request, we've also prepared all the documents naming you Erica's guardian and providing you conservatorship of all her finances."

"I'll need an audit of Erica's finances and the names of her various accountants and investment managers."

"We'll take care of that. You also need to know that Erica is not aware of any of this and you will need to inform her."

"No sweat. I've got it."

I was about to find out that wasn't going to be so easy.

I arrived at the hospital a little before three. The security for the prison ward was extensive. I got to Erica's bedside around three fifteen. She was in a ward with eight other women. The noise level was through the roof.

As I walked over to her bed, Erica turned her head and smiled. "Thank God you're here. I'm chained to this bed in a loony bin. You've got to get me out."

"I'm working on that. You shouldn't be here much longer. You're being transferred to a private clinic near Geneva, Switzerland."

She pulled on her restraints. "Why can't I go home?"

I wasn't sure how I should answer that. I'd have to do my best.

I said, "You're under arrest."

"Why?"

"Daphne pointed a gun at Detective Hannity and tried to shoot him."

"Why don't they arrest Daphne, then?"

I felt like I'd backed myself into a corner.

I said, "Do you remember talking to the psychiatrists?"

"Yes. I thought they would never leave."

"Do you know why they were here?"

"Not a clue."

Damn. I hoped they'd said something to her.

"They think you may be suffering from a mental illness."

"Is that why I'm restrained?"

"Yes, it is."

"I feel fine. Call a nurse and have them remove these restraints."

"I wish I could, but it's not as easy as that. Later this afternoon, a US Marshal is going to come here and escort you to the clinic in Switzerland."

"I don't care to go. I'd rather be with you."

"I'll be with you the entire time."

"What about your job?"

"I'm taking a leave of absence. I plan to stay with you in Switzerland."

Just then, a nurse came in to sedate Erica for the trip. As soon as she approached the bed, Daphne screamed, "What are you going to do, you bitch?"

She angrily pointed at me. "Why is that bastard here? Where are my glasses?"

The nurse left to get an orderly to help quiet her down.

I said, "Daphne, you've done a bad thing. You've killed Erica's mom and you've threatened Detective Hannity with a gun. Now you're going to face the consequences."

"I don't want to talk to you. Where's Anna? I can hardly believe the two of you are related. If I ever see you again, I'm going to kill you. You're going to die, you bastard. You're dead."

She violently struggled with her restraints. Two orderlies came in and held her down. The nurse added a sedative to her IV, which relaxed her muscles, and eventually knocked her out.

I went down to the cafeteria for dinner and asked the nurse to let the marshal know where I was.

About thirty minutes later, a tall, attractive blonde walked up to my table. She was in her early thirties, about five feet nine inches tall, with beautiful blue eyes and a figure that wouldn't quit.

She asked, "May I join you?"

I immediately replied, "Of course." *Was I the luckiest guy in the looney bin or what?*

She set her tray down and introduced herself. "I'm US Marshal Jennifer Shockley. I'll be escorting Erica to the clinic in Switzerland." She held out her hand, which I shook, and then she passed me her credentials. I examined them and handed the leather pouch back across the table.

She continued, "I've been briefed. Is there anything else you need to tell me?"

"I'm not sure what all you know. Erica and I are engaged to be married. Daphne wants to kill me."

"That's quite a conundrum."

"It's the most challenging situation I've ever experienced."

"I don't think you've got anything to worry about. Erica and Daphne both will be heavily sedated when we transport them to Switzerland. They'll be able to walk and physically function, but mentally they'll both be in another place."

"That's crazy."

"I know, but it works every time. I've never had a problem."

"I hope Daphne doesn't spoil your perfect record."

"I'm not worried."

I wished I shared her confidence. I asked, "How is this going to work?"

"Erica will be sedated. She'll be handcuffed to me. I'll take care of any of her needs. I'll have additional syringes of sedative on me if she starts to come around. We'll fly nonstop to Paris and then transfer to a local flight to Geneva. That's about it."

"Will you be armed?"

"No, I won't. Should the unthinkable happen, we don't want the fugitive to have access to a weapon."

"Good." I was comfortable with everything she said. Too bad that wasn't what actually happened.

# Chapter Forty-Seven

Everything went perfectly at the airport. Erica was out of it, but she could stand, walk and sit. She had no expression on her face. She stared straight ahead. Marshal Shockley was handcuffed to Erica. I would accompany them every step of the way.

We boarded the plane before the other passengers. Our seats were opposite the middle restrooms. After a while, all three of us fell asleep. I remember stirring slightly when the girls got up to go to use the facilities. I immediately fell back asleep.

The next thing I remember was a slight pinch on my thigh. I slept even more soundly after that.

Several hours later, a flight attendant shook me, and told me to wake up. I was groggy and it took me a minute to get my bearings.

I immediately looked at the two seats to my right. The marshal and Erica should have been there, but both seats were empty. I looked around and saw all the other passengers had deplaned.

I asked the flight attendant, "Have we landed? Where is everyone?"

The male attendant replied, "Sir, we landed almost an hour ago. We've been trying to wake you up for the last thirty minutes. Are you okay?"

"Where are the two women that were sitting beside me?"

"They probably got off the plane."

"They couldn't have. One was a federal marshal. The other was a fugitive. They wouldn't leave me here."

"And what's your relationship to these two women?"

"I'm the fugitive's fiancé."

"Why are you traveling with them?"

"The fugitive is suffering from a mental illness. The marshal thought my presence would calm her."

Just then, I noticed another flight attendant struggling with the restroom door. I stood up and asked, "Is something wrong?"

She tugged and tugged. "For some reason, I can't get this door open."

"Can I help?"

"Sure. Have a go."

I pulled the handle so hard it came off in my hand.

The attendant said, "The door opens to the inside."

"Good to know."

With that, I slammed my shoulder into the door with all my strength. The door opened a little, but something kept it from opening all the way.

The attendant looked in and screamed. I looked after she ducked out. All I could see was a woman's arm handcuffed to the plumbing under the sink. I thought it might be the marshal, but I couldn't see her face.

I requested a hammer so I could smash the hinges and remove the door. The attendant hesitated. I said that woman could be dying and she returned a couple of seconds later with a hammer.

I smashed the hinges and pulled the door out into the passenger compartment. The marshal sat on the pot, sound asleep. I shook her a couple of times.

She came to and asked, "What happened?"

I replied, "I have no idea, but somehow you and I were both knocked out."

"I should have a handcuff key in my pocket. Would you check?"

I rooted around in the pocket of her slacks. "I don't find it."

"Could you call airport security and have them bring me a handcuff key? Also, Mr. Sparrow, could you check the inside pocket of my jacket for the two syringes?"

I carefully explored the inside of her jacket. The syringes were both gone. No big surprise. That explained the marshal's and my deep sleep.

A few minutes later, an airport security officer arrived and unlocked the handcuffs. The marshal rubbed her wrist and stood up. She requested an urgent meeting with the airport's chief of security along with a senior local law enforcement official. She then called the embassy and asked them to send an FBI agent.

As we walked down the corridor, I said, "Please call me Jack."

She replied, "You can call me Marshal Shockley."

I was a bit put off. She went on, "Just kidding. You can call me Jen."

I asked, "What happened on the plane?"

"Erica had to go to the bathroom. I told her fine and we both got up. You were sound asleep and didn't seem to notice. I told Erica I wasn't undoing the cuffs so she'd have to sit with her one hand straight ahead. I said I'd close the door as far as I could against the chain between the handcuff on my wrist and the one on her wrist. She'd need to hold her handcuffed arm as close to the door as she could while she used the facilities. She thanked me."

"That all sounds reasonable. Did you suspect she had become Daphne?"

"No. Not at that point."

"What happened next?"

"The toilet flushed, water ran in the sink and then, a paper towel ripped from the dispenser. I felt the door start to open and released my hold on it. As soon as it was fully open, Daphne yanked me into the compartment and slammed the door shut behind me. Without a second's hesitation, she grabbed my head and slammed it against the mirror. I was out like a light. I didn't wake up until you shook me."

Jen was a mess. One side of her hair was matted down with blood. She moved her jaw back and forth to assess any further damage. Despite Daphne's brutality, she seemed alright.

# Chapter Forty-Eight

We continued walking down the jetway in silence. Our meeting was going to be in a conference room within the airport security center. When we entered the area, I was impressed. The center looked more like a war room than an office. Security monitors and computer screens were everywhere. All the officers manning them wore headsets.

We were shown into the conference room. Special Agent Harry Brock, Assistant Prefect of Police Claude Henri, and Chief of Airport Security André Étienne introduced themselves. Harry, Claude and André, got it.

Jen provided photos and background information on Daphne and Erica.

She asked me, "Does Erica have any friends or contacts in Paris?"

"I'm not sure. I can check with her people in New York and let you know."

"Great. Also, Anna needs to be on the next flight to Paris. She's the only person that both Erica and Daphne hold in a positive regard."

Jen then turned to André and Claude. "How much video surveillance is available on the airport grounds and throughout the city?"

André reported, "We have already traced Daphne's movement through the terminal building. Apparently, she picked up a random suitcase and climbed into a taxi long before either you or Jack regained consciousness. I have a call into the cab company, who should be able to give us a destination. Claude will be following up with them.

"I have also issued the French equivalent of an all-points bulletin to arrest Daphne on sight. She had taken Jen's passport and billfold. The two women resemble each other, but I'm not sure how far she will get with those.

Regardless, I have also included that information in the bulletin."

Claude added, "As soon as we have a destination, we'll close in on her. In addition, we've notified all hotels in the area to be on the lookout for this woman."

I reached into my jacket pocket. Both my billfold and passport were gone as well. I handed a note to that effect to Jen. She announced it to the group. Apparently, that gave Daphne quite a bit of additional money. She might also be able to use my credit cards. Either way, between Jen's and my cash and traveler's checks, she should have almost four thousand dollars US. That could be one more among an increasing number of problems we faced.

Later that day, the stolen suitcase was located at the Gare du Nord train station. Someone taped a sheet of paper with the word "BOMB" written in big, bold letters to the bag. That shut down the station for hours.

Police checked the security tapes and saw Daphne leave the suitcase. She appeared to then buy a train ticket with cash and disappear into the mass of humanity boarding various trains. Once again, she could be anywhere and we were no closer to finding her.

Anna arrived the next morning. I briefly updated her on the situation. She couldn't believe it. I'd called Detective Hannity to let him know what happened. He said he'd already been contacted and briefed. I asked him what he thought would be the easiest way to identify Erica's European friends. He told me the FBI should be working on that as we spoke. I touched base with Jen, and she agreed I was off the hook.

Anna had never been to Paris. Lilly and I had come many times. Since neither Anna nor I had anything to do, I told her I'd be her tour guide. She was thrilled.

Our first stop was the Louvre, historic home to French kings and queens and now a world-renowned art gallery. Anna was fascinated. We spent the entire day touring the galleries and gardens.

That evening, after several glasses of excellent French wine, I thought about what Daphne would be doing. I figured she had two options—fight or flight. She could go basically anywhere she wanted and no one would ever know. On the other hand, if she chose to fight, I knew she'd be coming after me.

I thought I should probably mention that to someone and called Jen. Voicemail answered and I left a brief message. She called me back about three hours later. I was sound asleep.

"Hello?"

"Jack, sorry I couldn't get back to you sooner. What do you need?"

I was only half-awake. "Who is this?"

"It's Jen. You called me and left a message. It's two a.m. What's up?"

"Thanks for calling. I had a thought about Daphne."

"Go ahead. We haven't had much luck with anything else. What's your idea?"

"I think there's a good chance she may still be in Paris."

"Why would she risk that?"

"The last time I talked to her, she said she was going to kill me."

"Do you think you're in danger?"

"Yes, I do. I can't think of much else she'd rather do."

"You don't think she'd try to escape?"

"To be honest, I don't see that as an attractive alternative. The only person in the world that she cares about is Anna, and we've flown her to Paris. How convenient for Daphne. The only other person she has feelings for is me, and she's pledged to kill me. I'm here as well. No doubt in my mind, she's in Paris."

All of a sudden, someone in my room said, "How perceptive, Jack. You hit the nail on the head. Now, please hang up the phone and get ready to leave."

Jen asked, "Who is that?"

"Daphne," I said and hung up.

"You are a clever boy. Now, get dressed. We're leaving."

"Where are we going?"

"You'll have to wait and see. René has Anna waiting in our car. Move along now."

Daphne waved a gun. I got dressed and walked down to the car. Anna and someone else—René, I assumed—were in the backseat. I sat in the front passenger seat and Daphne drove.

She said, "Jack, don't get any ideas. If you attempt to escape, René will kill Anna."

She then turned to Anna. "Sorry, love, but your dad is a hard man to control. We've got to play our best card with him."

Daphne drove for over an hour. As far as I could tell, we were in the middle of nowhere. Just as I thought she was lost, we turned into a driveway. Daphne got out and opened the gates.

After she drove through them, she stopped, closed the gates, and continued down the drive. Just ahead, the driveway encircled a beautiful fountain in front of a huge old estate. Apparently, René lived in an elegant French château.

Once inside, Daphne ordered me down into what appeared to be a medieval dungeon. She tied my hands to two large rings about seven feet off the ground. I asked what if I needed to go to the bathroom? She said here was fine. Probably hundreds of prisoners relieved themselves and worse right where I stood.

Later, I faintly heard Anna and Daphne yelling at each other. I hoped Anna realized the only way to get along was to go along—her best chance to free me would be to stay free herself. Whatever she had to do was more than worth the effort. She was my only hope.

Eventually, it quieted down upstairs. God, this place was cold, damp, uncomfortable, and stank to holy hell. I wasn't sure how long I could stand it. Once my eyes adjusted, I noticed two sets of skeletons against one wall. Not a promising sign.

At least Jen knew I'd been kidnapped (or killed) by Daphne. They might be able to get some good shots from the hotel cameras. I felt for sure we were in René's car, which should lead to René's house. Fingers crossed.

# Chapter Forty-Nine

Sometime in the middle of the night, Anna made her way down to the dungeon. She untied my arms. I rubbed and shook them to get my circulation going again. Damn, that felt good.

Anna said Daphne and René drank themselves into a stupor while she dumped her drinks into a convenient plant.

We quickly walked up the steps and just as we were about to open the door, a giant explosion knocked us both off our feet. Fortunately, we were able to catch ourselves before we tumbled down the long set of stairs and onto the hard dungeon floor.

The police shouted commands as they charged into the château. I suggested we hang around the dungeon until all the excitement was over.

After about twenty minutes, the upstairs door opened and Jen hollered down, "Jack? Anna?"

I acknowledged and she quickly rushed down the stairs, her flashlight and gun leading the way. She cleared the room, holstered her weapon, and gave us both big hugs.

She said, "We have Daphne and René in custody. The French police insist on charging them both with kidnapping. They'll be put in a French jail tonight."

I said, "That will further complicate things. What if I refuse to press charges?"

"Doesn't matter. The way the police see it—she broke the law and needs to pay."

"We've got to figure a way to get Erica to that clinic in Switzerland. She needs their help now more than ever."

"I agree. I'll talk to my superiors about it. Feel free to contact Erica's legal team. Maybe someone will have an idea how we can proceed."

Jen dropped Anna and me back at the hotel. We grabbed a bite, went to our room, and collapsed into our beds.

Later that night, I got a call from Claude with the Paris police. "Jack, we've got a big problem."

"What's that?"

"We have a woman in jail named Erica and she insists on talking with you. I've sent a car to pick you up. The driver will be there by the time you get downstairs."

A few minutes later, I was in the police car. The driver spoke almost no English. We had a quiet drive to the jail. I was searched and then shown to the visitors' center which was nothing more than a small, dingy room with three tables, each with two chairs. I was the only one there.

After fifteen to twenty minutes, Erica was shown in. She wore coveralls, handcuffs, and shackles. I stood and she leaned her body against mine. That was the best she could do with her hands cuffed and feet shackled. The guard separated us and said something in French that I assumed meant "No physical contact."

We both took a seat. Erica asked the guard if he'd remove the handcuffs. "*Non,*" he replied and walked to the nearest wall to talk with the other guard.

Erica whispered, "This place sucks. How soon can you get me out of here?"

"I have no idea. Everyone's working on it, including the Marshals Service."

"What did Daphne do to land me in here?"

"She kidnapped me and Anna."

"I'm so sorry. You've got to get me out. I don't know how much of this place I can take. Everyone speaks French and I don't understand a word. The guards are getting frustrated with me. I'm afraid one of them is going to hurt me."

"We can't let that happen. I'll talk with the prosecutor as soon as we're done."

"In that case, we're done right now. Go talk and good luck. I'll do the best I can. I love you."

"I love you. Don't worry. You'll be out of here soon."

Once I was reunited with my pocket trash, I asked to see the prosecutor. The guard told me that wasn't possible and showed me to the door. I called the embassy from the sidewalk and made an appointment to meet with the ambassador in thirty minutes. I was there in twenty. The ambassador welcomed me.

After pleasantries, I explained, "Erica Richards is the innocent victim of a psychological disorder. She suffers from Dissociative Identity Disorder. In order words, she has two personalities—one loving, one violent."

He asked me to elaborate. I said, "She was on her way to a Swiss clinic in the custody of a US Marshal, when her other personality initiated an escape.

"She needs to be in a hospital, preferably in Switzerland, where she can receive the highest-quality care."

He thoroughly agreed and scheduled a meeting with the prosecutor for both of us in an hour.

Fortunately, the prosecutor spoke reasonably good English. The ambassador explained the situation and urged him to recommend Erica be transferred to the hospital.

The prosecutor wasn't so sure. "I want to talk with Erica."

He called for her to be brought to his office. Unfortunately, they ushered Daphne through the door. She violently protested. We urged the prosecutor to keep Daphne in a holding cell until Erica could take over and he could talk with her. I was sure he thought we were nuts, but he agreed. The prosecutor said he would contact us after he talked to Erica and excused himself.

The next morning, the ambassador conferenced me into the call from the prosecutor. Once we were all on the line, he began, "I must tell you Erica is a delightful young lady. It's hard to believe she's the same person as Daphne."

I said, "I know. One wants to marry me, the other wants to kill me."

"In that case, you have a worse dilemma than I. I've talked with the judge that would handle this case as well as the assistant prefect of police. We all agree that Erica needs to be in psychological care, not prison. I've authorized our law enforcement to coordinate a safe transfer of Erica as soon as the details can be arranged. Thank you for bringing this to my attention. Please keep in mind that she could still face kidnapping charges at some future date."

The ambassador said, "We appreciate your consideration in this matter and will do everything we can to work with your people in effecting Erica's safe transfer to Swiss care."

And that was that.

Once we took custody of Erica, we headed to the airport. Our flying time was brief. No bathroom breaks on this one. We landed at Genève Aeroport outside of Geneva.

The last leg of the trip went much better than the first. To the best of our knowledge, we dealt with Erica the entire way. Unfortunately, sometimes it was hard to tell as Daphne had become quite effective at acting and talking like Erica. She'd certainly fooled Jen with the whole bathroom episode on the previous flight.

Our plane stopped short of the terminal. A set of steps was provided so Jen, Erica and I could deplane. After we left, the steps were pulled away and the door was closed and secured. The remaining passengers would deplane at the jetway in the terminal.

The Cantonal police put us into the back of a police van. A section of chain link separated us from the officers. The drive to the château took almost as long as the flight. When we finally arrived, we climbed out of the van and I looked around. We were in a valley surrounded by majestic snow-capped mountains. I've never seen a more breathtaking view.

# Chapter Fifty

The château was equal to its surroundings. The ornate architecture and beautiful gardens were more typical of a luxury estate than a mental hospital. I thought Erica could get the kind of care she deserved in a place like this. Hopefully they wouldn't have a problem controlling Daphne.

As soon as we transferred custody of Erica to the institution's staff, I asked to meet with the person in charge of patient care. His name was Luca Andreas. He greeted me in Swiss German. I knew a little German, but I had no idea what he said. I introduced myself in English and he quickly switched languages. I was surprised he spoke with a British accent, but he told me he learned English in Great Britain.

I told him a little about Erica and then said, "Daphne is one of the most violently aggressive women I know. She knocked the marshal out by slamming her head against a mirror. I can't think of any vicious action she wouldn't be capable of."

"We have several violent women here and we know how to deal with them."

"I understand that. But Erica, her other personality, is a tender and sensitive woman. I'd hate to see you treat her the same way you do Daphne."

"Right. What do you recommend? You can't have it both ways."

"That makes sense, but Erica is the one the psychiatrists are going to treat. I'm sure how you handle her will affect the degree to which she's willing to cooperate with the doctors."

"Are you saying we should go easy on Daphne?"

"Yes, to a certain extent. You also need to know Daphne can impersonate Erica."

"This situation sounds impossible. Did our management and doctors understand what they were getting into when they agreed to accept Erica as a patient?"

"I believe they did. Maybe we should expand our meeting to include them. Hopefully we can reach an amicable agreement on how to restrain and treat Erica."

"You're right. I'll try to set something up for nine in the morning."

Erica should be settled in by now and I hoped to be able to spend some time with her. I asked at the nurses' station about visitation. She said there were no visitors allowed at the clinic. That was not going to hack it.

I called Jen and she agreed to meet me before she left the clinic for her flight home. We got some coffee in a small reception area. I filled her in on what Luca and I talked about and my meeting in the morning. I then brought up the visitation situation.

She said, "My job ended when I turned custody of Erica over to the clinic staff. I'm getting ready to catch a plane home and get my next assignment."

"What about Erica?"

"I hope she gets the best care possible."

"What about Daphne?"

"I hope she rots in Hell."

"How do you reconcile those polar-opposite sentiments?"

"I don't. I'm done. Best of luck, Jack."

And with that, she turned and walked out the front door.

The clinic had a reception desk. I asked the girl manning it, "Is there anywhere nearby I could stay?"

"No. All the hotels are in Geneva."

"Is there anything at all closer?"

"No."

"I have a meeting first thing in the morning with the powers to be. If I stay in Geneva, I don't know if I'll be able to make it all the way back here in time."

"I'll check with the director. Please have a seat and I'll let you know what he says."

I sat down. Almost an hour later, she walked over to me. "The director said you can spend tonight in our orderlies' dorm and eat in their dining hall. You will need to leave immediately after your morning meeting. I will arrange transportation for you back to Geneva."

This was unacceptable. I was here to provide support and encouragement to Erica. That would require being able to talk with her. I also wanted to work closely with the doctors and provide any information they needed.

This was like a prison—with no visiting hours or areas. Anything could go on behind these walls. I didn't care how pristine it all looked. I knew nothing about these people. Nothing about their methods of discipline. Nothing about their therapy techniques. Nothing. Nada. Not a damned thing. I shuddered as a cold chill ran up my back.

Sure, Erica was one tough broad and she could take care of herself under normal circumstances. But if she were drugged or restrained, she'd be helpless. I'd say Daphne deserved whatever she got except she and Erica shared the same body and they would also share the same physical abuse.

As crazy as it sounds, I thought I might have to figure out a way to get Erica out of here. I decided to learn as much as possible about the layout of the place and the care they provided the patients. I asked which way to the orderlies' dorm and was given a map with my route outlined.

The map was invaluable. I explored as many corridors as I could. Each eventually ended at a locked door. Security passes were needed to proceed.

Small windows with crisscrossing wire strands provided a peek down the hallways beyond the door. I knew I'd need to find a way to check out the secure portions of the facility as well. That was going to be a challenge.

Oddly, I couldn't hear a sound—no pleas for help, no screams in terror, nothing. This place must have phenomenal soundproofing. That could definitely work to my advantage.

I knew eventually someone would ask me what I was doing here. Every time I passed a staff member, I shielded the area where my pass would have hung down. Eventually, I explored every hallway I could identify.

I tried my best to find my way back to the dorm. I had to ask a couple of people for directions before I located the large room with lockers and cots.

I walked in and asked the only guy there, "Can you tell me which cot isn't being used?"

He pointed to a cot with a bare mattress and a pillow. "You can take that one. The linens are in that cabinet over there."

After I made my bed, I went back and asked the same fellow, "How do I get to the dining hall?"

"I'm going there himself. You can tag along if you want. By the way, my name is Jonas."

He stuck out his hand and I shook it. "Nice to meet you."

We went through the serving line and grabbed a table.

I asked him, "What do you do here?"

"I'm an orderly. That's part guard, part escort, part helper, and part whatever else the boss asks me to do."

"Can you tell me about the patients?"

"Sure. We call them clients. Most of them are so heavily drugged they are oblivious to what's going on. We can do whatever we want to them and they never know the difference. Are you a new orderly?"

I proudly replied, "Yes, I am. I report for duty tomorrow morning."

"Welcome aboard. I think you're going to have some fun here. If you're ready, I can help you with your uniform and ID card this afternoon."

"That would be great."

We finished our meal and he took me to a room that had shelves full of white pants, shirts, belts, socks and shoes. I grabbed two of each in my size. He then took me to the security center.

The guard there asked, "What's your name?

I replied, "I'm not scheduled to report for duty until tomorrow."

"You must be Edmond Hooper."

"That's me."

He took my picture, had me spit in a test tube for a DNA sample, and fingerprinted me. A couple of minutes later, I had my lanyard and a keycard.

I asked, "Where can I go with this?"

He replied, "Everywhere." Problem solved.

# Chapter Fifty-One

Late that night, when everyone was asleep, I changed into my orderly uniform and grabbed a clipboard on my way out of the dorm. I'd circled the client quarters on my map and headed directly there. I used my new keycard to gain access.

As I walked down the corridor, I noticed a little brass placard with a name beside each door. I checked one after another until I came to Erica Richards. I used my keycard again to enter her room.

I quietly walked up to the side of her bed. "Erica. Wake up. It's me. Jack."

No response. I shook her. Nothing. She was restrained with two large leather straps across her body. I quickly undid the straps and tried to sit her up. She was dead to the world. I slapped her a couple of times.

Finally, she opened her eyes and yelled, "You slap me one more time, you son of a bitch, and they'll be scraping you up off the ceiling."

Great. I'd woken up Daphne. I tried to deal with her the best I could.

"I'm sorry, Daphne. I couldn't wake you up any other way. I need to get you out of this place."

She was groggy and didn't respond right away. After a minute or two, she said, "I couldn't agree more, but why would you do that for me?"

"If I get you out, I get Erica out as well."

She dozed off again. I shook her a little and she opened her eyes and said, "Good point. What's your plan?"

I lost her again. This time, I laid her back down, walked out into the corridor, and looked for a wheelchair. My plan was to wheel her out of this hellhole, find a vehicle, and take off.

I looked everywhere for a wheelchair and finally found one in an empty client room. I took it back to Erica's room as quickly and quietly as I could. Daphne was sound asleep. I moved her arms and she came back to life and said, "Love the whites on you. It's definitely your color."

I may have smiled. Then I asked Daphne where her stuff was and she said they'd taken everything. I told her that was fine and secured her in the chair. I took a blanket from the bed and draped it across her. I then studied my map and selected the exit that would put us closest to the garage.

No one was up and about this time of night. That would be a definite plus if it wasn't for all the cameras. I knew we were being watched every step of the way. I picked up our pace.

Finally, I made it to the exterior door. I unstrapped Daphne and told her to stay close. I knew as soon as I opened the door a deafening alarm would sound.

On the count of three, I threw the door open and we took off. The alarm shrieked loudly into the otherwise quiet night. The blaring noise brought Daphne to her senses and she began running beside me. I saw the vehicles and headed towards them.

I looked all around for a key box. I scoured the garage walls without seeing one key. Daphne opened one of the car doors and yelled the keys were in the cars. She quickly jumped into the vehicle, started it, put the car in reverse, and floored the gas. Before I could take two steps, she was out of sight. I opened the door of the next car and immediately heard automatic weapon fire as bullets danced around my feet.

I threw my arms up in the air and I was told to lie face down on the floor. I could feel my hands being secured behind my back and a hood put over my head. Someone roughly helped me to my feet and shoved me back into the building.

I was put in what felt like a small, dark room. My legs and arms were secured to a chair, which was bolted to the floor. Someone took off my shoes and socks. The hood remained on my head. Everyone suddenly left and the door slammed shut.

After a while, I fell asleep. I woke up when someone viciously slapped me.

I hadn't even heard them come into the room. My arms and legs were untied from the chair but another rope tightly secured my hands.

Two men grabbed me and hooked that rope onto something above my head and raised it slightly. My toes barely touched the ground. A large knife ripped my clothes to pieces. Within seconds, I was naked except for the hood.

Before I could take a deep breath, someone beat me with some type of wand. After ten to fifteen minutes of blows all over my body, they left. Every muscle hurt. Even with that, eventually, I fell back asleep.

These beatings continued every two to three hours without one word spoken. After the fourth beating, I was unchained from the ceiling and dragged outside. Every part of my body cried out in pain. They threw me on the ground and tied a heavy rope around my wrists. In a few minutes, I started moving. The rope must have been attached to a vehicle. I scraped along the ground and flew up into the air when I hit the occasional bump. After a couple of minutes, my mind could no longer deal with the pain and I passed out. I doubted I'd ever regain consciousness.

Much to my surprise, I awoke to the feel of snowflakes gently falling on my battered body. My shoulders hurt like hell and my arms were still tied together. The hood was over my head.

Every inch of my body screamed out in pain. All I could do was lay there. Before long, the snow totally covered me.

I tried to move but it hurt too much. After a great deal of effort, I was able to get the hood off my head. When I opened my eyes, I was blinded by the brightness of the sun reflecting off the snow.

Once I was able to focus, I noticed there were no signs of civilization—no roads, no buildings, no telephone poles, no nothing. I figured I was in the middle of nowhere.

I tried to look to the other side. The only way I could turn my head was to drag my face through the mud. When I finally had it turned, I had to spit the gooey dirt out of my mouth. That side was nothing more than a barren, white mountain slope.

After several hours, I got feeling back in my legs. First my thighs, then my knees, my ankles and finally my feet. As I moved my feet, I realized they weren't tied together. If I had any strength at all, I should be able to stand up, but I couldn't.

As the snow continued to accumulate, I licked it. The moisture felt good on my lips and in my mouth. I thought I should feel cold, but I didn't. The days of abuse to my body must have somehow desensitized my skin. To be honest, I was surprised I was even alive.

I slept, tried to move, licked snow, and slept. The sun set and rose again. The next day, I was able to rock my body a little from side to side. Even a slight movement made me feel better. I tried to lift my feet again but they wouldn't budge.

Later that afternoon, I thought I heard some faint far away voices, accompanied by a gentle swishing sound. They quickly got louder, closer. I thought they might be skiers. All of a sudden, I saw the snow fly into the air. The last thing I remember was a pair of skis crashing into me.

# Chapter Fifty-Two

When I woke up, I was lying in a bed. I looked to my side. Marshal Jen sat beside me, holding my hand.

She smiled, "Good morning, stranger. We weren't sure you were going to make it."

I coughed a couple of times. "Me neither. Where am I?"

"You're in a hospital in Lucerne, Switzerland. Do you feel like talking?"

"No. I want to go back to sleep. Maybe later."

Apparently, I dozed off so quickly I didn't even hear her response. I had no idea how long I slept. To be honest, I didn't care. They must have been giving me painkillers. When I finally woke up, much to my surprise, Jen was still sitting beside me, holding my hand.

I asked, "Have you been here the entire time I slept?"

"No. I needed some rest as well. Plus, you've been asleep for almost two days."

"I can't begin to tell you how much better I feel."

"I'm glad to hear that. Your injuries weren't as bad as they could have been."

"Tell me about them."

"Both your shoulders were dislocated. The doctors were surprised your arms didn't separate from your body when you were dragged behind the car."

"How did they know about the car?"

"The cuts and bruises on your body, the rope around your wrists and the fact that it was only a few feet long before it was frayed off."

"I'd also been beaten extensively."

"They knew that as well. Whoever beat you was an expert. Lots of bruises and some minor damage but no broken bones."

"Are they sure? I get shooting pains every time I breathe."

"That's from your bruised ribs. The skier hit you and did that damage with his skis and weight."

"Ugh. Do you have any idea how I got on the mountainside?"

"Once again, the doctors speculate the car went around a curve much too fast and the rope snapped. You went flying off the road, across a ditch and landed on the mountain slope."

"I must be a lot tougher than I thought."

"Apparently. Everyone here was surprised you survived."

"Me too. Have you heard anything about the clinic?"

"Nothing so far, but the police want to talk to you."

"Can you get them here right now? That place needs to be shut down before anyone else gets hurt."

"Sure. I'll give them a call."

And with that, Jen got out her cell phone and called the police. After she hung up, she said, "Two of their investigators should be here in about thirty minutes. You might want to think about what you're going to tell them before they come."

"No problem. I'm just going to tell them the truth."

# Chapter Fifty-Three

When the officers arrived, I was more than ready for my interview. They introduced themselves and pulled up chairs next to the bed. Their English was easy to understand.

The older officer said, "The clinic wanted us to arrest you for criminal trespass and kidnapping."

I replied, "That's pretty ballsy."

"I'm not familiar with that word—ballsy."

"Boldly aggressive."

"Got it. When we found you with your hands tied, a hood next to your head, and beaten and bruised within an inch of your life, we realized those accusations were ridiculous.

"Your injuries made us suspicious of the clinic and we got a search warrant. Our raid revealed numerous abuses. All the patients appeared heavily sedated. Many complained of sexual mistreatment.

"Management and senior staff had already fled. They must have been tipped off. The remaining orderlies and guards confirmed what we'd been told. Several were promised lighter sentences and confessed to participating in both patient abuses and the punishment you received.

"Although almost all of the surveillance recordings were destroyed, we did find a few that documented the abuses. We've made a number of arrests and shut down the clinic for good."

"Sounds like you have the situation well in hand. What do you need from me?"

"We have a couple of questions that should help our prosecution. We suspect you may have gotten some information from one of the orderlies that may have sparked your attempt to rescue Erica."

"That's correct. I think his name was Jonas. Basically, he told me the orderlies could take advantage of the clients drugged state and sexually abuse them."

They handed me a stack of pictures and I identified the man I'd spoken with.

The investigator continued, "Did you see any of the men that beat you?"

"No. I had a hood covering my head the entire time."

"Could you see anything looking down past the bottom of the hood?"

"Now that you mention it, yes. I saw a number of tattoos, watches, bracelets and rings."

"We thought you might have. We took pictures of the wrists and hands of all the male employees at the clinic. Do you feel you may have been beaten by any females?"

"No."

"Please take your time and carefully examine each of these photographs. Tell us if you saw any of these tattoos or jewelry. Did anyone speak during this time?"

"No."

"That must have been strange."

"Extremely."

I studied the pictures and set aside the ones with things I'd seen. Then, I went back through each one of those and carefully examined every detail. In addition to distinguishing jewelry and tattoos, I paid particular attention to the fingernails. Several of my abusers had missing or blackened nails. When I was done, I'd identified six suspects. The investigators were pleased.

Jen came back in and I asked her to get my doctor. A few minutes later, Jen and the doctor came into my room.

I asked him, "Can Jen stay while we discuss my situation?"

He replied, "No problem."

"Do you have any idea when I'll be able to check out of the hospital?"

"Anytime you like. We have reset your shoulders, bandaged your ribs and treated all your bruises and cuts. The only other problem you had was severe dehydration, and we have given you enough fluids to take care of that."

"Fine. I'll be leaving within the hour. I want to thank you and all your staff for the excellent care you've given me."

"I'll pass on your appreciation. I want you to know, it has been our pleasure to care for you, Mr. Sparrow."

As soon as he left, I asked Jen to excuse me a minute so I could change into the clothes she'd brought me. She was more than happy to step out into the hall.

Once I was dressed, I opened the door and requested a wheelchair. Jen left, got her car, and drove up to the discharge area. I gingerly got in the passenger seat. The hospital had given me a large bottle of painkillers to take as needed. As soon as I fastened my seat belt, I popped two pills in my mouth.

Jen looked at me. "Where to?"

"Wherever Anna is."

"She's back at the hotel and can't wait to see you."

"Let's go."

That was the best news yet. I wanted to see and talk with her as soon as possible. I was surprised she wasn't at the hospital. But I was sure there was a good reason she wasn't there.

# Chapter Fifty-Four

Our hotel was another beautiful château. Jen got one room for Anna and another for me. I was still a little shaky on my feet, so she helped me into the lobby, the elevator, and my room. She had moved all my personal items from Geneva.

I told her, "I need to see Anna."

"And she wants to see you. Before you do that, though, I need to tell you a little about what's happened."

"Is she okay?"

"Yes. She's fine, but she's had a tough time."

"What happened?"

"Daphne contacted her and said she wanted to see her."

"Oh God."

"You don't have anything to worry about now, but for a while things were a little precarious."

"Just tell me. The longer you dance around what happened, the more worried I get."

"Well, you know Daphne is in love with Anna and desperately wants the two of them to be together."

"Ugh."

Jen smiled. "Anna told me her relationship with Daphne was over and she was afraid of her.

"We told Anna she was our only hope to find Daphne. We assured her we would do everything we could to protect her. After some initial hesitation, she agreed to help.

"And?"

"Daphne contacted Anna and told her she wanted them to be together. She told Anna she would have a friend meet her at a certain time and place. Anna was to come alone and leave her cell phone at the hotel."

"Surely you had some sort of other tracking device on her."

"We did. When she met Daphne's friend, she was taken to a restroom and searched. They used a device to find the tracker and then destroyed it.

"The friend was furious. She called Daphne and recommended she forget about Anna. Daphne said no and told her to blindfold Anna and bring her. That was exactly what she did."

"Sounds like trouble."

"Definitely. When Anna arrived, everything was lovey-dovey. That didn't last long. Anna said Daphne's personality changed and she became much more suspicious and sinister. Daphne interrogated Anna about the tracking device, why she was there, and who she worked for.

"She hit and slapped Anna. This went on for a while. When Daphne was done, Anna was bruised and beaten. Daphne said she was sickened by the sight of her and told her friend to blindfold Anna and leave her by the side of the road somewhere."

"That's terrible."

"I know. The friend dropped off Anna far from Daphne's hiding place. Fortunately, Anna was able to find her way to a nearby clinic that treated her wounds, which were all superficial. She asked the clinic to call me, and as quickly as I could, I picked her up and brought her back here. She's been resting ever since. I'd say Anna and Daphne's relationship is definitely over."

"That's a silver lining. Can I see Anna now?"

"Of course. Remember, she's fine. Don't be too shocked by her appearance."

"Enough. Help me to her room."

"You two have connecting rooms. She's through that door. Let me give you a hand."

Jen got me up and over to the door. She knocked. Anna opened the door. I was shocked. Anna had two black eyes in addition to the cuts and bruises over all the visible parts of her body. I was sure Anna was just as upset to see me. Together, the two of us looked pathetic. Anna and I hugged and then she helped me to a chair.

I filled her in on the details of what happened. She was surprised I'd survived. Then she filled me in on the details of what happened to her.

Daphne was one mean, heartless bitch. I wanted nothing more than for her to be arrested, convicted of murder, and thrown in jail for the rest of her life.

I suggested the three of us go down to the bar for some drinks. Everyone was on board and we headed to the hotel lounge. We all got comfortable at a small table. I ordered a Corona; Jen, a scotch on the rocks; and Anna, a piña colada.

After my beer, I switched to scotch. We drank, laughed and told each other a little more about ourselves. Jen had wanted to be a US Marshal since high school. Her school held annual career days which gave the kids a chance to talk with a good number of adults who pursued a wide variety of careers. One year, Jen met a man who was a US Marshal. He told her about his work pursuing fugitives and she was hooked. Ever since that day, she knew exactly what she wanted to do.

She enrolled in the University of Tennessee and earned a degree in criminal justice. The day after graduation, she applied for a job with the Marshals Service. That was a little over ten years ago.

During her time on the job, she'd found and arrested hundreds of fugitives, from low-level felons to international drug dealers. She said she never had a dull day at work. I could tell Anna was interested. Maybe, she found her career. We'd just have to see.

The more we drank, the more personal we got. Anna excused herself and said she needed to get some sleep. Jen told me how challenging her job was in terms of maintaining relationships.

She said, "I've had several boyfriends but nothing serious."

I tried to reassure her. "You're young and beautiful and eventually the right man will come along."

Jen put her arm around my shoulder and moved a little closer to me. She looked into my eyes. "Maybe he already has."

My first thought was, what could this amazing young woman possibly see in me? My second thought was Erica and I planned to get married. That thought didn't ring as true to me now as it once had. Either way, I knew this was my cue to excuse myself and go to sleep. We both got up and she walked me to my room.

We stood at my door and Jen said, "Thanks for listening to my frustrations tonight."

I smiled. She kissed me on the cheek and went to her room. I stumbled into my bed and slept like a baby.

# Chapter Fifty-Five

I didn't wake up until ten the next morning. After I cleaned up and got dressed, I knocked on Anna's door. She opened it right away. I invited her to join me for breakfast and we both hobbled down to the hotel coffee shop.

After we finished our meal, I asked Anna how she was doing.

She replied, "Alright. I'm bummed out about Daphne. The last time we were together, I'd thought she'd lost her mind."

"Imagine how I feel. That crazy bitch has done nothing but give me hell six ways to Sunday."

"Do you think this will ever end?"

"I hope so."

"Do you remember when you told me Daphne was in the living room while Erica and I were making love?"

"I'd forgotten all about that but now that you mention it, I do."

"We now know, that could have never happened. Why would Daphne ever say that?"

"She probably knew I'd tell you and wanted to get under your skin."

"Clever. What do you think really happened?"

"Chef Louie may have told Daphne you had been in town and she made up the rest."

About then, Jen joined us. After she sat down, I asked, "Any news?"

"As a matter of fact, there is. The Swiss police think they've zeroed in on Daphne's location."

"That's great. How did that happen?"

"The local police showed Daphne's picture around and got a hit from a delivery driver. They plan to raid the house this afternoon."

"Can we watch?"

"Sure. I'll need to be there anyway to file an extradition order with a local judge."

We arrived at the police station a little after two and met the commander who reviewed the entire operation with us. They planned to have everyone in place by three thirty and move in at four.

Jen, Anna and I could watch the video feeds at the command center. Each assault officer would be wearing a body cam. Assuming no serious injury, Daphne would be brought to the jail down the hall. If she required medical attention, she would be transported to a nearby hospital.

Time crept by. We definitely had front-row seats and were ready for the action to begin.

As the clock struck four, the officers stormed the house. They encountered two people who swore no one else was there. They handcuffed them and proceeded to search the entire house room by room. Several officers remained outside to preclude Daphne's escape.

When they got to the main bedroom bath, the door was locked. They'd brought a battering ram, which they'd already used on the front door. The bathroom door was hardly a challenge. Several officers rushed into the small room. Daphne was taking a bath.

They ordered her to stand up and put her hands on her head. After she stepped out of the tub, one officer offered her a bathrobe. Once she'd secured that, they handcuffed her and led her outside.

Jen immediately left to file an extradition order. Anna and I didn't know what to do, so we just stayed put.

The body cameras remained on. I tried to determine from the conversation whether the woman was Daphne or Erica. With them speaking Swiss German, I didn't know what was happening. I suspected the woman was Erica because she wasn't acting wild and crazy, but in reality, I couldn't tell.

As soon as the whole group entered the prisoner processing area, we went back out into the waiting room. Anna and I were both anxious to meet with Daphne.

Jen came back into the station and told us she was going to talk with her superiors in Washington about how they planned to handle the return trip to New York. She disappeared into an office.

After a couple of hours, an officer said we could meet with Daphne. The visiting area was as barren as any I'd seen. The prisoners remained behind a sheet of plexiglass and spoke through an opening about mouth high.

The guards led Daphne through a door. They then let go of her and she sat right in front of Anna and me. She looked like shit—hair a mess, no makeup and big black bags under her eyes.

Once we sat down, Anna said, "Daphne?"

She smiled. "No, Erica, sweetie. Let me talk to Jack."

With that, Anna got up. I sat down and said, "I've been worried sick about you."

"Thank you. I did nothing to deserve this kind of treatment. I was simply enjoying a warm bath and the next thing I knew, I was handcuffed and riding in the back of a police car."

"I know none of this makes any sense. Daphne is to blame for everything bad that's happened."

"I know she is but I'm getting sick and tired of it."

"I can't begin to imagine what you've been through, but that's all behind you. Has anyone told you what to expect?"

"No. Do you know?"

"To a certain extent. The Marshals Service has chartered a private jet to take you, me, Anna and Jen back to New York. You'll then be transported to the prison psych ward at Elmhurst Hospital for treatment."

"Hopefully that will be better than what I got at the Swiss clinic."

"I'll do everything I can to make sure that's the case."

"I know you will, Jack. Thanks for everything. I love you and can't wait for the time the two of us can be together once more."

"Me too. Love you."

That was nice. I couldn't remember the last time Erica and I had a pleasant conversation. I was about to give up on her but felt much better about our relationship after that brief exchange.

We had a couple of weeks to kill until our jet arrived. The police decided to provide Erica some psychiatric help. The doctor asked about her childhood. She told him about the heartbreaking death of her little sister, Daphne. The doctor tried to help Erica find a way to work through that trauma. He told Erica her other personality, Daphne, was her way of dealing with that loss. Only when she could come to terms with the death of her sister could she expect her other personality to go away. Sounded simple enough. It was anything but.

Erica felt good about working with this particular doctor and asked if he could come with her to New York and continue his talk therapy. The doctor said he would if she paid his normal rates and if he could bring his family with him. She agreed to both conditions and even offered Daphne's condo as a comfortable place to stay. He said he'd have to talk it over with his wife. All that sounded like a great idea to me until I met him.

Dr. Heinrich was about my age and height. He was also ruggedly handsome with an athlete's body. Could there have been more to Erica's invitation than psychological care? I hoped not but I was more than a little concerned.

Jen thought the doctor had already made good progress with Erica and tried to pull a few strings so he could travel with us on the jet. The more Erica talked with him, the less frequently Daphne appeared. I thought she'd be totally gone before we knew it.

Jen, Anna and I continued to have dinner together. We'd often go to one of the restaurants the girls discovered online or one that someone told them about. Tonight was Indian food. I couldn't help but think of the movie *Along Came Polly* with Ben Stiller and Jennifer Aniston when they went to an Indian restaurant and he got terribly ill. As I recall, he broke out in a sweat, turned bright red, threw up, and had the runs. Not a great first date. I'd be a little more cautious with my meal.

Jen and I turned out to be great drinking buddies. We had a ton of fun after Anna left us each night. Some nights we danced, some we sang karaoke, and some we just drank. We got pretty cozy with each other, but I wasn't going to let it go too far.

By the time we boarded the jet, we were the best of buds. The doctor had accepted Erica's offer and would be flying with us. I definitely felt better with him here. If we had any problems with Daphne, I was sure he would have a good idea how to handle her.

Miraculously, Daphne didn't materialize on the flight. Erica asked me to help get the psychiatrist settled in Daphne's condo. I wasn't thrilled, but what could I say? At least he would soon have his family with him and Erica would be detained in the prison ward.

Back in New York, Erica, once again, had one of nine beds in the psych ward at Elmhurst Hospital. This place was still a madhouse. I tried to visit her every day, but it was almost more than I could handle.

# Chapter Fifty-Six

Anna and I stayed in Erica's condo. We dined almost every night with the good doctor. He said he was amazed at Erica's swift progress. In all his years of practice, he'd never seen anything like it.

After a few days, Anna wanted to get back to Franklin and plan her classes at UT. Jen knew most of the professors and all of the classes and volunteered to help with her schedule.

I called the airport and asked them to refuel my plane and reposition it in a parking spot. The hangar charges were exorbitant. Fortunately, Erica's money took care of them.

Paying her routine bills turned out to be a major undertaking. I decided to hire a bookkeeper in New York to take care of the day-to-day financial transactions. Erica's investment advisor recommended two firms. I interviewed both and hired the one I thought would do the best job. That took a huge weight off my shoulders.

My next challenge was to say goodbye to Erica. I knew she'd be angry I was leaving. But, I didn't think I could stand spending much more time in the psych ward. I tried my best to explain that to her. She replied since she had to be there day and night, I was getting off easy. I told her I loved her and would be back to see her soon. I couldn't think of anything else to say.

The next day, we packed and got a car to the airport. Our flight home was quite a relief after all Anna and I had gone through in Europe. Neither of us could wait to sleep in our own beds.

After a couple of days of rest and relaxation, Anna called Jen to get some help with her schedule. Jen said she was staying with her family in rural east Tennessee and offered to drive over and sit down with her. Anna was thrilled. I hated to admit it, but I looked forward to seeing Jen as well.

She arrived the next afternoon and helped Anna knock out her classes in short order. I suggested we celebrate with a night on the town. I wanted to show Jen all my favorite hangouts. Anna volunteered to be our designated driver. We started at the Bluebird Café and then moved our celebration to lower Broadway in downtown Nashville. I had a number of honky-tonks there I enjoyed. Jen shared my pleasure. Being an East Tennessee girl, she was a huge country music fan.

After more than a few drinks, I asked her, "Did you grow up with indoor plumbing?"

Anna was shocked by the question. "Where the hell did that come from?"

"I knew several men that grew up in rural Tennessee who didn't have that luxury."

Jen jumped in. "No problem, Anna. I'd had bathrooms, but a couple of my friends didn't."

Anna was surprised. She thought, how is it possible for anyone growing up in the United States not to have indoor plumbing? Now she knew.

Jen and I both loved to dance. We did the Texas two-step, line danced and generally had a ton of fun. Anna finally accepted an invitation from a handsome young wrangler to hit the dance floor as well.

By the time we got home, Jen and I were both more than a little tipsy. Jen said she planned to get a hotel room, but I invited her to stay with us. She quickly accepted. Anna got her set up with everything she needed to be comfortable.

I told the girls goodnight, started a fire in the hearth, and had a nightcap. When I was about to head upstairs, Jen came down in a one of my shirts, unbuttoned halfway down. I asked her if she wanted a robe and she said she was fine, but she'd like one of whatever I was drinking. I poured a brandy for her and another for myself.

We both sat on a sofa in front of the fire. She rested her body against mine. We didn't say anything at first, and then she said, "Do you ever think about Erica?"

"I do."

"What do you think?"

"This isn't kind, but I think it's good she's nuts or she'd certainly go crazy in a place like that."

"That's terrible," Jen said and picked up a pillow off the sofa and hit me with it. I tried to protect myself but soon realized she wouldn't stop until I physically restrained her. I grabbed both her arms and held her still.

Her breathing was heavy. She looked into my eyes, lifted her head to mine, and kissed me. That was all it took. The kissing led to caressing. The next thing I knew, neither one of us could stop ourselves.

I was frustrated. I knew I should be able to resist, but somehow I wasn't. I was terribly attracted to Jen and we'd definitely gotten close over the last couple of months. But there was no excuse for this.

I was still engaged to Erica. Granted, I'd stopped seeing a future with her when I'd left the psych ward, but technically, we were still engaged. I didn't think it was fair for me to break off our engagement because of her current circumstances. That would be insensitive.

And now this thing with Jen. Where was that relationship headed?

# Chapter Fifty-Seven

Rob's graduation from Duke was a huge affair for the entire family. The event was held on campus at the Wallace Wade Stadium. This year's speaker was none other than Hillary Clinton, former Secretary of State and 2016 presidential candidate.

I immediately called Detective Hillary Clinton in New York. I had the wild idea that she'd enjoy attending the ceremony as our guest.

After hellos, I said, "Hillary Clinton is going to speak at my son's graduation."

"That's exciting. You probably aren't too surprised to hear that I've never met my namesake."

"So, you were named after her?"

"I was. My parents are lifelong Democrats and I'm sure they hoped I would follow in Secretary Clinton's footsteps."

"Did you ever consider a political career?"

"Nothing more political than the New York City Police Department."

I'm sure that could be tough enough.

"The graduation's the weekend of May twelfth through fourteenth. We'd like you to be our guest."

"That's so kind. Thank you. I'd love to hear Secretary Clinton speak."

"I doubt you'll have a chance to meet her, but I think it's worth a try."

"That would be a huge honor."

"Certainly."

This could be interesting.

I reserved three rooms for the weekend—one for me, one for Anna and one for Hillary. Rob could stay with me or in his off-campus apartment. Anna and I flew in from Nashville and we both picked up Hillary at Raleigh-Durham International Airport.

The next day, the weather was beautiful. The commencement ceremony went off without a hitch, and then Secretary Clinton walked up to the podium.

My expectations were quite low. I knew she was an accomplished attorney who served as First Lady, senator from New York, and most recently Secretary of State. She'd also run for president against Trump, and we all know how that turned out. But I read about her White House years in a couple of the tell-all books and they weren't complimentary.

Secretary Clinton surprised me with her speech. I actually found it quite inspirational. I was sure it also hit the mark with the graduates.

Detective Clinton stood, clapped and shouted after the address. We all wandered down to the football field as things broke up. Secretary Clinton talked with students and professors.

Detective Clinton walked right up to her. "I'm Hillary Clinton and my parents named me after you."

Secretary Clinton replied, "I'm honored. Thank you for making your way down here. What kind of work do you do?"

"I'm a detective third class with the New York City Police Department."

"I know that's dangerous and demanding work. Thank you for the sacrifices you make to serve our fine city. So nice to meet you."

With that, she was pulled into another conversation and we left. Detective Clinton was so elated after talking with Secretary Clinton that she was on cloud nine for the rest of the day. I knew we'd made a friend for life.

On the way to the airport the next day, Detective Clinton said, "I wish I'd had a picture taken with the Secretary."

Anna said, "I took several with my phone. I can text or email them to you."

The girls quickly exchanged numbers and Anna sent the pictures. Rob wanted to stay in Durham until he nailed down a summer job. Anna flew back to Nashville with me.

Life returned to normal. A few days later, Anna said Rob left an excited message that he had some big news to share with both of us. We didn't have any idea what it could be. I called him and put the phone on speaker so Anna and I could both hear.

After pleasantries, Rob said, "Dad, you're not going to believe what's happened."

"I hope it's good."

"It's better than good—it's stellar."

"Anna's here with me, tell us the news."

"Okay. Here goes. I've been accepted at the University of Michigan Law School."

"That's one of the best law schools in the country."

"I know. BOOM. I'm sure it helped that you and Mom went there."

"Possibly. At least your mom put that degree to use. She would be so proud of you, Rob."

"She's the reason I applied."

"Congratulations on yet another academic achievement. We'll plan a celebration when you come home. Do you have any idea when that will be?"

"I'm still working on an internship for the summer. I'll let you know."

"Congrats, son. Take care of yourself."

"Will do. Bye."

Anna said, "Well, everyone's life seems to be finally falling into place. Rob's going to Michigan Law School, I'm starting my criminal justice studies at UT and I'm through with Daphne."

I was tempted to mention Jen, but I didn't want my life to be too much of an open book where my kids were concerned. A little mystery was always helpful.

# Chapter Fifty-Eight

Summer was relaxing and enjoyable. Jen became a frequent houseguest, Rob got an internship with the U.S. Attorney in Nashville, and Anna worked with the Williamson County Sheriff's Department. Just before school started, I flew the kids and their stuff to Knoxville and Ann Arbor.

I'd tried to call Erica at least once a week. Our conversations were strained. She didn't think it was fair I hadn't been to see her. Quite honestly, I didn't think there was any point in making the long trip.

You can imagine my surprise when she finally called one day, as happy as a lark. She exclaimed, "Jack, the most wonderful thing has happened."

She hadn't been this excited in months.

"I'm so glad. Tell me all about it."

"I'm home."

What? How is that possible?

"That's great. How did that happen?"

"Well, Freddie—I mean, Dr. Heinrich—has been making incredible progress. Daphne is all but gone. Once he thoroughly talked me through my childhood trauma, my Daphne personality almost totally disappeared."

"And they released you?"

"Not exactly. I'm still under arrest, but now it's at home. I have to pay for a series of full-time guards that stay here twenty-four seven. I also wear an ankle bracelet."

"Has Dr. Heinrich gone home?"

"Not at all. He's still right next door. His family had to leave, though. The kids needed to get back to school. Isn't it all wonderful?"

"Yes, I'd say it is. How are you feeling?"

"I feel great. I can't wait to see you. They say you can visit anytime you want. I don't know when I've been so excited."

"I've wanted to talk with you. How about this weekend?"

"Talk? That's all? Talk? How about a little sex? No. How about a whole bunch of sex?"

"Right. But we need to talk through some things first."

"Jack, I'm getting a bad feeling. Do you still love me?"

"Of course I do. I'll see you Saturday afternoon."

"Alright. Bye."

I could tell she was disappointed. I might have burst her bubble, but I didn't know any other way to approach it. I couldn't imagine a future with Erica. I felt Daphne would always be on the sidelines, waiting to ruin any fun we might have. Sure, maybe "Freddie" had performed a miracle, but in my experience, miracles were few and far between.

I'd fly up Saturday morning. I called Anna and talked with her about my dilemma with Erica. I was surprised she answered the phone. Most times, I got her voicemail, which I knew she rarely checked, so I usually just called back.

"Anna, I've got something I need to run past you. Do you have a few minutes?"

"Sure, Dad. What's up?"

"Erica called and she's been released to guarded house arrest. She wants me to come up so we can rekindle our relationship. I'm not so sure that's what I want. I don't see a future with Erica. I can't picture a scenario where she doesn't end up in jail or a mental hospital."

"That's what I'd always thought. How is it she's home?"

"Dr. Heinrich. Apparently, he's quite a miracle worker. She's almost totally cured."

"I doubt that."

"As do I. That's part of my dilemma. The other part is the feelings I have for Jen."

"I know. Isn't she the best?"

"She is. I'm literally torn between two amazing women. I can't figure out how to handle things with Erica."

"All I can say is be honest with her. Talk about your concerns. I'm not so convinced of her miraculous recovery, but if she's doing half as well as she says, she ought to be able to deal with the truth."

"I hope so. Thanks, Anna."

I was surprised by Erica's call on Friday night. She asked if I could come up the next weekend instead. I said sure but was wondering what was up with that. I'd just have to wait and see.

Work picked up. My weekend and following few days were extremely busy. On Friday, I double-checked with Erica. She said she was excited to see me, but her police guard said I couldn't stay with her and I would need to get a hotel room. I said fine but continued to wonder what was up.

Saturday morning, I flew to New York, took a car to my hotel, dropped my bags, and grabbed a cab to Erica's. She greeted me as her elevator doors opened at the penthouse level. She was holding hands with Freddie and as bubbly as I'd ever seen her.

She exclaimed, "Jack, I've got the best news. Freddie and I are in love. Can you believe it? We're so happy."

I didn't get off the elevator. Erica handed me our engagement ring. I smiled, pushed the button for the lobby, then the one to close the doors, and rode the elevator back down. I felt like I'd been slapped in the face on the outside, but I was overjoyed on the inside. My problems were solved. Dr. Heinrich definitely was a miracle worker.

My phone rang in the lobby. It was Erica. I didn't answer it and permanently blocked her number. I'd call her sister in the morning and tell her I was resigning from the conservatorship. I felt so much better. I couldn't wait to call Anna and Jen. Since I didn't plan to fly home tonight, I decided to stay in the city and celebrate the fact that Erica was no longer my responsibility.

I probably should have called Jen before I started drinking. Oh well, hindsight is twenty-twenty. When I finally got in touch with her, my speech was a little slurred. She asked if I'd been drinking. I said yes.

Jen then said, "Have you been drinking with crazy Erica?" That was what she called her now. Probably not fair, and definitely not kind, but I could certainly understand where she was coming from.

"No. Erica and I are through."

"Really? What happened?"

"She's got a new lover."

"How's that possible?"

"It was bound to happen. Dr. Heinrich is her new main man."

"I'd say he's not as smart as we thought he was."

"I agree. Surely he understands what he's getting into. But I can tell you from experience, Erica's charms are hard to resist. She's probably pulled the wool over his eyes."

"I don't want to assume anything. Does this mean that Erica is totally out of your life?"

"Yes, it does. I got my ring back and blocked her on my phone."

"When can we get together and properly celebrate?"

"I'll be in Franklin tomorrow night, so any time after that."

"Great. I'll call then."

I continued my celebration—dinner at what I considered the finest restaurant in the city and drinks late into the night at my favorite jazz club. I slept well into Sunday.

I updated Anna from the cab to the airport. She was as relieved as I was. I then called Erica's sister, Kathleen, and relayed the latest developments. I told her I'd be sending a letter of resignation and recommended she continue with the same bookkeeper. She thanked me and said she greatly appreciated everything I'd done.

I made my way home at a leisurely pace. All's well that ends well, and this chapter of my life certainly had. At least, that was what I thought.

# Chapter Fifty-Nine

Jen surprised me when she showed up at my door on Sunday night. I was delighted to see her and told her I was making one of my favorite dinners—chicken pesto.

Anna, Jen, and I all enjoyed the meal and our evening. We had a ton of laughs and ended the night on a high note. Sometime in the middle of the night, there was a knock on my door and Jen slipped into my room. We barely sleep all night.

I felt like, for the first time in ages, I had my life together. Jen continued to get Anna excited about the Marshals Service. My work was more rewarding than ever, and I hadn't heard anything from New York for several weeks.

Then, much to my surprise, Detective Hannity called. I hadn't talked with him in months and I'd really never expected him to call.

I answered, "A voice from the past."

"Too bad we can't keep it that way."

I didn't know how to take that and simply let it pass. Obviously, something had happened.

I asked, "Is there a problem?"

"You could say that."

"Anyone I know?"

"You're kidding me, right?"

"Erica?"

"No, Daphne. Did you know Dr. Frederick Heinrich?"

"Yes. Is he alright?"

"Would I be calling if he was alright?"

"Guess not. What happened?"

"As best we can tell, Daphne took a big kitchen knife and stuck it clean through his heart."

"Oh my God, that's terrible."

"You're not kidding. What a mess."

"Where did you find the body?"

"In the middle of Erica's bed. He was totally naked."

"What about the police guard?"

"Daphne was having sex with her and slipped her a downer that night, rather than the upper she usually gave her."

"And the ankle bracelet?"

"Some time later, Daphne removed it and was able to secure it to a homeless man. Do you have any idea how far those guys walk in a day?"

"I don't."

"That guy walked almost twenty miles before we were able to run him down."

"Did he have any information?"

"No. He had a hard time completing sentences. We think the bracelet may have been put on him while he was passed out the night before."

"Any leads on Daphne?"

"Not really, but from what the guard told us, she might be heading your way. She seems to hate you and Anna with a passion and promised to kill you both."

"Oh shit."

"Right. Good talking with you, Captain."

"Thanks, Detective."

I hung up and dialed Jen. She answered on the second ring.

She said, "I was getting ready to call you. Have you heard the news?"

"Yes."

"I need to get you and Anna protected."

"What do you have in mind?"

"I'd like you to fly to Knoxville, pick Anna up, and then fly to Baltimore, Maryland."

"Why Baltimore?"

"I live and work there. I'll put together a plan and muster the resources we'll need. We should be ready as soon as you arrive."

"What about my house in Franklin?"

"I'd like you to leave a key with a neighbor, so local law enforcement can stake it out in case Daphne shows."

I went over the name and address of the neighbor, walked next door, and gave her a key before I left. I called Anna on my way to the airport and told her what was up. I only had to say it once and she was ready to roll. We both knew what a serious threat Daphne was.

Anna alerted her friends and roommates to be on the lookout for Daphne. If she showed, they were to contact Marshal Jen. She made sure each girl had her number.

# Chapter Sixty

We were both pretty tired by the time we landed in Baltimore. Jen joined us for dinner. We talked, laughed, and enjoyed each other's company like nothing at all was wrong.

Jen and I told Anna goodnight and walked down the hall to my room. I unlocked the door and we both went in. My bag was sitting beside the desk and another bag I wasn't familiar with was next to it. I looked at Jen.

She whispered, "I didn't think you'd mind if I spent the night."

"Of course not, but I'm not sure clothes are going to be necessary."

"I hope not." With those words, Jen slowly unzipped her tight-fitting dress and let it fall to the ground. She wore nothing beneath it. For me, this was like the starting bell at a horse race. I sprang into action. Sometime around three in the morning, we both decided we needed a little sleep. Our wake-up call came sooner than we would have liked at six a.m.

Anna joined us for breakfast. We were scheduled to meet with the group of marshals at nine. Jen was tight-lipped about what we could expect to hear at that meeting. We asked her repeatedly, but she said we needed to wait until nine and then all our questions would be answered.

Jen drove us to the Marshals' Baltimore headquarters. We met in a conference room.

She introduced us to everyone. I didn't bother trying to remember all the names because I didn't think I'd need to. Jen told the marshals a little about Anna and me and our lives back in Tennessee.

Then she turned to us. "Basically, I'm going to present you with the two alternatives that give you and Anna the best chance of surviving. Number one, we can give you new identities and relocate you until Daphne is behind bars or dead."

"How long do you think that would take?"

"You and I both know Daphne is quick to act. She's not one to think things through or otherwise deliberate. I'd say not long. Maybe not much more than a nice vacation for the two of you."

"And number two?"

"Number two is much riskier. With that, you wouldn't go into hiding at all. We'd simply provide you both with a group of protection agents and hope they could head off any attack by Daphne."

"That sounds much more dangerous."

"It is. I strongly recommend number one."

"Anna and I will have to talk this over. Can we get back in touch with you later this afternoon?"

"You can, but we'd prefer you don't leave these offices."

"No problem. We just need to be able to talk in private."

"We can arrange that."

Jen told us she would have lunch delivered. Besides that, we were left alone.

I asked, "Anna, what's your feeling?"

"I'd like to get back to class. I don't feel I can afford to miss many days. How about you?"

"I'm extremely busy at work and now is not the time to take a vacation."

I called Jen on my cell and told her we'd made our decision. She said to sit tight until she could get everyone back together. Anna excused herself to use the restroom.

Shortly after Anna left, Jen came back and asked where Anna was. I told her the restroom. She panicked.

She exclaimed, "You mean you let her go to the restroom by herself?"

"That's been the case since she turned two."

I don't think Jen appreciated my attempt at humor and charged from the room. I quickly followed but stopped when she entered the ladies' room. I could hear Jen yelling and slamming stall doors.

In what seemed like two seconds later, Jen ran out, radio to her mouth. "I need the entire building locked down right this second. No one enters or leaves. We have a missing protectee—Anna Sparrow. She's late teens, five six, a hundred and twenty pounds, shoulder-length brown hair with blue eyes. She was last seen wearing a dark blue knit shirt and blue jeans. Please detain her and anyone with her. Consider anyone with her armed and dangerous."

# Chapter Sixty-One

A loud alarm sounded and red lights flashed in all directions. Jen grabbed my arm. "We've got to get you someplace safe."

"You lost Anna?"

"Yes."

"How could that possibly happen? You've got your own building, your own guards, your own security system—how could anyone sneak in here and grab someone?"

"We don't know. We're checking the security tapes now. All we know so far is that we cannot find Anna anywhere."

"That's ridiculous. She went to the potty. One door in—same door out."

"There's a window in that restroom."

"A window? We're on the third floor, for God's sake."

"I know. It's unlikely but not impossible. We've had prison escapes under similar situations."

I was frustrated by the ineptness of the marshals. I could feel my face turning red as I clenched my fists.

Jen acknowledged my obvious concern. "Jack, I know you're upset. We all are. Now is not the time to point fingers. Our one and only priority is to locate and rescue Anna."

That hit a nerve. I took a deep breath and calmed down. "You're right. I don't know what got into me. What can I do to help?"

"We're going to pull out all the stops in our search for Anna. To do this, we need to know you're safe. We don't want any concern about you to distract us from finding Anna."

"Agreed. What do you have in mind?"

"We're going to lock you in an interview room."

"Are you serious?"

"Yes. They're totally secure. The only way out is through the door, which will be padlocked and guarded."

"What if I get hungry, thirsty?"

"We'll provide drinks and snacks."

"What if I need to go to the bathroom?"

"You'll be accompanied at all times by an armed guard. He'll never let you out of his sight."

"Okay. But you need to come up with something better long-term."

"We will, but in the short term, it's all about Anna."

I reluctantly agreed to my temporary confinement. Jen walked me to an interview room. She told me she'd be back soon. After she closed the door, a padlock engaged. That was the last sound I'd hear for what seemed like an eternity.

After several hours of not being able to see or hear a thing, I felt like I was going to go nuts. I paced awhile and then sat at the small table. A camera was mounted close to the ceiling in the far corner. The red light was on. I gave whoever was watching the finger and threw a chair at it. Nothing happened. They were probably used a little bad behavior.

I must have dozed because I abruptly woke up to the sound of someone jiggling the lock on the door.

I said, "Hello?"

Someone on the outside said, "Shut up, asshole. We should have you out in a couple of minutes."

I thought I recognized that voice—female, a little husky, abrasive.

I tentatively asked, "Daphne?"

"Good guess. Now sit down and relax, we've almost got this off."

I repositioned myself directly in front of the camera and waved my arms, yelling, "Daphne's on the other side of this door. She's about to get the lock off. Please send armed assistance immediately."

Daphne yelled, "I told you to be quiet, dipshit. I'm going to make you pay for all your misbehavior."

I thought, *She can only kill me once. How bad could her punishment be?*

"I know what you're thinking. I don't just want you to die, I want you to suffer beforehand. I want you to watch me slowly kill your beloved daughter. You can't imagine how miserable the last few hours of your pathetic life are going to be."

As soon as she said that, the door flew open. Behind Daphne, a group of marshals rounded the corner. They immediately opened fire. I flipped the table over and hid behind it. Bullets flew everywhere. I got as flat on the floor as I could while still staying behind the table.

Almost as quickly as the shooting started, it stopped. A marshal said, "You can get up now, Mr. Sparrow."

I quickly checked to make sure I hadn't been nicked by a stray bullet. After I determined I was uninjured, I asked, "What about Daphne?"

"She got away."

"How's that possible?"

"I wish I knew. I thought we had her dead to rights. One second she was here, the next she was gone."

"Did you capture any of the women with her?"

"We shot one up pretty badly. We're not sure she's going to make it."

"Let's hope she does and that she knows where Anna is."

About then, Jen walked into the room.

I looked at her. "You haven't found Anna?"

She replied, "No."

She couldn't help but notice the bullet holes in the table, chairs and especially on the back wall.

She asked, "What the hell happened here?"

I replied, "Daphne."

"Daphne?"

"She snuck into your offices, overpowered your guards and destroyed your lock. I'm lucky she didn't get me. Were the marshals able to capture her?"

"I'll have to find out."

"Jesus. Are you serious? You lost Anna and then you let Daphne get away. I'm losing confidence in the Marshals Service. What's happening?"

"We're aggressively pursuing both people. You need to relax and know that the Marshals Service almost always gets their man, or woman."

"Thanks. I know I should have more confidence, but after everything that's happened today, I'm really shaken."

"I can understand. Daphne returning for you was quite a shock."

"You're telling me."

# Chapter Sixty-Two

Neither one of us said another word for the next few minutes.

Finally, Jen ventured, "What's on your mind? You have that faraway look in your eyes, like you're deep in thought."

I shook my head. "Right. Sorry. I was thinking about Daphne. I'm having a tough time accepting she and Erica are the same person. Daphne is so, so bad. I'd really say downright evil. And Erica is so, so good. I don't think I've ever heard her utter an unkind word about another human being."

"I know. It's almost incomprehensible. Maybe you could use some therapy."

"I'm sure I could. I'm having a tough time coming to terms with everything. I barely know Daphne, but I detest her. I've known Erica intimately and I've loved her deeply. There's no way I could reconcile those two diametrically opposed feelings."

"I understand, but we need to know what you and Anna have decided to do about the two choices I gave you earlier. Have you decided?"

"Yes, the second one. We want to be available to help you anyway we can."

"You do realize that could put you in great danger?"

"I do, but I've already lost so much—first Lilly, then Erica. I think losing Anna would devastate me. I want to help anyway I can. Disappearing isn't going to do any good."

"I understand. We'll arrange the best protection money can buy. I'll be your liaison with the investigation into Anna's abduction. Any questions?"

"No. I need some nourishment and sleep."

"That's fine. We have a cafeteria here and also some guest quarters. You can stay until your protection is in place."

"I don't feel too safe here. You know, with Anna disappearing and Daphne appearing."

"You've got nothing to worry about. We've redoubled our security. Also, we believe Daphne had some inside help. We are reviewing the backgrounds of all our employees and will be interviewing them individually. Each one will have to take a polygraph test.

"Guilty parties tend to split once we start. We should know relatively soon who Daphne recruited from our ranks. Identifying that person will probably provide our first lead to finding Anna."

"I hope so. I don't intend to spend more than twenty-four hours here."

"That should be enough time. Get some food and rest. Call me when you wake up."

Jen assigned a marshal to stay with me. I felt like I had a babysitter—not a great feeling. I ate and went to sleep.

Sometime in the middle of the night, I was startled. Daphne was sitting at the foot of my bed, holding a large kitchen knife.

I sat straight up. "How did you get in here?"

She laughed. "It's not what you know but who you know. Why did you think you'd be safe here?"

"I thought the Marshals learned from their earlier failures."

"Really? I'm surprised you have that much confidence in these losers."

Daphne then threw back the bottom of my bedcoverings and slashed both my feet.

I screamed in pain. "What the hell are you doing?"

"I'm going to make sure you don't run away. Now, turn over on your stomach so I can tie your hands together."

"Why should I?"

With that, Daphne put the bloody knife in her right hand and used her left to slug me in my face as hard as she could. My lip started bleeding and I thought she might have loosened a couple of teeth.

"Now, turn over onto your stomach."

I complied. She tied my hands together, rolled me back over, and put the knife back in her left hand.

"Stick out your tongue."

"Why?"

"Just do it."

I opened my mouth and she pulled out my tongue. "I'm tired of all your verbal abuse. After this, you'll never be able to say one more word to anyone."

As she brought the knife towards my tongue, I struggled and screamed. The next thing I knew, the marshal shook my shoulders.

He yelled, "Wake up, Jack. Wake up!"

I opened my eyes and was totally confused. My hands weren't tied together and my tongue was intact.

I said, "Quick, check my feet. I think the bottom of my feet have been slashed with a knife."

The marshal complied. "Jack, you're fine. You must have had a bad dream."

That was terrifying. Everything seemed so real. Thank God it was just a dream—or should I say nightmare? I didn't think there was any way I could go back to sleep, but somehow I did.

# Chapter Sixty-Three

The next morning, Jen met me for breakfast in the cafeteria. As soon as she sat down, she said, "I've got a ton of news."

"Do you have Anna?"

"Not yet, but we're getting close."

"Tell me."

"Daphne was able to seduce two of our newer employees. As soon as we started the polygraph tests, they both took off. In no time, we located and arrested them.

"We've already met with the district attorney, who gave us a great deal of latitude in making a deal with one of these women. We told them what charges they faced and how long they could expect to be in prison.

"Not surprisingly, they both wanted the deal. We said we would give it to the one that gave us the best information. They immediately spewed everything they knew.

"The information they shared was great as far as it went. We understood how Daphne got Anna out of the building and how she snuck back in. What we don't know is where she was holding Anna.

"One of the women, Claire, volunteered to go undercover for us. We gave that a great deal of consideration. We told her how dangerous that could be. After a lot of back and forth, we decided to give her a chance.

"We told her if she provided us with a location and subsequently helped us rescue Anna, we'd settle for a guilty plea with a sentence of probation rather than prison time. Claire couldn't have been more motivated to help. Or, so we thought."

She told Jen she might have met some of the other women helping Daphne. That was another lie. She knew exactly who aided Daphne and precisely where Anna was being held.

As soon as Claire was released, she took the battery out of her phone and walked to a friend's apartment. She told the friend she was having her car repaired and needed a vehicle for the afternoon. The friend gladly lent her a car.

Claire was certain there was a tracking device in her vehicle and never intended to take her car anywhere near Daphne. She then asked her friend for a change of clothes—something more casual, she said—and again the friend complied.

Claire took her driver's license out of her purse and put it in her pocket. She left the purse behind with her clothes. She was relatively certain she couldn't be tracked. She thanked the friend and drove to Daphne's lair.

By the time Claire arrived, the sun had set. She parked and ran into the house. One of the women told her Daphne was asleep and she ran upstairs to the main bedroom.

Daphne was out of it. Claire said something but didn't get a response. Then she grabbed and shook Daphne's shoulders, still with no response. Finally, she threw back her hand and slapped Daphne as hard as she could.

Daphne reached up, grabbed Claire's arm and hit her on the side of her head with a heavy glass ashtray from the nightstand. She was out like a light.

Erica looked around and had no idea where she was. She got out of bed, looked for a phone, and found one with a battery lying next to it. With some difficulty, she installed the battery and called Jack.

"Hello?"

"Jack, I don't know where I am."

Jack quickly told Jen it was Erica on the phone and she needed to trace this call. She ran from the room to get that started.

"Hello, Jack? Are you there? Jack?"

"Yes. Sorry. We're trying to get your location right now."

"What's going on?"

"Daphne kidnapped Anna. She's probably somewhere at your location.

There's undoubtedly a couple of women there helping her."

"Oh my God! That's terrible. What can I do to help?"

"I'm going to ask Jen. She should be back in a minute. How are you?"

"Alright. Some woman slapped me really hard to wake me up. I was so pissed I knocked her out with an ashtray."

"You need to see if you can find something to tie her up and gag her."

"Right. I'm looking now."

"Gag her first."

"Okay. I think I've got what I need. I'm setting down the phone."

I waited. It seemed like several minutes, but I'm sure it wasn't. Erica finally came back on the phone just as Jen walked up.

I asked Erica to hold on a minute. Jen told me they knew her location and had dispatched local law enforcement. She grabbed my arm and said we needed to walk while we talked. I asked her what Erica should do. She told me to hand her the phone and she put it on speaker.

"Erica?"

"Yes."

"This is Jen. You've done great so far. Local law enforcement will be establishing a perimeter around the house. If possible, we'd like you to get Anna and leave."

"How would I do that? I don't even know where she is."

"Do you think you can impersonate Daphne?"

"Well, I've definitely got the looks. What does her voice sound like?"

"Like your voice, but a little more gravelly."

"Gravelly?"

"Deeper, rougher, but just a little. Don't overdo it."

"Got it."

"You will need to go downstairs and find the other women. When you do, tell them, in your best Daphne voice, to get Anna and bring her to you.

"Once you have Anna, order the women to stay put. If they object, be as rude as you can, just like Daphne would."

"I don't know what Daphne is like."

"She's rude and authoritative. She's the boss, no questions asked."

"Good. I can do that. Then what?"

"Start walking down the driveway until you encounter the police."

"Will do. Wish me luck."

Jen and I both said, "Good luck."

Erica mustered every ounce of courage she had and headed down the stairs. Sure enough, she found two women in the kitchen.

Erica said, in her best Daphne voice, "Get Anna and bring her to me."

The women snapped to it. They both headed down the basement stairs and returned two minutes later with a tired and haggard Anna.

"I'm taking her outside. You two need to stay here."

All of a sudden, a loud, pounding noise came from upstairs. It sounded like someone was kicking the wall.

One woman asked, "What was that?"

Erica replied, "Beats me. Why don't the two of you go investigate? I'll be back with Anna in about thirty minutes."

She roughly grabbed Anna's arm. "Come with me, you worthless piece of shit."

# Chapter Sixty-Four

With that, Erica and Anna made it out the front door. The two other women cautiously walked up the stairs, their guns at the ready. As soon as Erica stepped onto the driveway, she told Anna to run. Anna hesitated.

Erica said, "Anna, it's me—Erica. The police are at the end of the driveway, let's move it."

They both took off running. Even with her arms tied behind her back, Anna ran surprisingly fast. When they reached the street, a police matron greeted both women and led them to a nearby ambulance.

With Erica and Anna safe, the police officers cautiously advanced on the building. The front door was open and the policemen entered the structure. Two officers cleared the downstairs while two more went upstairs.

Standing at the top of the stairs, they heard nothing—total silence. One officer indicated he'd clear the rooms on the left and the other officer could do the rooms on the right. They quietly worked their way through one room after another.

When the officer on the left got to the main bedroom, the door was ajar. He slowly opened it and stuck his revolver into the room. All hell broke loose. The gunfire was deafening. He was hit in the hand and dropped his gun. Before he could move, he was hit two more times in his side. The bullets passed through the wall like it was made of warm butter.

The other officer responded immediately with a barrage of gunfire through the same wall from one end of the room to the other. After that, everything was eerily quiet. He radioed the officers out front to send two EMT's with a litter upstairs and to be on the lookout for anyone escaping out a window. He slowly entered the room.

His first indication was three women, all dead. He kicked a weapon away from the first body and then the second. When he looked to do the same with the third, she raised her arm into the air and fired three quick shots into his face and neck.

Claire then grabbed his gun and any spare ammunition she could find. The officer's radio exploded with concern from his buddies outside. She quickly made her way down a back stairway and out into the backyard. A minute later, she was deep into the woods.

Just about then, Jen, a contingent of US Marshals and I drove up to the ambulances. As we got out of the car, Erica and Anna ran over and locked me in a three-person embrace.

They talked so fast, I couldn't understand what they said. Jen and the other marshals went over to the officer in charge.

I told Erica, "You did a great job."

"I can't stop shaking."

"That's the adrenaline wearing off. You'll be fine in a few minutes."

I gave Anna another hug. A huge wave of relief washed over me. I was so glad she was alright.

I asked her, "Are you okay? What did Daphne do to you?"

"I'm fine, and all Daphne did was tie me up and put me in the basement."

"What did you think when you saw Erica?"

"I thought she was Daphne and I was terrified. She told me she was Erica as we left the house, but I really didn't believe her until we were rescued."

"I understand. Daphne's fooled a lot of people by pretending she's Erica."

"Exactly. I'm worried about the police officers that risked their lives to save me. Would you check with Jen to make sure everyone's alright?"

"Sure." I walked over to Jen and asked her.

She said, "One of the officers was killed upstairs. We think Claire shot him. She's the only person that's not accounted for."

I was sure there would be huge repercussions within the Marshals Service if that was the case. I dreaded telling Anna. She was so sensitive and caring.

Before I could say anything to her, Jen walked up to Erica with another marshal. "Erica, you were a true hero. You saved Anna's life. I'm sure that will help you in court."

Erica looked confused. "Court? What are you talking about?"

Jen replied, "I feel terrible doing this but, Erica Richards, you are under arrest for the kidnappings of Anna and Jack Sparrow and the murders of Dr. Frederick Heinrich and Harriett Richards. Please put your hands behind your back."

Jen handcuffed her. She then helped her to a car, protecting her head as she put her inside. Erica looked at me just before Jen closed the door. Tears streamed down both cheeks. At that moment, I felt incredibly sorry for her.

I put my arm around Anna and hugged her. She cried as well. I couldn't begin to imagine how this mess would be resolved. I was about to find out.

# Chapter Sixty-Five

Somehow, life returned to normal. Anna studied criminal justice at the University of Tennessee in Knoxville, Rob buckled down on his law studies in Michigan, and I worked out of my home office in Franklin. I had a long list of workshops and talks.

These past couple of years had been one disaster after another. But, for once, I felt all that was behind us. Jen visited me often in Franklin and we occasionally met while we traveled. Daphne was locked up in the prison ward at Elmhurst Hospital, awaiting trial.

Erica received limited psychiatric therapy. Nobody felt there was much that could be done at this point. Her lawyers repeatedly petitioned the court for relief. The court would have no part of it. They weren't taking any more chances with this deeply disturbed psychopath.

About six months after the arrest, Jen called with what she described as great news.

I asked, "What's up?"

"We captured Claire."

Amazing. Claire was particularly good at escape and evasion. She had actually made it to number three on the FBI's ten most wanted list.

"That's great news. How did you get her?"

"As often happens, we got lucky. Claire is taking an uncommon medication for a condition she's had since birth."

"I'm surprised Claire didn't realize that could be a problem."

"But she did. She would pay various women to order the drug in their names. Claire had a pile of prescriptions from a shady doctor and she would merely fill in the appropriate woman's name.

"If we were alerted to someone new buying that drug, we would stake out that person's house and wait for Claire to show. She slipped past us on two previous occasions.

"The last time, she came close to eluding us again. Claire didn't pick up the pills right away.

"After about a week, the woman that ordered the prescription drove to a park in the middle of the little town where she lived. She sat down on a bench and wedged the prescription bottle between the legs and seat of the bench. A couple of days later, Claire came to pick it up and we arrested her."

"That's amazing. I can't believe Claire was so devious."

With all that behind us, Jen and I were ready to get away. We cruised the Caribbean and Central America. Occasionally, we ventured a little further from home.

We went to Paris twice and even explored Vietnam. My dad served there during the war. We invited him to join us, but he said he had no interest. He never talked much about his time there and I respected that.

# Part Six

# Trial

# Chapter Sixty-Six

Erica had been in jail almost fourteen months. Her trial was due to start in less than thirty days. The media circus was rapidly building to a crescendo.

Jen planned to attend the entire proceeding. Since Anna and I were scheduled to testify, we were both banned from the courtroom. We were similarly instructed not to watch the live broadcast on Court TV.

I could hardly stand the suspense. Jen recommended we both go about our daily studying and working routines. She explained that as soon as we finished our testimony, we could join her in the gallery. That sounded good but never actually happened.

Judge Herman Weber called his courtroom to order and quickly laid down the law on how his trial was going to proceed. Erica Richards was being tried for the murder of Dr. Frederick Heinrich.

The judge asked all the attorneys to introduce themselves. The lead prosecutor was none other than District Attorney Tom Randal. He was assisted by two other lawyers from his office. At the defense table, Erica sat between the two members of the defense team. Her lead attorney, Sam Roosevelt, sat to her right.

The defense strategy was twofold. Number one, Sam intended to prove that Daphne Erwin was a separate and independent person from Erica Richards. And number two, he was going to substantiate that Erica Richards had no participation in, no knowledge of, and no motive for Dr. Heinrich's murder.

The prosecution wanted to establish Erica and Daphne were the same person and subsequently prove Erica murdered Dr. Heinrich in cold blood.

They intended to seek the maximum penalty of life without the possibility of parole.

This case received an unprecedented amount of publicity. To think one of the most successful women in the world was being tried for murder was almost beyond belief. The vast majority of prospective jurors were familiar with one aspect of the case or another.

Jury selection took almost three weeks. Juror after juror was disqualified or challenged. At one point the judge considered a change of venue but both groups of attorneys wanted the trial held in New York City.

The defense thought there would be more sympathy for Erica among the people of this community. She had been generous with her donations to the arts, addiction agencies, and other nonprofit groups. Her attorneys felt she was generally highly regarded by the citizens of New York.

The prosecutors, on the other hand, believed that everyday New Yorkers would not be able to relate to this wealthy and somewhat aloof woman. She lived in a lavish penthouse high above the streets of New York. She spent more time traveling around the world than she did in the city. She never drove herself around town and rarely walked. She had nothing in common with the average New Yorker. The prosecuting attorneys felt she already had one strike against her. Only time would tell which side was correct.

The jury selection process was tedious and painfully slow. Eventually, though, a group of twelve jurors and two alternates was chosen.

All the players were now in place and everything was set for the trial to begin. Judge Weber pounded his gravel one time. "Ms. Richards, please stand."

Erica rose. She was handcuffed and had shackles on her ankles.

The judge turned to the bailiff. "Please remove Ms. Richards' restraints." He complied.

Weber read the charges and then asked, "Ms. Richards, how do you plead?"

"I plead not guilty."

"Thank you. You may sit down. Let the record show the defendant pleads not guilty."

With a nod from the judge, the prosecutor rose and approached the jury.

Tom Randal gave his opening statement. "Ladies and gentlemen of the jury, the people intend to prove, beyond a reasonable doubt, that this woman, Ms. Erica Richards, did willfully and viciously murder Dr. Frederick Heinrich early in the morning of the third of October, 2018. Dr. Heinrich was found naked in Ms. Erica Richards' bed with a large kitchen knife driven through his heart."

An image of the naked doctor appeared on a large screen to the left of the judge. The knife in his chest and a large pool of blood under his body were clearly visible. Nothing was obscured or blurred on his body. Members of the jury either took offense or were fascinated by the graphic display of the doctor's manhood. Some felt a little of both. The prosecutor noted this and quickly turned off the slide.

"Dr. Heinrich treated Ms. Richards for Dissociative Identity Disorder, or DID. That disease is more commonly known as multiple personality disorder. A person suffering with DID exhibits two or more different personalities. We will be going into this disease in more detail throughout the course of this trial.

"Ms. Richards was under Dr. Heinrich's care for almost a year. He initially diagnosed her condition and began treatment in Switzerland. He continued her therapy at the prison ward of Elmhurst Hospital here in New York.

"After several months, the court believed Dr. Heinrich had made such significant progress that they released Ms. Richards to her New York City condo and placed her under house arrest with a twenty-four-hour guard. Dr. Heinrich stayed in an adjoining condo the entire time he was in New York.

"We will prove that early in the morning of the third of October, 2018, Ms. Erica Richards drugged her guard and went to her kitchen to get the largest knife she could find. Dr. Frederick Heinrich was sound asleep at that time. Ms. Richards returned to her bedroom and drove that knife all the way through Dr. Heinrich's heart and into the bed. The only fingerprints found on the knife belonged to Ms. Richards and her kitchen staff. Once she killed the doctor, she escaped, and was apprehended by authorities at a later date. Thank you."

The judge invited Sam Roosevelt to make his opening statement.

Roosevelt began, "Daphne Erwin committed the crime the prosecutor just described. She drugged the guard and her fingerprints were on the knife.

"Dr. Heinrich and Ms. Richards' relationship started as strictly professional. Over time, they became friends and, ultimately, lovers.

"We will establish through a number of witnesses that Dr. Heinrich and Ms. Richards were deeply in love. We will also show Erica is a gentle person—not prone to anger, much less violence. Ms. Richards has never raised her voice to Dr. Heinrich and has never said an unkind word to or about him. The thought of Ms. Richards killing Dr. Heinrich is absurd.

"Ms. Richards is one person. She is a kind and giving individual. Erica has provided extensive support to local charities, youth programs, and eldercare initiatives. She has led a responsible life filled with kindness and generosity to her fellow New Yorkers. Erica is not a murderer.

"On the other hand, Daphne Erwin is a totally different person. Ms. Erwin is a cold-blooded killer. She should have been charged with this murder.

"Daphne Erwin and Erica Richards have never met each other but are aware of each other's existence. These two people do not live together or even have the same sexual preferences. One is good, the other is evil. You will learn over the course of this trial that there are multiple and significant differences between these two women. They are definitely not the same person.

"When you accept that, you will have no choice but to acquit Erica Richards of this horrendous crime. Thank you."

# Chapter Sixty-Seven

Sam Roosevelt took his seat at the defense table. District Attorney Tom Randal then stood. "The people call New York City Coroner, Dr. Sidney Rubenstein, to the stand."

Dr. Rubenstein testified he supervised the removal of Dr. Heinrich's body from the crime scene as well as the autopsy.

Randal continued. "Dr. Rubenstein, were you able to determine the time of Dr. Heinrich's death?"

"Yes. He died between one and one thirty a.m."

"Was there anything besides the vicious stab wound that contributed to Dr. Heinrich's death?"

"No."

"Did he have any drugs or alcohol in his blood?"

"No drugs but a slight evidence of alcohol—probably a glass or two of wine."

"Thank you, sir. No further questions."

As Randal took his seat, Sam Roosevelt stood up to cross-examine.

He asked. "Dr. Rubenstein, were you able to determine whether or not Dr. Heinrich had sex the night he died?"

"As a matter of fact, we did observe physical indications that would support that assumption."

"Thank you, sir."

Randal's next witness was Patrick Hannity, Detective First Grade, New York City Police Department. Hannity took the stand and was sworn in. The prosecutor established his qualifications and began his questioning.

"Detective Hannity, please relay the events of the third of October, 2018, relating to your response to a 911 call from the residence of Ms. Erica Richards."

Hannity pulled out a small notebook he kept in his pocket and flipped through a couple of pages. "Sure. I responded to a 911 call from one of Erica Richards's guards, Ms. Stephanie Wheeler, regarding a homicide at that address. When I arrived, the elevator was at the lobby level."

"Is that significant?"

"Yes. It meant no one had gone to the condo since the last person left."

"Please continue."

"As soon as I arrived, Wheeler showed me the victim in Erica Richards's bedroom. She had been told that a forensics team, the coroner, and a detective were on their way."

"Were you the first to arrive at the crime scene?"

"Yes."

"After you saw the body, what did you do?"

"I searched the entire condo to make sure no one else was there."

"What did you find?"

"Ms. Wheeler, myself and Dr. Heinrich were the only people in the condo."

"What did you do then?"

"I asked Wheeler if she had any coffee. She brought me a cup. Then we sat down in the living room."

"You didn't think you should more closely examine the scene?"

"Excuse me, counselor, who's the detective here?"

"Right, please continue."

"I asked Wheeler to describe the events of the previous night."

"Please share with the court the information she provided."

Randal hoped to disguise his question and slip it past the defense. Unfortunately, he had no such luck.

Defense counsel, Sam Roosevelt, stood up immediately. "Objection. Hearsay."

The judge sustained the objection. The prosecutor continued. "Detective Hannity, did you see any evidence of forced entry into the condo?"

"No. In fact, I reviewed the visitors' logs from eight p.m. until I arrived and no one signed into the building between those hours. The only person that left was Daphne Erwin at one twenty-six a.m."

"Does a doorman maintain those logs twenty-four hours a day?"

"Yes. No one comes or goes without an entry being made."

Randal had a quick thought. This was a chance to establish that Erica Richards was the only person in the condo at the time of the murder capable of killing Dr. Heinrich. He felt a slight tinge of exhilaration at the thought of eliminating any other possibility from the jury's mind. Now was his chance to strike.

"Based on that information and the fact that the guard was unconscious and the doctor was dead, Erica Richards is the only person that could have possibly killed Dr. Heinrich. Was that your conclusion?"

Sam had a good feeling how Hannity would respond and decided not to object on the basis of leading the witness.

Hannity surprised the DA. "No, not at all."

Randal was taken aback. He'd thought he had Erica dead to rights.

Cautiously, he asked, "How can you say that?"

"Easy. One of two possible people were in the condo at the time of the murder. Either one could have killed Dr. Heinrich."

"And who could the second person have possibly been?"

"Why, Daphne Erwin, of course."

"Are Daphne Erwin and Erica Richards not the same person?"

"No. Not by a long shot."

Randal felt a debilitating wave of anger and frustration wash across his body. To disguise it from the jury, he turned and slowly walked back to the prosecution table. He casually picked up and examined a meaningless sheet of paper. When he felt himself calming down, he turned and walked back to the witness stand.

He continued his questioning. "Did you determine that a knife was missing from the block in the kitchen?"

"Yes. I further matched the brand and style of the knife in Dr. Heinrich's chest with the knives in the kitchen. It was a perfect match."

"Did you find any indication of a struggle in the bedroom where Dr. Heinrich was brutally murdered?"

"No. He appeared to be sleeping and died immediately when the knife pierced his heart."

"Is it common in a stabbing death to have one single wound in the victim?"

"No. Most often, a victim is stabbed multiple times."

"Do you have any theories on why that wasn't the case with Dr. Heinrich?"

"Objection. Calls for speculation." Sam had quickly jumped to his feet.

"Sustained."

Randall decided he was done with Hannity. He wanted to ask if the single wound suggest premeditation but quickly realized that would prompt another objection.

Erica Richards's guard, Ms. Stephanie Wheeler, was the next scheduled witness, and the prosecutor was anxious to move on to her and get her testimony on record.

In the course of his cross-examination, Sam Roosevelt asked Hannity, "Had you been to the Richards condo previously?"

"Yes, on two occasions."

"What was the reason for your first visit?"

"Mr. Jack Sparrow filed a complaint against Ms. Daphne Erwin, who he claimed threatened him with a gun."

"Who is Mr. Jack Sparrow?"

"At that time, he was Ms. Richards' boyfriend."

"What was the result of that investigation?"

"We dug a bullet out of the wall behind the bed and matched it to a pistol owned by Erica Richards. Mr. Sparrow said that Ms. Richards was out of town at the time and invited him to stay in her condo while he was in New York. The complaint indicated Ms. Daphne Erwin threatened Mr. Sparrow with a gun and fired it one time over his head."

"Did you recover the gun and examine it for fingerprints?"

"We did. The only fingerprints we found belonged to Ms. Erica Richards."

"Did you also dust the room for fingerprints?"

"Yes. We found prints for Mr. Sparrow, Ms. Richards, and her maid."

"What did you conclude from that information?"

"That Ms. Erwin must have worn gloves."

"How did the bullet from the police lab firing compare to the bullet dug out of the wall?"

"They both came from the same gun."

"Did you investigate Ms. Daphne Erwin?"

"We did."

"What did you discover?"

"She's a ghost—no birth certificate, no Social Security card, no driver's license, no tax returns, absolutely no indication she exists as a living, breathing human being."

"Isn't that unusual?"

"Not really. In my line of work, we come across ghosts more often than you'd think."

"Detective, did you have any other encounters with Ms. Daphne Erwin?"

"Just one more."

"When was that?"

"On my second visit to Ms. Richards' condo."

"Tell us why you were there and who was with you."

Hannity flipped through his notebook until he found the date in question. He reviewed his notes and said, "We were there to tell Ms. Erica Richards her mother had been murdered and to ask her to voluntarily submit to a psychological examination. Accompanying me were my partner, Detective Hillary Clinton, supervisory psychiatrist, Dr. Farley Hammond, and Ms. Richards' public relations coordinator, Ms. Patsy Herrington, as well as Ms. Anna and Mr. Jack Sparrow."

"That's quite a group."

"I know. I'd taken Jack Sparrow so he could break the news to Ms. Richards. He requested his daughter, Anna Sparrow, and Ms. Richards' public relations advisor, Ms. Patsy Herrington, accompany him."

"And exactly what happened?"

"We expected Erica's total cooperation because that was the kind of person she is. We handled everything low-key.

"Jack held Erica's hands and broke the news. She was extremely upset, but everything went as well as could be expected until Daphne let go of Jack's hands, jumped up, and pulled a gun on everyone. I was close enough I thought I could easily neutralize the weapon.

"Unfortunately, before I had possession of the gun, Daphne managed to fire one shot which nicked the side of her own torso. Once I had the weapon, I cuffed her and called for an ambulance. They took her to Mount Sinai Hospital where her wound was treated.

"I then accompanied her to the prison ward at Elmhurst Hospital for psychiatric evaluation. When I got back to the station, I laid charges against her for menacing a police officer and discharging a firearm."

"Thank you, Detective."

# Chapter Sixty-Eight

The prosecutor then called his next witness, Ms. Stephanie Wheeler, a guard with the Department of Corrections.

Ms. Wheeler was sworn in.

Randal began, "Ms. Wheeler, please state your full name, profession, and your duties in regard to Ms. Erica Richards."

"Stephanie Anne Wheeler, correctional facility guard. I was one member of a three-person team that kept Ms. Erica Richards under continuous observation. I generally worked the night shift from midnight to eight a.m."

"And where were you during those hours on October third, 2018?"

"I was on duty, guarding Ms. Erica Richards at her Central Park condo."

"Can you tell us about your interaction with Ms. Daphne Erwin?"

"My legal counsel has advised me to respectfully refuse to answer questions of that nature on the grounds that it might tend to incriminate me."

"Did you and Daphne have a sexual relationship?"

"My legal counsel has advised me to respectfully refuse to answer questions of that nature on the grounds that it might tend to incriminate me."

"Did Daphne drug you that night?"

"My legal counsel has advised me to respectfully refuse to answer questions of that nature on the grounds that it might tend to incriminate me."

"Fine. No more questions, Your Honor."

The defense counsel began his cross-examination. Sam Roosevelt asked, "Are you still employed by the Department of Corrections?"

Wheeler responded with yet another, "My legal counsel has advised me to respectfully refuse to answer questions of that nature on the grounds that it might tend to incriminate me."

"Your Honor, I fail to see how Ms. Wheeler could incriminate herself by answering this question."

The judge said, "You will answer the question, Ms. Wheeler."

"No, I am no longer employed by the department."

Sam Roosevelt was done. "That's all I have, Your Honor."

Ms. Wheeler was excused and Detective Hannity was recalled.

Prosecutor Tom Randal picked up the questioning. "Detective Hannity, please tell us about your interview with Ms. Stephanie Wheeler on the morning of the third of October, 2018."

Hannity pulled his little notebook out again and flipped through the pages. He stopped when he found the page he was looking for. The defense chose not to object to this third-party testimony.

Detective Hannity began, "Ms. Wheeler brought me a cup of coffee. I asked her what happened last night. She said Ms. Daphne Erwin and she were lovers. Before they had sex, they would each take a pill that would heighten their experience. On that night, Ms. Wheeler took the drug and that was the last thing she remembered until around six the next morning.

"When she woke up, she was slightly disoriented. Once she got her bearings, she checked on her prisoner, Ms. Erica Richards, and discovered the body of Dr. Frederick Heinrich naked in Ms. Richards' bed. She screamed. After she recovered, she called 911. Then she called the staff and told them not to report for work."

"Detective, I see you're referring to notes you've made. Do you have her responses word for word in your notebook?"

"Somewhat. I try to write down the significant information verbatim. Some of the other stuff, I summarize."

"I'd like to make photocopies of the pages that reflect the testimony you just gave. Would that be agreeable to you?"

"I guess so. I also have some personal information in the notebook, so I don't want you or anyone else to look at any of the other pages."

"Agreed."

Detective Hannity handed over the notebook and copies were made of the relevant pages and entered as evidence. The defense had no additional questions for the detective.

The next prosecution witness was a toxicologist. She testified that she analyzed Ms. Stephanie Wheeler's blood and observed a high quantity of fentanyl, a popular sedative. The defense attorney had no questions.

# Chapter Sixty-Nine

Prosecutor Randal wanted to get an assessment of Erica's psychological condition on the record. Since Dr. Heinrich was the victim and would not be able to testify, Randal called the supervising police psychiatrist, Dr. Farley Hammond, to the stand.

"Dr. Hammond, have you reviewed Dr. Heinrich's notes regarding his treatment of Ms. Erica Richards?"

"I have."

"Could you briefly describe the process Dr. Heinrich undertook and the results he achieved?"

"I can, but I'm not so sure how brief it will be."

"Just do the best you can."

"Thank you. Dr. Frederick Heinrich is—I mean was—one of the world's leading psychiatrists in treating Dissociative Identity Disorder. He successfully treated many patients over his twenty-year career."

"Doctor, I apologize for interrupting, but I understood that positive results from treatment of this disorder are rare."

"That is generally true, but Dr. Heinrich was the exception. I'm sure that's why Ms. Richards hired him."

"Please continue."

"Thank you. Dr. Heinrich treated Ms. Richards for well over a year."

"Did he also treat Ms. Daphne Erwin?"

"No. Ms. Erica Richards was the one with the disorder."

"Are you saying that Ms. Daphne Erwin and Ms. Erica Richards are the same person?"

"No. Daphne Erwin is a second personality of Erica Richards."

"As such, does Erica control Daphne's actions?"

"No. Daphne controls everything she does. Erica merely provides the body. The mind is Daphne, the body is Erica."

That wasn't at all where the district attorney hoped to go with that line of questioning and he abruptly changed gears.

"Was Dr. Heinrich able to identify the cause of this disorder?"

"Yes. Erica had a traumatic experience when her younger sister, Daphne, and father, Erwin, were struck and killed by a drunk driver. The talk therapy revolved around resolving the trauma Erica experienced as a result of that incident."

"That sounds pretty straightforward."

"Well, it's not. That's why so few cases are cured."

"What progress did Dr. Heinrich report?"

"He felt he was getting closer and closer to success. He reported the Daphne Erwin personality had all but disappeared."

"Is that why they released Erica from the prison ward at Elmhurst?"

"Yes. In his final two reports, he claims Erica was totally cured."

"But that wasn't the case?"

"No. Not at all. Daphne found a way to mask her personality. She could do it so well that Dr. Heinrich believed he was always speaking with Erica. I've never known of a second personality that could do that."

"How are the people that you know taking Dr. Heinrich's death?"

"Not well. He was highly respected and well regarded. His death came as a total shock to everyone. We all heard how violent Ms. Erwin was, but most of us felt she was no longer a threat. We couldn't have been more wrong."

"Thank you, Doctor."

Sam Roosevelt took the cross-examination. He asked, "Doctor, you got to know Dr. Heinrich quite well over the time he treated Erica. Would you happen to know who his closest friends were?"

"I would definitely say his wife, Dr. Henry Young, and Dr. Peter Carlisle."

"Where are they located?"

"His wife is in Switzerland and the two doctors work in his Paris clinic. His wife spent the entire summer in New York and the two doctors visited him frequently. In fact, we all went to lunch numerous times."

"Do you think the doctors would be willing to come and testify to Dr. Heinrich's character and share anything he may have said to them about Erica?"

"Certainly. I can contact them later today."

"Your Honor, I would like to add those two doctors to my witness list."

"Agreed. Are you done with the witness?"

"No. I'd like to explore his beliefs concerning Erica's control or influence on the Daphne Erwin personality."

"Continue."

"If I understood you correctly, you said Erica had no control over what Daphne did."

"That's correct."

"Did Erica have any knowledge at all of Daphne's actions?"

"None whatsoever."

"From what you're saying, Ms. Erica Richards had no knowledge of or participation in this murder."

"Correct."

"She couldn't have initiated it and couldn't have stopped it."

"Correct."

"In other words, you're saying Ms. Erica Richards is totally innocent of these charges."

"Correct."

"Would you please state your conclusion for the record?"

"Ms. Erica Richards is innocent of the charges against her concerning the murder of Dr. Frederick Heinrich."

"Had you become friends with Dr. Heinrich?"

"I did over the course of his work with Ms. Erica Richards."

"What kind of person was he?"

"He was one of the most brilliant psychiatrists I've ever known."

"And what were his chances of helping Ms. Erica Richards?"

"Exceptional. He was her best shot at a complete recovery."

"Are you saying Ms. Richards' future happiness depended on the success of Dr. Heinrich's treatment?"

"Totally. Without him, she would have few prospects to lead a happy and fulfilling life."

"His death, then, was the worst possible thing that could happen to Ms. Richards."

"That is correct."

"Can you imagine any possible motive Ms. Richards would have to kill him?"

"No. She had a much stronger motive to keep him alive."

"Let's talk about Ms. Daphne Erwin."

"Fine."

Tom Randal stood up and yelled, "Objection."

The judge inquired, "On what grounds?"

"Relevance?"

"Overruled. Continue, Mr. Roosevelt."

The jury hung on every word of this testimony. In just a few short questions, Roosevelt proved Erica's complete innocence.

Randal didn't have any legal reason to object. He just wanted to vent his frustration at the defense attorney's success with a prosecution witness. When he sat down, he looked like he was ready to pound his head against the table.

Sam resumed. "Was Ms. Erwin capable of this murder?"

"Yes."

"On what do you base that answer?"

"Dr. Heinrich interviewed Ms. Erwin a number of times in the initial months of his treatment of Ms. Richards. He wanted to understand what she was capable of and how strong her motivation was to take violent action."

"How did Dr. Heinrich characterize Ms. Erwin?"

"He said she was a cold-blooded killer. She had no moral compass whatsoever. She responded to any perceived threat with extreme violence."

"What kind of threats did she feel she faced?"

"Her main concern was exposure. She became extremely worried that someone might discover who she really was."

"Did she actually know who she was?"

"She may have had a sense of it."

"What did she sense?"

"To understand that, you need to realize she was extremely paranoid. She constantly felt people were out to get her."

"Was she threatened by Dr. Heinrich?"

"Definitely."

"How so?"

"If Dr. Heinrich was successful, Ms. Erwin would cease to exist."

"How was she threatened by Ms. Richards' mother?"

"Ms. Richards' mother had all the information she needed to expose Daphne for who she was. Daphne couldn't let that happen."

"How about Jack Sparrow and his daughter, Anna?"

"Same thing."

"Let me summarize what you've told us. Based on Dr. Heinrich's work papers and the debriefings he gave you, there is no possible way Erica Richards could have murdered Dr. Heinrich."

"That's correct."

"At the same time, based on that same material, Daphne Erwin had the motive, the means, and the opportunity to murder Dr. Heinrich. Finally, Erica Richards and Daphne Erwin are two separate and distinct people who have no knowledge of and no influence on each other's actions."

"That's correct."

"Thank you, Doctor."

"Your Honor, I make a motion for a summary dismissal of the charges against Ms. Erica Richards based on the testimony and conclusions presented by Dr. Hammond."

Judge Weber replied, "It's not going to be that easy, counselor. Motion denied. Your next witness, Mr. Randal."

"Your Honor, the people rest their case."

# Chapter Seventy

Defense attorney Sam Roosevelt stood up and called his first witness, Mr. Jack Sparrow. I was sworn in and took the stand.

"Please state your full name."

"John Henry Sparrow."

"And you go by Jack?"

"Yes."

"What is your relationship with Ms. Erica Richards?"

"At one time, she was my fiancée."

"Are you aware of any of the proceedings of this trial?"

"No."

"Had you been in love with Erica Richards?"

"Yes. With all my heart and soul. We planned to get married."

"Do you still love her?"

"No."

"What happened?"

"She fell in love with Dr. Heinrich."

"Did you have hostile feelings towards Dr. Heinrich?"

"No. I was relieved."

"How's that?"

"Daphne's unrelenting efforts to intimidate me and ultimately kill me became more than I could handle."

"Did she intend to physically harm you?"

"I sincerely believe she had both the desire and the capability to kill me."

"How is it you're still alive?"

"Law enforcement and the grace of God."

"How would you describe Daphne?"

"Pure evil."

"And Erica?"

"Pure goodness."

"Do you believe they are the same person?"

"I do not."

"But they both occupy the same body."

"That's insignificant. It's like saying they both drive the same car. It means nothing."

"When did you first meet Ms. Daphne Erwin?"

"At my wife's funeral."

"What was she doing there?"

"My wife and I had gone on a twentieth-anniversary cruise. She became terribly seasick. I tried my best to help her, but she just wanted to be left alone.

"After a few days, my wife complained that a woman, Daphne Erwin, gained access to our cabin, drugged and raped her. Daphne denied the rape accusation and said she and my wife were madly in love. Daphne was overcome with grief at the funeral."

"Did you have words with her at the funeral?"

"I did. I was mad as hell at her. I told her I should have her arrested. We quickly got into a yelling and shoving match. Eventually, she tripped and fell to the ground."

As soon as I said those words, Daphne jumped to her feet and screamed, "Lilly and I were madly in love, you low-life piece of shit."

Judge Weber pounded his gavel and instructed her to sit down. She had other ideas.

Daphne yelled, "Who the hell is this little prick in the black robe? Is it Halloween? If you keep that up, I'm going to shove that gavel up your ass."

Judge Weber instructed the deputies, who were already trying to corral her, to restrain and remove her from the courtroom.

Not surprisingly, Daphne put up quite a fight. Both deputies went flying across the room. She knocked over tables and chairs and headed towards me and the jury.

She reached out her hand to grab me by the neck. Just before she got hold of me, the bailiff tased her. She collapsed at my feet.

The deputies immediately reattached the handcuffs and leg irons. Once Daphne regained consciousness, she yelled obscenities, insults, and threats. They dragged her from the courtroom kicking and screaming.

The judge tried unsuccessfully to reestablish order. Finally, he just pounded his gavel one time. "This court is recessed for thirty minutes."

After the jury was escorted out of the courtroom, the tables and chairs were turned upright and put in their proper places. The jury was shown back into the courtroom and the attorneys took their seats. The bailiff then led me to the witness stand.

Exactly thirty minutes later, the judge returned to the bench, and pounded his gavel. "This court is back in session."

The judge then nodded for the defense attorney to resume his questioning. Sam stood and walked towards the witness stand.

He asked me, "Who was that woman?"

"Daphne Erwin."

"Is she prone to violence and threats?"

"Yes."

"What has she done to you?"

"She fired a gun at me and warned me not to interfere in her relationship with my daughter, Anna."

"Did you file a police report?"

"Yes."

"Anything else?"

"She's kidnapped me several times and has repeatedly threatened to kill me."

"Are you scared of her?"

"Yes. I realize what she's capable of."

"And what is that?"

"Murder."

The prosecutor objected—conjecture on my part. The objection was sustained. The jury was instructed to ignore my response.

"Do you notice a resemblance between Daphne Erwin and Erica Richards?"

"No. Not at all."

"No physical similarities?"

"Sure—height, build, hair color—but that's it. They're totally different people."

"In what way?"

"Erica is caring and kind. Daphne is cold-blooded and vicious. Erica prefers relationships with men; Daphne prefers women. Erica has perfect vision; Daphne requires a strong prescription for nearsightedness. I'm sure there's many more differences, but those are the ones I'm aware of."

"To your knowledge, have the two women ever met?"

"No."

"Are they aware of each other's existence?"

"Yes."

"Have they communicated with each other?"

"Yes."

"How have they done that?"

"They have passed notes under each other's door."

"Have you seen those notes?"

"Yes."

"Is the handwriting similar?"

"Not at all."

"No further questions, Your Honor, but I reserve the right to recall this witness at a future time."

The prosecutor chose not to cross-examine.

Weber said, "Mr. Sparrow, you are excused. You'll need to wait outside the courtroom until such time as you may be recalled."

# Chapter Seventy-One

Anna was called as the next witness. She was sworn in and took her seat on the witness stand.

Sam began the questioning. "Please state your full name for the record."

"Anna Marie Sparrow."

"What is your occupation?"

"I'm a student at the University of Tennessee, studying criminal justice."

"What career do you intend to pursue?"

"Law enforcement. I want to be a US Marshal."

"Very good. What is your relationship to Jack Sparrow?"

"He's my father."

"To Erica Richards?"

"She's my dear friend."

"To Daphne Erwin?"

"She is my former lover and current mortal enemy."

"That's from one extreme to the other."

"Is that a question?"

"No. Who did you meet first, Erica Richards or Daphne Erwin?"

"Daphne."

"When and where did you first see her?"

"About two and a half years ago at my mother's funeral."

"Why was she there?"

"She was distraught and said she loved my mother."

"Loved in a spiritual or physical sense?"

"Both."

"How did you feel about that?"

"I was disgusted."

"Why's that?"

"First of all, because she was talking about my mother. I'd never been comfortable with the sex lives of my parents. Secondly, I wasn't ready to accept a physical relationship between two women."

"Have you changed your mind on your second point?"

"I have. I didn't realize how deep, how complete, and how passionate a relationship between two women could be."

The gallery became alive with whispered comments. Judge Weber pounded his gavel once and told the gallery they would be removed if there were any further outbreaks. He glanced over at the jury to judge their reaction. They took everything in stride.

"When was the next time you saw Daphne?"

"When my aunt, two girlfriends, and myself stayed in Erica's condo about seven months later."

"Tell us about that encounter."

"Dad called Erica for some recommendations on things to do and see in New York. She was leaving the next day for a photo shoot in Cuba. She invited us to stay in her condo while we were there. We were thrilled.

"The first night of our stay, Daphne had a party. Erica's butler, Oliver, told us Daphne invited the girls and me to join her. I ended up spending the night. Our relationship took off after that."

"When was the next time you saw Daphne?"

"A couple of weeks later. She came to spend some time with me at college."

"How did she seem?"

"Just fine. We were both madly in love and had a couple of incredibly passionate nights together."

"Only a couple?"

"Right. My dad flew out to see me and Daphne left."

"Did your dad have any particular reason to visit?"

"Yes. He wanted to tell me about his encounter with Daphne."

"What about it?"

"Daphne threatened him with a gun and told him not to interfere in our relationship."

"How did you feel when you heard that?"

"Concerned. I understood how Daphne felt about Dad, but I didn't think her actions were necessary or appropriate."

"Did it affect your feelings towards her?"

"Not really. I still loved her as much as ever."

"When did you see her next?"

"A few weeks later. We met for spring break at the Greenbrier in West Virginia."

"Who paid for that vacation?"

"I guess Daphne did. I know I didn't pay anything. I'm just a broke college girl, after all."

"And how was that time with Daphne?"

"Heavenly. I was on cloud nine when she left."

"You felt your relationship was solid at that point in time?"

"I did."

"And then what happened?"

"I quit school and moved in with her. Shortly thereafter, she invited my dad to a dinner party we were hosting."

"How was that?"

"Amazing, as always."

"Then she surprised you at Erica's place. What happened?"

"She pulled a gun on me."

"Why did she do that?"

"My dad was comforting Erica after he'd told her her mother had been murdered. Then, without any warning, Daphne pushed my dad away and pulled a gun."

"That's fine. Detective Hannity has already testified about what followed. Your next meeting?"

"In Switzerland. Daphne escaped from the clinic and she was anxious to be with me. She had a friend, René, pick me up. At the same time, the two women kidnapped Dad. Daphne and I argued about that all night. Before long, the police rescued both Dad and me."

"Did Daphne seem to treat you differently after she told you she had your dad?"

"I was the one that changed. We argued. I told her in no uncertain terms that she needed to release my dad and forget about him. Daphne said she couldn't do that and as long as my dad was alive he was a threat to our relationship. I told her if anything ever happened to my dad, she and I were through. That's when the real argument began."

"Was that the end of your relationship?"

"Definitely. A couple of weeks later, Daphne escaped again. I agreed to wear a tracking device and hook up with her. One of her accomplices found the device and Daphne realized I could no longer be trusted."

"Did she mistreat you?"

"Yes, she restrained and beat me. Fortunately, she didn't do any serious damage."

"You've seen both sides of Daphne's personality."

"Yes."

"Can you think of any circumstances where she should be released back into society?"

"No. Only at the time that personality ceases to exist should Erica be released."

Anna was excused from the witness stand. The defense recalled Dr. Farley Hammond. A deputy brought him back into the courtroom and he took the witness stand. The judge said, "Dr. Hammond, you are still under oath."

Defense attorney Sam Roosevelt began, "Dr. Hammond, several witnesses have testified about Daphne Erwin's erratic and violent behavior. She seems to be able to go from tender and loving to vicious and dangerous at the snap of a finger. Is that unusual in Dissociative Identity Disorder cases?"

"Yes, but not totally unheard of. The first personality is built on a lifetime of personal interaction with other people. That personality has figured out how to maintain an even keel even in challenging situations.

"That's not the case with this second personality. She has had little life experience to help her deal with the difficulties she encounters. She is easily threatened and can occasionally overreact in response."

"One last request. I need you to confirm it's not uncommon for one personality not to have any knowledge of the actions of the other personality."

"That's correct."

"Thank you, Doctor. Your Honor, I wish to reserve the right to recall this witness should it become necessary."

"Granted."

# Chapter Seventy-Two

When the attorneys took their seats the next morning, Erica was already sitting at the defense table. She hadn't been there since Daphne's outbreak. The judge didn't want to take a chance on something like that happening again. This morning, though, he had no choice. Erica was on the docket as the opening witness.

Defense attorney Sam Roosevelt knew putting the accused on the stand could be a risky proposition. Not only did she have to answer all his questions, but she'd also have to honestly respond to everything the prosecutor asked. In addition, there was always the possibility Daphne would rear her ugly head at some point during the testimony, which Sam believed could work in his favor.

Once the judge took his seat, pounded the gavel, and declared the court in session, Sam called Erica to the stand. She was sworn in.

Sam began, "Please give your full name."

"Erica Grace Richards."

"Ms. Richards, please tell us about your family."

"My younger sister, Daphne, and my father, Erwin, were killed by a drunk driver when I was a child. My mother, Harriett, was murdered last year. My older sister, Kathleen, is married with three children and lives in rural Vermont, outside of Stowe."

"The loss of your sister and father must have been extremely difficult for you."

"It was. I'd adored Daphne and always thought of her as my baby. I changed her diapers, gave her bottles and often rocked her to sleep. As she grew into a toddler, we were closer than I'd ever been to another human being.

When she was killed, I was devastated. I didn't know what I was going to do. I felt my life had come to an end."

"Did your mother put you in counseling or therapy?"

"Years of it, but it didn't seem to make much difference."

"Is this difficult to talk about now?"

"Not so much. I've talked about it quite a bit with Dr. Heinrich."

"Did that help you?"

"Tremendously."

"Have you ever talked about it with anyone else?"

"Just the therapist I had as a child."

"Tell us about Daphne Erwin."

"Not much to tell."

"Why do you say that?"

"I barely know her."

"But she lived next door to you."

"It didn't seem we were ever there at the same time. I'd leave and Daphne would arrive. Similarly, I'd come home and she would have already left."

"A previous witness testified you passed notes back and forth."

"That's correct. But it could be weeks before I'd receive a reply."

"You said she lived next door. Did she own that property?"

"I'd always thought she did until Jack told me I owned it."

"Jack is Jack Sparrow?"

"Yes."

"What did you think when he said that?"

"I thought it was ridiculous."

"How's that?"

"I don't remember buying it."

"Why would you let Daphne Erwin live rent-free in a condo you owned?"

"I can't imagine I would. I had no clue that place was mine."

"Are you aware the police were unable to locate any fingerprints for Daphne Erwin?"

"I've been told that."

"They checked your gun, the knife, and your condo from top to bottom.

They couldn't find one fingerprint that was unaccounted for."

"I didn't understand that at the time but I do now."

"Jack Sparrow also testified that you've never seen Daphne Erwin, never spoken to her or had any direct contact with her whatsoever—either personal or business-related. Is that correct?"

"Yes."

"Didn't you wonder about Daphne—who she was, what she does, that sort of thing?"

"No. I had no interest."

"Let's talk about Dr. Heinrich. Did you love him?"

"Yes. More deeply than I'd ever loved before."

"Did you love Jack Sparrow?"

"Yes. We planned to get married."

"What happened?"

"Dr. Heinrich touched me in a way no human being has ever touched me before."

"In a physical sense?"

"Well, that too, but what I was referring to was spiritual. He understood me. He got me. Our love grew from that."

"How did you react to his death?"

"Not well. I was heartbroken and felt hopeless and lost. I didn't know where to turn for comfort."

"What happened then?"

"I was reincarcerated. I've been receiving treatment in the prison ward at Elmhurst Hospital ever since."

"Has that helped you?"

"Yes, it has. I'm much better able to accept and deal with Dr. Heinrich's death."

"Thank you, Ms. Richards. Your Honor, I reserve the right to recall this witness."

The judge granted his request and turned the witness over to the prosecution.

The prosecutor, Tom Randal, began his questioning. "Ms. Richards, you know now that you and Daphne Erwin are the same person."

"No, that's not correct. We couldn't be more different."

"Alright. Let me rephrase that. You and Daphne Erwin occupy the same body."

"That's true to a certain extent."

"And how's that?"

"She needs glasses and I don't; she's left-handed and I'm right-handed; she prefers women and I prefer men. Even physically, we are different."

"You and Daphne both must experience huge gaps in your everyday life."

"No. I don't think so."

"For a week, you're Daphne, then for a month, you're Erica. Erica is missing a week, Daphne is missing a month—huge gaps in your life."

"No. That's not the case. I can't speak for Daphne, but my life seems to run along fairly consistently."

"That makes no sense."

"Maybe you're the one that needs therapy."

Tom took a two-minute break in his cross-examination and reconsidered his line of questioning.

Finally, he took a deep breath and continued, "How does Daphne feel about these gaps?"

"I don't know, you'll have to ask her."

"I am asking her."

"No, Mr. Randal, you're asking Erica Richards."

"No further questions, Your Honor."

# Chapter Seventy-Three

All of a sudden, the woman on the witness stand came to life. She blurted out, "Don't you want to ask me any questions, dickhead?"

Prosecutor Tom Randal spun back around. "And you are?"

"Daphne Erwin, shit for brains."

The defense counsel shouted objections. The judge pounded his gavel.

Randal ignored all that and calmly asked, "Tell us about the night you killed Dr. Frederick Heinrich, Ms. Erwin."

The entire courtroom suddenly went silent.

"Sure. First thing, I had to get rid of the dipshit guard, so I gave her some fentanyl. She thought we were going to have sex, but took a nice long nap instead.

"Then I went into the kitchen and grabbed the biggest knife I could find. I marched into Erica's bedroom. Freddie boy was passed out on her bed. As usual, he was naked as a jaybird.

"I grabbed the knife with both hands, raised it high above my head, and brought it down with all the force I could muster. For a second, I thought it was going to go clear through his body but it stopped when the handle hit his chest."

As soon as she finished, two deputies grabbed her and dragged her out of the courtroom. As usual, she was kicking and screaming a string of profanities. The judge tried to restore order.

After a couple of minutes, he declared a thirty-minute recess and immediately left the courtroom. The jury was abuzz with conversation. The defense was overjoyed; the prosecution, concerned.

Once the trial reconvened, Sam was ready to move on to the next step in his strategy—to further establish the differences between the two women. He felt this was crucial to creating reasonable doubt in the minds of the jury.

"The defense calls Erica's chef, Louie Dubois."

The chef took the stand and was sworn in.

"Chef Dubois, did you work for Erica Richards?"

"*Oui.*"

"English, please."

"Yes."

"How long did you work for Erica?"

"Approximately twelve years."

"Did you work for Daphne Erwin?"

"Yes."

"How long did you work for Daphne?"

"Approximately one year."

"Did Daphne pay you?"

"No. Erica was my primary employer and was the one that always paid me."

"Have you seen and interacted with both women?"

"Yes."

"Have you ever thought they could be the same person?"

"No, never."

"Why is that?"

"They were as different as night and day. Each woman liked different foods and had different ideas about when and how food should be served. Erica and Daphne couldn't have been any more dissimilar."

"Thank you, Chef Dubois."

The prosecutor wanted to cross-examine the chef.

Tom Randal asked, "Chef Dubois, what was your reaction when you heard about the murder of Dr. Heinrich?"

"I was shocked. He was a fine and thoughtful man. I also had a chance to get to know his wife and children. They were all quite charming."

"Thank you, Chef."

Sam's next witness was the doorman.

"Sir, did you know both Erica Richards and Daphne Erwin?"

"Yes."

"Would you tell us a little about each woman?"

"Certainly. Erica was a kind and considerate lady. Daphne was much more abrupt. She never even tried to be pleasant around me."

"Do you believe they are the same person?"

"No. That's impossible. They are much too different."

"Thank you."

Tom didn't care to cross-examine this witness.

After another day and a half of testimony, the defense rested their case. The prosecutor only had another couple of hours of rebuttal witnesses. No new information was offered. The last day was merely a reaffirmation of points already made. When both sides were done, the judge called for closing arguments. The prosecutor, Tom Randal, went first.

"Ladies and gentlemen of the jury, thank you for the time and attention you have given this capital case. Murder is the most serious crime on the books. The finality of death is a given.

"The guilt of the accused is anything but. The job of the prosecutor is to prove that guilt beyond a reasonable doubt. I believe I have done just that.

"We have the testimony of the murderer. You heard, in her own words, how Erica Richards committed the crime on the night in question. I read from the record, please excuse the language:

"'First thing, I had to get rid of the dipshit guard, so I gave her some fentanyl. She thought we were going to have sex, but she took a nice long nap instead. Then I went into the kitchen and grabbed the biggest knife I could find. I marched into Erica's bedroom. Freddie boy was passed out on her bed. As usual, he was naked as a jaybird. I grabbed the knife with both hands, raised it high above my head, and brought it down with all the force I could muster. For a second, I thought it was going to go clear through his body but it stopped when the handle hit his chest.'

"Yes, we understand Erica suffers from a mental illness, but the defense has never presented that as a reason to acquit her of this crime.

"They would have you believe Erica and Daphne are different people. That's ridiculous. Anyone can clearly see they are the same person. Erica is Daphne and Daphne is Erica. Several have testified Daphne does not exist as a human being.

"Since Daphne doesn't exist, who could have killed Dr. Heinrich? Erica Richards is who.

"Was anyone in that condo that night besides the guard and the doctor? Erica Richards was the only other person there.

"Besides the kitchen staff, whose fingerprints were on the murder weapon? Erica Richards's fingerprints were the only other prints.

"Clearly, Erica Richards is guilty of the murder of Dr. Frederick Heinrich, beyond any reasonable doubt. Thank you."

Sam Roosevelt gave the closing argument for the defense.

"As you saw and heard, Erica Richards did not make that confession. Those were the words of Daphne Erwin, the actual murderer. Erica Richards is innocent of this crime. She played no role whatsoever in the brutal murder of the man she loved, Dr. Frederick Heinrich.

"Daphne Erwin has confessed and is guilty of that murder. Unfortunately, she has not been accused, but Erica Richards has.

"I emphatically state you have no choice but to acquit Erica Richards of the murder of Dr. Frederick Heinrich. Witness after witness has testified that Daphne Erwin and Erica Richards are two different people with no knowledge whatsoever of the other person's actions. Erica has no hand in anything Daphne does. Erica Richards couldn't have possibly killed Dr. Heinrich. She was madly in love with him and her future well-being totally depended on him. His death was a tremendous loss to Erica. Nothing in her could have possibly caused her to murder him.

"Ladies and gentlemen, I encourage you to listen to the experts. They are all telling you Erica is innocent. Whatever you do, do not convict an innocent woman of this crime. Acquit Erica Richards. Thank you."

# Chapter Seventy-Four

The judge gave the jury their instructions and they retired to the deliberation chamber. They elected Harold Adams foreman. All twelve members made it all the way through the trial.

Adams's first official act was to ask for a vote. Slips of paper were passed around the table. All the jurors wrote their verdicts and passed the slips back to Harold. He read each verdict aloud—guilty, not guilty, guilty, not guilty—and so on. When he was done, he tallied six guilty ballots and six not-guilty ballots.

Adams observed, "We're not off to a great start. In fact, we're not even close to a verdict. We're split right down the middle. Let's each share our thoughts on the case."

He pointed to the woman on his left. "Lisa, you don't have to say how you voted, but I think your assessment of the case would be helpful. I'd like to go all the way around the table and get everyone's perspective on the trial."

Lisa began, "I've never heard of a case like this one. The fact that it involves a well-known and highly regarded woman makes it that much more disheartening. I think we can all agree Daphne planned and executed the murder."

She stopped and looked around the table. Everyone's head nodded.

She continued, "The problem we have is that she is not on trial. Erica Richards is charged with the crime. I don't know about anyone else, but I believe Erica had no knowledge whatsoever of the killing. I believe she played no part in the brutal attack. Does that make her innocent? I believe it does."

She turned to Richard sitting beside her. "What do you think?"

"I think we need more information on the law. Let's put together a series of questions to ask the judge."

Again, twelve heads nodded. Harold asked, "What questions does everyone have?" Adams rolled up his sleeves. He knew they'd all be there awhile.

Javon suggested the first question. "If the accused has no knowledge of or participation in a crime, can they be convicted of that crime?"

Emily added, "What is the standing of Dissociative Identity Disorder in terms of the law? Is that illness acceptable as a defense? What are the standards of guilt and innocence under these circumstances?"

Lisa asked, "Does having that disorder meet the insanity standard?"

Pepper, the youngest member of the jury, little more than a youngster herself, said, "Do you think we're going to be able to wrap this up before dinner? I kind of have a date tonight."

Walter, the oldest member, was quick to respond, "Sorry, honey, but I don't think you'll be making that date. We're sequestered until we reach a verdict."

Pepper looked confused. "What does that even mean?"

Javon replied, "We're going to be locked up like prisoners—no outside contact until we decide."

"That sucks."

Harold said, "Let's get on with the task at hand. This chitchat is wasting time."

Pepper was hurt. Nobody else cared about her problem.

Richard observed, "I got the impression Daphne confessed. In fact, she described the murder in gruesome detail."

Leeroy jumped in. "I remember that, but the judge didn't seem to think that was significant."

Harold wrote down, "What was the significance of Daphne's confession?"

Leeroy continued, "I believe the prosecutor proved, beyond a reasonable doubt, that Erica killed Dr. Heinrich."

Everyone had something to say. Some agreed with Leeroy. Some not so much.

Leeroy finally said, "Her prints were on the knife and she didn't have any alibi for that night. I say case closed."

Lisa asked, "What would her motive have been?"

"Lovers' quarrel?"

"Really? With a huge knife through the heart? Erica has no history of violence whatsoever."

"Daphne, then. Can we connect the two? Maybe they were in cahoots."

"Are you serious? Did you not hear the testimony? Daphne and Erica had no contact except for the occasional note. Plus, Daphne was the one Wheeler told Detective Hannity was in the condo that night."

Harold interrupted, "Let's get back to our list of questions. What else do we have? I'd like to get these to the judge before dinner."

Richard hoped someone else would reach the same conclusion he had, but at this point, he couldn't see any indication that anyone was even close to his way of thinking.

Finally, he asked, "Does anyone think we should delve further into Erica's mental illness?"

Lisa quickly jumped on that. "Exactly. This case isn't about guilt and innocence. It's about the responsibility a person with mental illness has for something done as a result of that illness."

Leeroy said, "Make some sense, girl. We're here to decide guilt or innocence. The doctors can address mental illness. That's not something we could even begin to do."

Lisa responded, "That's correct. But personally, I believe Erica is innocent of the murder. Her mental illness has resulted in the creation of Daphne Erwin, who I believe is one hundred percent guilty of the murder. We have no way of punishing the guilty person without administering the same punishment to the innocent person. We can recommend a mistrial and ask the judge to order psychiatric treatment for Erica until such time as Daphne is no longer a factor."

Leeroy said, "More nonsense. Erica is clearly guilty under the law and I don't see how we can overlook that."

Harold thought now was his chance. "Why don't we add the possibility

Lisa suggested to our list of questions for the judge? In other words, is there a way for us to avoid ruling on Erica's guilt or innocence while ensuring she remains incarcerated and that she receives ongoing psychiatric care and treatment?"

Leeroy latched onto that. "We can assure incarceration by simply declaring her guilty. What could be simpler?"

Lisa jumped in. "We're not looking for an easy way out here, we're seeking justice. Our duty is to ensure justice is served."

Javon added, "That's right. We have a solemn responsibility. We can't look for a quick fix. We must assure we arrive at a fair and just verdict."

Leeroy snapped, "Bullshit. Guilty. What's for dinner?"

Richard couldn't let that pass. "We've got serious work to do here. We're talking about a woman's life."

Leeroy was ready to take a swing at Richard. "Listen here, shithead…"

Harold firmly cautioned, "Leeroy."

Javon tried to settle things down. "Let's go ahead and order dinner and get back to our list of questions after that."

Everyone agreed. The bailiff brought in menus, which the jurors studied. Orders were placed and small talk followed as they waited for their meals.

Harold didn't feel his job as foreman was to lead the discussion. He thought he needed to make sure the discussion moved along to a conclusion the group could agree on. Now, he thought that was all but impossible, but he promised himself he would never stop trying.

# Chapter Seventy-Five

Eight days later, the bailiff led the jury back into the courtroom. The foreman gave him a folded sheet of paper, which he handed to the judge, who read it twice.

Weber then queried the jury, "Have you reached a verdict?"

Harold replied, "No, Your Honor, we have not, but with the court's permission I'd like to read a statement every member of the jury has signed."

Judge Weber replied, "This is extremely unusual, but I'm going to allow you to read your statement into the record."

"Thank you, Your Honor. 'We, the members of the jury, have deliberated eight days and nights. We've repeatedly sent questions to the judge, who has been thorough in providing his responses. We've also requested testimony to review to ensure we didn't overlook or misunderstand anything. The reason we couldn't reach a verdict has nothing to do with guilt or innocence.'"

With those words, the prosecutor jumped up. "Your Honor, the only question put to the jury is guilt or innocence. There is nothing else for them to decide."

The judge looked at the prosecutor and asked, "Are you objecting to something?"

"No, Your Honor, I'm not."

Harold, the foreman, continued, "Based on the testimony of Dr. Hammond, we all believe Ms. Richards is suffering from a mental illness known as Dissociative Identity Disorder. We also believe from his testimony and the testimony of others that she has no knowledge of anything her other personality, Ms. Daphne Erwin, has done. As such, we can't imagine how she could possibly be held accountable for those actions.'"

Tom jumped to his feet but said nothing. The judge gave him a look and he sat down.

Harold concluded: "'At the same time, Dr. Frederick Heinrich is dead. Daphne Erwin has admitted to killing him. But who is Daphne Erwin? She is nobody. She does not exist. Your Honor, this is the strangest case we could have ever imagined. Half of the jury cannot convict Ms. Richards and the other half believes she is guilty. We recommend you declare a mistrial.'"

The judge interrupted, "That's my decision to make. The jury's role is not to make recommendations but to determine guilt or innocence."

"I understand, Your Honor. After more than a week of deliberations, the jury was unable to agree on a verdict. Both the initial and final vote was six guilty and six not guilty."

"Thank you, ladies and gentlemen of the jury. I need to ask each of you a couple of questions. The first is do you believe you could have reached a decision if you'd had more time?"

Each juror individually responded no.

"Second, do you believe you could have reached a decision if you had more information?"

Each juror individually responded no.

Judge Weber pounded his gravel and announced, "I hereby declare a mistrial in the case of the State of New York versus Erica Grace Richards."

He then turned to the jury "I want to thank each and every one of you for the thoughtful and dedicated service you have given this court in hearing an extremely complex case. This jury is dismissed." Gavel pound.

Weber then turned to the attorneys. "I want to meet with both attorneys in my chambers immediately following the conclusion of this case.

"This court is dismissed." Another gavel pound.

The judge, defense attorney, and prosecutor retired to the judge's chambers.

As soon as everyone was seated, the judge turned towards the prosecutor. "I am going to issue an order to immediately commit Erica Richards to psychiatric care at a mental hospital administered by the New York penal system. The care is to continue until she is determined to be cured of Dissociative Identity Disorder by three independent psychiatrists.

"I also recommend that, should she be unequivocally cured of this disorder, the murder charges against her be dropped."

The prosecutor objected immediately, "Your Honor, you know her continued prosecution is a decision that I, as district attorney, will make at the appropriate time."

The judge quickly responded, "I realize that. I'm merely expressing my opinion on the matter."

"I understand. We will certainly take your opinion into consideration, although I'm sure I speak for everyone here when I say it's highly unlikely Ms. Edwards will ever be cured."

"I agree. That's all I have. I thought you both did exemplary jobs in service to your client, Mr. Roosevelt, and the State, Mr. Randal. I look forward to seeing each of you in my courtroom again."

# Chapter Seventy-Six

For what seemed like forever, Anna and I have been sitting on a bench outside the courtroom waiting to be called back to the witness stand. Finally, we were told the case had gone to the jury. The two of us retired to our hotel with the occasional outing to nearby restaurants. We couldn't even begin to think about work or school.

Eight days later, Sam called and told us the court was reconvening. We hustled over to the courthouse as quickly as we could. When I opened the huge doors to the courtroom, we were overcome by a loud roar with reporters pouring out through the opening.

I quickly learned a mistrial had been declared. If I was honest with myself I couldn't really imagine any other outcome.

Convicting Erica would be a total miscarriage of justice. Acquitting her would be even more egregious. To my way of thinking, a mistrial was just about right. When I learned of the judge's subsequent order and recommendation, I couldn't have been more pleased.

That said, I asked for and received a transcript of the trial proceedings. When I finished reading, I felt sorry for Erica but was pleased she was not convicted and that she was receiving the treatment and care she needed.

The appearance of Daphne in the courtroom was terrifying. I was glad I'd only been there for the first outbreak. I hoped I would never see or hear from that crazy bitch again.

At the same time, I was disappointed I'd probably never be with Erica. I loved her and truly missed her, but the Erica currently a prisoner of the New

York penal system was not the same woman I'd fallen in love with.

*Goodbye, beautiful lady. I'll never forget all the unbelievable memories we made together. The lady in white will always hold a special place in my heart.*

# Acknowledgments

One night, my wife and I were on a Caribbean cruise. As we walked through the Atrium, something caught my eye—the lady in white. We whisked past her and I never saw her again.

Months later, I thought I could write a story about the woman I'd barely even seen. That fleeting look was all I had when I started writing.

A number of people helped with this book and I'd like to thank each and every one of them. First of all, my wife, Pam, and her brother Jim. They both read my first draft and made suggestions and recommendations that contributed to a much more enjoyable read. Also, our son, Braden, and neighbor, Bob, who patiently proofread the finished book.

Next, I want to thank my editor, Eliza Dee with Clio Editing. Once again, she's done an incredible job pointing out numerous typos, grammatical errors, omissions, and things that didn't logically follow one another.

Thanks as well to my professional proofreaders—Donna Rich and Nancy Brown—and my formatter—Jason Anderson with Polgarus Studio.

Last but certainly not least is my cover designer Chris Andruskiewicz with Sparrow Graphics. Did she do an amazing job or what? I couldn't be more pleased.

Special thanks as well to Rick, Randa, and Becky who charged my iPad with their gas generator when Hurricane Ian knocked out our electricity for five days. With their help, I was able to finish my final review of *Lady in White*.

I also want to thank you, the reader. I hope you enjoy reading this story as much as I enjoyed writing it. I look forward to hearing your comments at dmccurrach@gmail.com.

As always, I take full responsibility for any mistakes or anything else that isn't quite right.

Thank you.

David McCurrach
North Fort Myers, Florida
December 1, 2022

# Author

David has enjoyed writing his entire life. This work is one of six novels he has completed. Prior to those, he published three non-fiction books dealing with the financial education of children.

Late next year, he plans to release his third novel, *A New Life*. Be sure to sign up on his website, davidmccurrach.com, for prenotification when that book is about to be published.

David and his wife, Pam, live in North Fort Myers, Florida. He has five children, fifteen grandchildren and three great-grandchildren who live all across the country.

# Books by David McCurrach

*Lady in White*

*Death Needs No Invitation—A Tommy Boyd Adventure*

*Allowance Magic—Turn Your Kids Into Money Wizards*

*Kids' Allowance—How Much, How Often and How Come*

*The Allowance Workbook—For Kids and Their Parents*

www.ingramcontent.com/pod-product-compliance
Lightning Source LLC
Chambersburg PA
CBHW061948170626
46813CB00006B/2568